DEPTHS

Steph Campbell

Liz Reinhardt

Copyright © 2012 Steph Campbell & Liz Reinhardt

All rights reserved.

ISBN-13: 978-1482719765

1 COHEN

It's surreal sitting here on my bed, listening to my girlfriend talk, because I'm pretty sure she's breaking up with me— while wearing my favorite Dodgers t-shirt.

The same one she pulled on after she screwed my brains out and collapsed on my chest, sweaty and giggly, before falling asleep in my arms last night.

"What the hell are you talking about?" I ask, sitting up straighter in the bed and watching her pile all her silky hair on top of her head as she looks at herself in the mirror.

She actually takes a second to check herself out from the side before she bothers to turn and acknowledge me again. Not that I can blame her, since she's hot as hell, but can the girl focus for two seconds?

"Kensley, I don't even understand what you're saying. Last night you were on top of me in this bed telling me how much you love me and now it's all over? I'm…this makes no damn sense. At all. So explain it to me."

She comes over to the bed and sits on the edge carefully. She looks at me, her big brown eyes wide and innocent. It's a face she makes when she feels guilty.

Come to think of it, it's a face she made last night. When she stripped her black lacy bra and panties off and pushed

3

me back on the mattress. Just before she straddled me, asked me to talk dirty, then slid my dick into her, whispering that she loved me and always would, she flashed me that *sorry* look.

My mind flips back to a few hours before.

"Cohen," she panted, her hips pumping up and down, her gorgeous tits shaking with every bounce. "I'll never forget you."

I thought it was a weird thing to say, but my mind wasn't really focused on her words. I was reaching up to feel the soft, full swell of those perfect tits. Sometimes Kensley says crazy shit. She wants to be an actress, and she's into role playing and all that, so I basically ignore most of what she says because we both tend to get wild in the sack. I say lots of things no one who knows me from work or general life would imagine me saying when I have a beautiful girl in bed with me.

"Cohen." She takes my hand and looks up, every move so deliberate, it's like she rehearsed it all.

Fuck.

"Last night was…it was my way to say goodbye," Kensley explains, her voice soft. Theatrically soft. Like she's gunning for best sympathetic break-up with a pathetic boyfriend.

DEPTHS

Double-fuck.

"Good-bye?" I sputter. "Really? Good-bye? We looked at puppies last week. This week you're ready to say good-bye?"

"Let me go down on you," she offered. It was a nice gesture, but Kensley didn't go down on me unless she was saying sorry or she wanted something.

Since I wasn't pissed at her, I asked, as she sank to her knees, "What do you want, babe? I know you made that registry at the jewelry store that friend of yours owns a while ago, but our anniversary is in a few weeks. I promise, you'll be happy."

Her eyes flipped up to my face and she looked...guilty. "Can't I just do this to be nice?"

I wasn't going to say no to that. "Of course. And th-th-ank...good freaking God, Kensley."

And then I didn't say anything else, because my girlfriend's tongue was doing crazy, amazing things to my dick, and I wasn't about to stop that.

"You know I've been wanting to move to Hollywood. Now's my chance, and I know you're not into it—" She lifts her hand when I open my mouth to protest. "Saying you'll give it a few months isn't good enough. I need you to be two-hundred percent behind me. Actually I don't know if

5

that would even be enough. I guess I really just need to be on my own to pursue my dream."

"I get that, Kensley," I say through gritted teeth. "But I don't get why you think breaking up is going to make things easier. What about having me around makes things harder for you in any way?"

"It's really not even you," Kensley says. I'm trying my damndest not to roll my eyes at the clichéd breakup that is happening. Right now. To me. "Don't roll your eyes."

I guess I didn't try hard enough.

"I don't understand then. If it's not me...We've been together for years. Since high school. I told you my dad had a store branch near Hollywood, if you want to go. I've said that for years. What's so wrong about things now?"

Kensley pushes her hand into her hip and puckers her mouth, twisting it around like she's thinking about how to say whatever it is just the right way.

"Fine," she says, stepping forward and putting her palms on my chest. It feels weird, because she's closer and touching me, but, at the same time, I feel like she's pushing me away. "It's not just the Hollywood thing. This hurts me to say, Cohen, but...it *is* you. You just...you haven't grown since we were in high school, that's what it is. We eat at the same restaurants, we go to the same movies, we go to your mother's— Every. Single. Sunday. We watch the same shows on that damn DVR religiously. You just…you never want to try new things. And what I'm about to do, who I'm about to be? That's going to be nothing but new experiences. And I just don't feel like…you and I don't *fit* anymore."

I can't help but think of just how well we fit last night.

And apparently, won't ever again.

"Kensley, I just got back from a goddamn real-life treasure hunt. How much more adventurous can you get than that? And what's wrong with my mom? She makes a killer matzo ball soup and carne asada that will change your life. How much more excitement do you need out of life than a half-Jewish, half-Mexican household? And if we move, there will be new places to eat, new things to see, and I'll try them. You and me, being together, *that's* the adventure. What more could you want?"

"I don't know. But I do want more. And you're not giving it to me."

"Is there someone else?"

She takes three steps back. One for each letter of the answer she's working up the courage to give. Because I can see it in that faux tortured look on her face that there's more to this than me not wanting to go bungee jumping off the Great Wall.

She waves her hand around like she's brushing off the question as ridiculous.

"So, there is?" I push.

"Not exactly. But there could be. And I need to be open to that. Not stringing you along when neither one of us are happy."

"I'm happy," I say. And I am. Things aren't a thrill around my place, I'll give her that. But I work long hours at the furniture store my family owns—it's a nice, comfortable, stable life. I'm hoping to keep saving and have a nice, comfortable, stable future. Until five minutes ago, I thought Kensley was part of that future.

"Cohen…Don't make this hard. Please. I want us to stay—"

"Don't say it. Don't say friends." I wipe my palms on my jeans. I'm a man, I'm not going to cry, but I'd be lying if I said I wasn't shaken up. "We're done here, Kensley. I've got to go to work."

I half expect her to try to stop me. But when I'm all the way to my car, hand on the door handle, and she hasn't so much as called my name, I realize that I just did her a major solid by walking away. I made it easier for her. There was no chance I was going to be able to change her mind. Kensley was already gone before we woke up this morning.

I took her to dinner after work last night. And then the whole foods store where we stocked up on all that clean-eating crap I'll never touch. Then we went back to my place for the night. I guess she did me a solid, too. She knew she'd be breaking it off with me and we still had incredible sex. One last time before what I'm sure will be a long, dry spell for me.

A pity fuck before she left, stomping on my heart on the way out the door.

I look back and squint so I'm able to see through the high sun, looking for Kensley. But she isn't there.

The bell above the door jingles as I push through it and I want to rip it down and stomp on it until it stops being so damn cheery.

"You're late," my drama-queen younger sister, Genevieve says. She flips her long, dark ponytail over her shoulder and raises her eyebrows at me, and I know one wrong word can send her into a hissy fit or make her burst into tears. We usually all walk on eggshells around Gen, but I'm not in the mood to deal with her today.

"Sue me," I say, ignoring the way her jaw drops open. Despite her crazy mood swings, she and I have always gotten along okay at work, mostly because I pretty much ignore her when she's being a pain in the ass. Today's just not a good day for me already.

"Just go clock in, Cohen. We've got inventory to do." She's younger than me, but she rides my ass like she's the older, more responsible sibling. Probably because she secretly wants to get the same respect our older sister, Lydia does in our family. Ever since I dropped everything last year to go sail the Pacific Ocean with my best friend Deo, Genevieve acts like she's the only stable thing this family has got. Which is hilarious, since she's the one of us best known to fly off the damn handle. "And consider shaving! Mom would be pissed if she knew you were talking to customers with that crap on your face."

I rub my hand against my cheek. There's a day's worth of stubble, but that's it. It's been a day since I've shaved. *One. Get over yourself and your sense of authority, Gen.*

I toss my keys and iPhone under the register and go to the back room to punch my time card. I went to school and got a degree to end up working for my folks at their furniture store. It wasn't the plan, but they needed me, and for now at least, it isn't half-bad. The hours are good, there's a decent benefits package, and my place always has nice furniture…to impress all the women that aren't there.

I slide the card stock into the time clock and chuckle, as I

DEPTHS

do every morning, like a ritual. It's an ironic kick in the balls that my own parents make me a slave to the man.

The phone is ringing when I turn the corner back into the showroom and Genevieve is showing some newlywed-looking assholes the mattresses and I want to tell them to run, that once you're with someone too long, they get tired of you. They want more. Even if the sex is earth-shaking, and you help them with their car payments, and even pick the onions out of their enchiladas because they claim to be allergic. But none of that is *adventurous* enough. Fuck my life. So instead of breaking their love spell, I jog up to the front counter and grab the phone.

"Hello, Rodriguez Family Furnishings," I say.

"Hello, Cohen Rodriguez," the familiar voice replies. It's Maren, this girl who works in our warehouse site.

"Hey," I say. I talk to Maren daily. Sometimes, more than a few times a day. She's always helpful and polite, but her voice is a little too raspy— a little too sexy to have me totally convinced that she's all good-girl. In my mind, she's got this rad pin-up vibe going. You know, the whole curves for days; thick, gorgeous hair; silky lingerie that's meant to be seen. Course, I've never seen her. In reality, she could be six-foot-four and have a mean five o'clock shadow.

"Are you guys busy over there today?" she asks.

"I'm not sure, I just got in."

"Ah, must be nice to be the bosses' son and just waltz in whenever you feel like it," she jokes. "I bet you were out all night, barely able to drag yourself to the showroom today, huh?"

"What can I say, my life is one big party," I lie. I pull my iPhone out from where I'd stashed it earlier and check to see if Kensley has called.

She hasn't.

DEPTHS

2 MAREN

Pathetic as it is, Cohen's voice is the sexiest thing going on in my life.

I really need to call Jason back, even if he did stand me up on our last date. I'm an independent, modern woman, and if I need sex, I should go ahead and get it, no strings attached.

I shake thoughts of one-night-stands with dangerously sexy assholes out of my head and wrap myself back in the comfort of work.

And Cohen. A smile curves on my lips when my brain bumps over his name.

"Well, I appreciate yesterday, party boy. You saved my life scanning those documents at the eleventh hour. I hope I didn't make you late for any big plans."

I bite my lip, sensing that he's distracted, not really listening to me. He just got in, which sucks. I love my chats with this guy, but I obviously called a little too early, and now I'll have used up my one call for the day and it's going to be a rushed one. Suckity.

"Nah. Nope." There's a long pause before his deep voice grates across the phone lines again. "Not a problem. There's

13

no problem." The bite of his words lets me know this probably doesn't have anything to do with the scanning.

"Listen, you sound swamped. I needed to run some shipment times by you, but I can totally call back later if you want, alright? It really is no problem."

I stare at the hideous peach walls of my tiny office and twirl in my chair while I wait for his answer, closing my eyes because I hate looking around while I'm in this tiny office.

The lady who worked here before me was with the company for almost twenty years, and she got a little crazy with the personalized decor. The peach walls are just the beginning; there are also thick, lacy cream curtains on the windows, doilies everywhere, silk plants in dusty baby blues at the window ledges, and prints of kids in floppy clothes pretending to be grown-ups cluttering the walls.

I should take some of this down, just to neutralize it back to a business-like work environment. But doing something like that would mean admitting that I'm staying here, and I have other plans, bigger plans for my life.

Eventually, anyway.

So I just try not to acknowledge the fact that I basically exist in some sappy old lady's pastel nightmare and focus on the good parts of this job. Like phone calls to sexy-voiced guys I do business with.

Cohen takes another few seconds to answer me, and, much as I love his sharp wit and delicious voice, this is getting obnoxious fast.

"Sorry, Maren. I'm…Can I transfer you to the phone in the back?"

"Sure." I pick up a doily with the end of my pen and shake some of the dust out of it. There's a lot. Enough that I cough, then sneeze twice.

Okay, whether I stay here very long or not, I should de-clutter just so I don't wind up with a respiratory infection.

When Cohen picks up again, there's a still quiet on the other end that lets me know he's somewhere private. "I'm sorry, Maren. My dipshit little sister just agreed to stay out on the floor, so I won't get interrupted again, I swear. You were saying we needed to go over some shipments?"

I like his business voice. Cohen gives off this very laid-back, sweet vibe when we're just chatting, but when it's time to get work done, he's totally alpha about everything. It's a damn sexy mix.

I wonder if he's like that in other ways? Sweet on the street, alpha in the sheets…

So inappropriate! I self-lecture.

I need to get laid immediately. And get back to the

conversation at hand.

"Don't be too hard on poor Genevieve. I heard she's having a rough time at school," I scold, smiling at his chuckle.

"She whined to you, too? Maybe if she actually did some of her work and paid attention in lecture, she'd pass something."

I kick my pinchy heels off my feet and wiggle my toes to get the blood flowing. "Hey, we can't all be dean's list every semester like you were. Your dad never fails to mention it." I love how the Rodríguezes give each other shit all the time, but they're also fiercely loyal and proud of each other.

Even Cohen and Genevieve, who always seem to be at each other's throats.

"Speaking of dean's list, how are your classes going, Mare?" When I'm quiet for a minute, his voice drops. "Maren? Don't tell me you went through with dropping them. I told you if you needed a loan—"

"Cohen," I plead. Because if he gets me thinking about it all, the education classes I bailed on, the professors I let down, the roommate I left high and dry, I will lay my head down on this desk and cry my eyes out. "You know I can't borrow money from you. It's…it's not right. I mean, I so appreciate your offer. It's beyond sweet. But this is my problem. And you know how things are with my dad. Even if I stuck it out this semester, it would be more of the same or worse next semester. So, there's that."

I squeeze my eyes shut and try to ignore the images of my dad, red-eyed, stinking of sweat and whiskey, sobbing so hard, drool drips down his chin. Just when I think I've seen him at his drunkest, he ups the ante and shocks me with fresh lows I never dreamed were possible.

This month it was two DUIs, back to back. I can't even think of where I'm going to get the money to pay for a lawyer. And it was almost a relief when he lost his job. He has no excuse to drive without work, so he stays home watching talk shows and the soaps my mom and sister used to love so much.

I wrestle with the tears, digging my nails into the grainy desk in an effort to win the battle with my overactive tear ducts. And I do win.

Yay me.

Cohen makes a little strangled sound in the back of his throat. "So you bailed him out again?"

"Don't you dare lecture me about helping family." I singsong to disguise the tremble in my words. I'm so damn good at pretending everything is cool with everyone but Cohen.

Or maybe Cohen is the only one in my life who, for whatever reason, doesn't assume I'm happy with things the way they are. He's the only one who ever asks what I want. And I love him for that. But I also hate him for it. Because he acts like it's so damn easy.

And it just...it just isn't.

"I know you love your dad, Maren. I know that. But what you're doing, it isn't helping him or you and I just think—"

"I think we should get back to business," I say, hating how icy my voice is. I shake my head, disgusted at the fact that I'm so cold to Cohen when he's nothing but good to me.

It makes no sense at all. How you tiptoe so carefully around the people who use you like an emotional punching bag, but the people who want to help? It's nothing to throw their kindness right back at them. I drag the breath into my lungs in deep gasps, because I'm so close to crying, I'm not going to be able to hold back soon.

"Okay." Cohen speaks carefully. "If that's what you want, I'll drop it. But let me say this," he rushes. "If you need anything, I'm here. Okay?"

A nice, normal person would say 'okay' back. Or, better yet, 'thank you.'

But I'm not a nice, normal person. I'm a thoughtless asshole running scared, so I talk about spreadsheets and sales. Like a coward.

"I emailed you a spreadsheet. Can you check the next two weeks against your sales' dates? Last month we got our wires crossed and I had fountains coming in when you guys were having your rug sale. I know how crazy that must have been, and I don't want anything like that happening again."

I hold my breath and bat back the words that threaten to spill out.

Words like, *Help me, Cohen.*

Words like, *Forgive me for being a bitch. If I didn't have your voice some days, I know I'd sink under the pressure of it all and drown.*

Words like, *I imagine running away with you, and I've never even seen your face. Because, even though we've never met, we know each other. And I'll never say that out loud, because it makes me sound like a lunatic.*

His chuckle is low and deliciously rough, and my entire body relaxes. Cohen, awesome Cohen, just let it go like he always does, ready to make me happy, even if what I'm asking him is so stupid and cowardly.

"It was pretty crazy, but we actually wound up making a great profit on those fountains. I think we did better with them than with the rugs, so, you know, as usual, even when you make a mistake you're brilliant."

I feel a hot flush spread over my chest and neck, and I button and unbutton the top button of my crisp, professional white dress shirt, which is feeling very constricting all of a sudden.

No one compliments like Cohen Rodriguez. No one.

"You're just trying to butter me up, because you know damn well it was still a mess-up, and I hate making them. I'm afraid I'll lose my spot as your dad's favorite shipping coordinator."

If my voice sounds a little high and breathy, I don't think he notices. I can hear him tapping on the keyboard, and I imagine him squinting at the screen.

With gorgeous blue eyes, framed by eyebrows that are always pressed a little low. I also imagine that he has shiny brown hair and a strong jawline.

That's what I daydream he looks like…but he could be a troll with a wart on his nose and a constant lip-licking habit for all I know. Our relationship is strictly phone-only.

"No worries there. You have my dad wrapped around your little finger. I've only ever seen him act the way he acts with you when he's with my sisters. He actually says you're as smart as my sister Lydia, who my parents think is the world's smartest person just because she's a lawyer, so, trust me, he loves you."

It's silly, but I feel proud about that. My dad loves me fiercely, but I feel like he hasn't noticed me for years, no matter what I do or how much I achieve. Feeling like I have a place in the Rodriguez family, even a totally unimportant place, is a little lifeline I can grab onto during the hurricane that currently defines my life.

"Well, I don't want to take any chances," I insist. "Look it all over, Rodriguez, and tell me if I screwed up."

"Everything looks great. I can't even imagine how you manage to coordinate all of this. You know we know how lucky we are to have you, Maren. My dad would throw a tantrum if you ever left. Priscilla was sweet and all, but she could never pull everything together like you can."

How can such simple words pack such a punch? Maybe because there's just the clean, sweet honesty of his words and my realization that he's saying them because he absolutely means them.

And that means everything to me.

"Well, I'm glad to help."

Glad to help, loving the compliments, but cursing my own efficiency. If I hadn't done such a thorough job, I'd get a few more minutes on the phone with him to break up this dreary, boring day before my lonely, depressing night.

There's a long pause, and Cohen clears his throat. "Yeah,

so I guess I better get going. This morning has been insane—
"

"Of course. You had all those customers when I first called and Genevieve is probably talking them into crazy art deco pieces we'll just have to return later." I pretend for his sake and mine that I'm just as eager to get off the phone now that the business is all handled.

"Actually, I wish it was just customers." His words come to a dead stop, and I realize that this can go one of two ways. I either get him off the phone and keep everything simple.

Or…

I roll my desk chair to the door of my office, which is partially ajar, and swing it shut.

"It must have been pretty bad if you're wishing for customers, Cohen. What's our mantra again? 'If it wasn't for the customers, this job would be amazing?'"

His laugh is grainy and not totally happy. "Sad but true, right? Look, I don't want to dump on you, but, uh…this is weird. Um, Kensley broke up with me this morning and I was pretty much blindsided by it, so if I'm a little out of it. Yeah." He sucks a long breath in. "Shit. That's the first time I said it out loud. I know it's so fucking cliché, but it made it feel more real, you know?"

I feel an instant, righteous anger, which is ridiculous.

Maybe stupid, asshole Kensley had excellent reasons for breaking up with Cohen. Like I said before, I know him from business calls and our phone friendship, which means that I actually know nothing at all about what he's like as a real life friend or a boyfriend. She could be unequivocally justified in letting him go.

But I doubt that with every cell in my body.

"Oh, Cohen. That sucks. And don't even talk to me about anyone dumping on anyone. You've listened to me whine and cry so many times. I'm just…I'm so sorry."

I'm sorry for his idiot ex. She's going to regret what she did. I wouldn't be surprised if she called him back by tonight. They'd been an item for years, and guys like Cohen just don't come along every day.

I could say all these things, but…

A teeny, tiny part of me is hoping that I'm wrong. A tiny part of me hopes that she's way too stupid to realize what she lost, because he deserves better than someone who'd let him go like that. So much better.

"I guess I just feel…I don't know. Kind of pissed. I mean, I think I'm more pissed than I am hurt or sad or whatever." He laughs a little at this confession. "She said I wasn't exciting enough. Seriously?"

"That's ridiculous!" I seethe on his behalf, though, again,

honestly, I have no clue if she's dead-on in that regard. He's an amazing conversationalist, and I'm not even bored when we're talking straight business. But we've always had a natural ease with each other, so maybe I'm biased.

"And the worst thing is, now that she said it, I can't shake the idea that maybe…maybe she's right, you know? I mean, I know *you* get it. What it means to work hard, to put yourself out there every day because you have a job to do, because other people depend on you. She never got that. To tell you the truth, she had the luxury of doing whatever the hell she wanted because her parents totally spoiled her and gave her everything. It's not like that for me. I've always had to work hard for what I have." He lets out a long, frustrated breath.

"Well, I may be overstepping but—"

His laugh cuts me off. "You're not. Trust me. I'm the one using up your time whining about my pathetic love life. And I really respect you, Maren, so if you have any advice for me, I'm all ears."

A tiny coil of warmth unfurls low in my stomach and knots my tongue. "Oh. Cohen, it's just, um…thank you. I, um, don't claim to know much about, you know. Love. And all that. But, I think that this was a good thing. If you think you are maybe…taking things too seriously…with your life, what better time than now to put yourself out there? Make a bucket list and start crossing things off. You're always telling me to do things for myself. Well, take you own advice. Get out there!"

For a minute there's nothing but silence on the other end, and I'm scared I really did overstep. I should have just stuck with sympathy; I suck at advice.

Then his voice rings out, excited. "Maren, you're a damn genius! This is great. You know what? This is perfect." He's getting louder and more energized with every word. "I love this. You're right! Maybe this whole thing was a blessing in disguise."

"That's right," I rally him. "And, look, Cohen, if that was the only problem, I think it was crazy that her solution wasn't just to do more exciting things with you. You are freaking amazing. Trust me, good guys like you are few and far between."

He's quiet, I assume thinking over what I've said. I chew on my bottom lip, hoping I haven't crossed any lines.

"Hey?"

"Yeah?"

"You're making me blush," he says, and I laugh with pure relief. "I really…it means a lot. To me. What you think of me. But Mare?"

"Mmm?" I don't manage an actual word, because my heart is in my throat.

"Right back atcha. You're…There's no one quite like you, cheeseball as that sounds. And you deserve the best. You know that, right?"

"Thank. You," I say slowly, because I want to say so much more that I'm chicken shit to even think. So I hide behind a stupid cop out.

Basically my MO.

And I guess my general lameness snaps Cohen out of talking about how cool he thinks I am.

"Listen, Maren, I seriously can't thank you enough. I really needed to hear that this morning. I'm going to get off so I can do some work and let you get some done, but I plan to make that list. You can hold me to it. And I'm gonna cross things off. All because of you. So thank you."

His voice is so sincerely grateful, it flattens my lungs free of any spare oxygen. I manage to gasp out some fumbling, awkward words. "You're so welcome. I'm really… I'm glad I could help. You deserve to be happy. And if you ever need to just talk, you don't have to wait for a shipment to come in or anything. I'm here. Whenever you need. If you do. Not that you will!"

I shake my head and clamp a hand over my own stupid

running mouth. What the hell am I saying?

"That means a lot. Really. And it goes both ways, okay?" The rumble of his voice sets my heart racing and tripping over itself.

Before the stretch of silence after his words gets too long and awkward, I rush to fill it in. "Okay. Well, we should get back to work, I guess. I hope your day gets better, Cohen."

"It already did. It did the minute I heard your voice, Maren. I hope your day is great."

I squeak out a goodbye just as Jacinda, the accounts payable girl, knocks on the glass of my door. I slam the phone down, feeling guilty even though there's no reason at all for me to feel that way.

"You look like you're up to no good," Jacinda says as she breezes in and collapses on the chair across from my desk. "Are you secretly a phone sex operator moonlighting as a nice, organized secretary?"

Just to irritate me, she peels off three post-it notes and sticks them on the edge of my desk.

My fingers twitch with the urge to rip them off, but I control my anal retentive leanings. I hate it when people touch my office supplies.

Hate it.

I'm going to jack her parking spot tomorrow to retaliate.

I also blush hot imagining what phone sex with Cohen would be like. He is newly single after all, so it's not like it's imposs—

Ugh! Jacinda is always the worst interrupter of my day.

Well, after Cohen. But I actually enjoy being interrupted by him. It's different.

"*I* am getting work done, unlike *you,* and, no, my work does not involve moaning and panting into the phone. Unlike your work, as far as I can tell. By the way, it's great you have a new boyfriend, but you should really close your office door when you, um, entertain him on his breaks." Her smile is completely smug, not even remotely embarrassed to know the entire office overheard her amorous conversation. I raise my eyebrows at her. "Why are you bothering me already?"

She snaps out a new business card, and I try to suppress a groan.

"No. Not again. I had to give scented candles as gifts to every single person I knew for an entire year. And the Tupperware? It's still in the packages. And the freaking muffin mixes and salsas and dips…okay, those were delicious, but I had to get a gym membership because I gained *fifteen pounds*. Stop. This. Madness. These get-rich-quick schemes don't work for you." I push her hand back, but she's unfazed and keeps pressing it in my face.

"The other things didn't work because I had no personal investment in them. I don't really like candles, and I hate cooking, so it should have been obvious that those were going to be duds. But *this* is something I can totally get behind." She lays the card down on my desk, and I gasp and shove it under my appointment book.

"Jacinda," I hiss. "I thought you were joking when you asked about the phone sex. What the hell are you thinking?"

"Don't be such a prude," she whines, sitting up straight, her bleach-blond bob swinging back as she raises that pointy chin of hers. "It's business."

"It's smut," I object, flipping the card back at her. "Where did you even find someone to print these cards up? They're…they're porn!"

She laughs, her slight frame shaking. "They get your attention, right? Don't get all uptight. It's not only sex toys. Look, I bet you have fourteen pairs of white undies and a couple of nude bras in your drawers. I'm selling lingerie, too, and you could use some."

I clutch at the top of my shirt. My underwear are *not* all white. They have colors and designs. I mean, they're also cotton, but that's not necessarily a bad thing. They're comfortable, and when I put them on, I immediately forget about them. Which is kind of the point of underwear as far as I'm concerned.

"I don't need new underwear, especially from whatever trashy catalog you're ordering from now," I gripe.

Jacinda raises one dark, over-plucked eyebrow. "Can I interest you in a vibrator, then? It's been two months since you went on that date. And I assume from your stories about his rancid garlic breath and clammy hands that it didn't end with a hot, body-shaking orgasm?"

I point at the door. "Get out."

"Oh! Is it back on with Jason?" Her eyes go wide. "I know he's a jerk, but, good Lord, he is hot sex on a stick! And there's a sweet little set on page forty-three, one of those thongs with a bow that makes your ass look like a present. I bet Jason would unwrap you the minute he saw it, if I you know what I mean."

"Out!" I point a finger to the door.

"Think about it." She gets up and straightens her too short skirt with a quick tug. "It might be fun. Fun…hmmm. Do you know what that word means anymore? Because you used to be fun. Lots of fun. Remember? And then you got…so adult."

"We *are* adults, Jacinda," I sigh.

Has it really been two months since my disastrous date

with that idiot whose name I can't remember? Maybe that's why I'm thinking about seeing Jason again. I'm turning into a cobwebby old spinster.

Cohen's voice spins in my head.

You deserve the best. You know that, right?

I think about another night with my dad passed out drunk in his recliner, some tasteless dinner and boring TV show all I had to distract me from the pile of bills I don't know how to pay.

I deserve…something else. Something fun. Just for the night.

Jacinda senses the fact that I'm considering her stupid idea, and she bounces on the balls of her feet, anticipating my cave-in. I slide the card out from its hiding place, and the image of the entwined bodies makes me blush. And feel a little…horny. What business do I have advising Cohen to seize the day when I'm spiraling into such a sad, boring state of loserdom?

Maybe this office isn't the present I can barely endure: maybe it's the future I'm barreling towards without even realizing it. That clinches it for me.

"Fine."

"Fine? You'll come?" She claps her hands a little. "Can you bring someone? I can get you a discount if you bring someone!"

"Get out," I groan. "I have work to do. Work that doesn't involve selling flavored lube." I glare at her, but Jacinda is unruffled by my disapproval.

"Bring a friend! My place, eight sharp on Friday. I'm glad you're finally dusting off your lady parts and getting back in the game." She trills this lovely observation at the top of her lungs as she exits into the main office hallway.

I sprint to the door and slam it shut, contemplating co-worker murder. I cram the scandalous card in my purse and put it and all things sexy out of my mind so I can get some work done without X-rated thoughts gyrating through my head.

3 COHEN

"What are you doing here, man?" my best friend Deo stands in the open doorway. I lean against the doorframe and close one eye to steady myself and to help focus on him, since the earth spun the entire walk over here.

"I couldn't make it all the way to my place," I say. I can hear myself slurring, but I'm powerless to correct it.

"Do you want me to drive you home?" Deo asks.

I shake my head. Then realize that was a bad idea. More spinning.

"No cars. Too much movement. Can I just crash here?"

"Oh, let him in for fucks sake, Deo!" Whit, his hot-as-hell girlfriend calls from behind him. Deo smirks at me before stepping aside to let me pass. I take the four longest steps of my life, then collapse onto his sofa, face first.

"I take it you had a little too much to drink?" Deo laughs.

"Fuck off," I mumble. I think I'm drooling on their couch. I sort of don't care.

"Cohen, you want something to eat? We had chicken and rice," Whit yells from the kitchen.

"You cooked, Whit?" I pick my head up just a bit at

the mention of home-cooked food. I'm not too drunk for that.

Deo snorts. "Please. Whit brings the sexy to this relationship. I'm the domesticity."

He hands me a glass of some thick, red shit that I know will perk me right up. We've shared pitchers of this mystery concoction before. No telling what's in it, but it'll sober you up and cure any hangover. I hold my breath and chug the gritty sludge as fast as I can, then lay back and wait for the mystery potion to work its magic.

"So, what's with you trying to out-drink the frat house?" Deo asks as he sits down on the arm of the red sofa.

"Kensley. She broke up with me."

Deo sucks in a quick breath through his teeth. "Ouch. Sorry, bro."

"She said I'm not impulsive enough or some crap like that. What does that even mean? I'm bo-hoodles of fun." No one says anything, and it's like total confirmation. "Right?"

"Please, you're super predictable and responsible and stable and all the things that a girl doesn't want in a guy at our age, Cohen," Whit says. She's standing next to Deo and he's rubbing his hand up and down her thigh while she talks, and I can't help but want to roll over and cry like a man-baby at the sight of the two of them. "She wasn't good

DEPTHS

enough for you anyway."

"She was way out of my league," I say.

"Wrong. You're just feeling sorry for yourself right now. Once you sober up, things will look different," Deo says.

"I've got to go to work, boys." Whit takes Deo's face in her hands and kisses him for a long few seconds.

"Damn, I wanted you to stay here and hold me, Whit," I say just to break their little love spell. Deo reaches over and smacks me in the back of the head.

"I'll give you that one because you're drunk, but Whit doesn't spoon with anyone but me," Deo says. He smacks Whit on the ass as she walks by to get her coat and she giggles and swats at him. "You want me to drive you, baby?"

"No thanks, I'm fine. You guys have a good night," she says. She leans over me and kisses me on the temple. "Hang in there, Cohen."

"Sure thing," I say. But I don't want to hang in. I want my girlfriend back. I want to be at home right now, in front of the TV, eating takeout with Kensley. I want to go through our nightly routine. Head to bed after *The Daily Show*, freakishly good- albeit predictable sex, coffee in the morning. What was so wrong with that?

Apparently everything.

35

"Your girlfriend is a fox," I say after Whit's closed the front door behind her.

"I told you, Cohen. You got one shot. Don't make me have to kick your ass right now, when you're practically crippled."

"Maybe Kensley was right," I say.

"Maybe Kensley is a bitch." Deo was always pretty cool about not throwing how much he hated Kensley in my face when she drove me crazy, but they had never liked each other. I guess now he's not going to hold back.

It's not exactly like he's wrong.

"Possible. But also, maybe she was on to something. Maybe I could change and she'd want me back."

"Dude, why would you want to change for her? For anyone?"

"Whit changed you," I say. And it's true. Deo went from this slacker, freeloading hippie to a full-on respectable adult all in the name of love and Whit's fine ass.

"True. But the difference is, Whit never asked me to change. And she was worth it. You just need to find someone who's worth it. Then it'll all fall into place."

"Like who? The only women I interact with are at work, and they're usually buying recliners for their husbands." I pinch the bridge of my nose to relieve the last of my headache, but the mystery sludge has already made me feel a hundred times better.

"I don't know, man. I can see if Whit can think of anyone to set you up with."

"What about…what's her name? I saw you talking to her at Rocco's place the other day? She came in for some ink. You used to date her."

"Claire?" Deo says, his eyebrows raised in disbelief.

"Yeah, what about setting me up with her?" Claire was hot as hell.

"No way." Deo crosses his arms and shakes his head.

"Come on, man. She looked super put-together. I was actually surprised to see her in there getting a tat. What'd she get anyway?"

"A bird. Tramp stamp, obviously."

"I'd like to see that," I laugh.

"I'll think of someone else."

"Why? Are you weirded out that you dated her first? Because I'm cool with it," I say, even though I'm not entirely. But these are desperate times, plus Deo dated half the local population before he met Whit and got tamed.

"Nope. I just don't think you'd be a good fit. Besides, she gave shitty head." Deo makes a grimace I'd never expect any guy to make in connection with the thought of a girl going down on him.

"No such thing," I protest.

Deo laughs. "Trust me, dude. You don't want any of that."

"Challenge accepted."

***

It was Whit who finally helped set me up on the date with Claire. Most of her hottie friends from college were already hooked up, so it wasn't like there were tons of alternatives.

"You look great," she sighed after I asked her for the third time. But she did get up to unbutton the top button on my new shirt. "Did you iron this?" Her eyes are so dark I can't really tell, but I think she's teasing me.

"Too much? God, I'm such a dork, right? It's just been years since I was on a first date with a girl, and I don't want her to think...I don't know what the fuck I want her to think." I push a hand through my hair, then groan, realizing I just undid all the time I spent in the bathroom trying to make it look half decent.

Whit's laugh isn't reassuring. She grabs my wrists and pulls my hands down, then musses my hair more. "Stop. Worrying. And loosen up. All this gel and starch is going to make you look nervous, then you'll feel nervous. You're amazing, Cohen. If I wasn't with Deo, I'd snap you up in a second."

"Stop torturing me, or I might push him off the side of his boat just to take you up on that."

She squints at a piece of my hair, moving it back and forth like it matters, then grins. "I'm way too mean for you, Cohen. And you and Deo are—and it hurts me to say something this cheesy, but it's so true—you guys are like peas and carrots."

"Am I the peas or the carrots?" I smile when she shakes her head.

"The peas, buddy. You're so the peas." She glances over her shoulder when Deo comes in and her whole face goes bright.

"So what are you? Cause you guys look pretty peas and carrots to me," I say as Deo practically runs over, grabs Whit around the waist, kisses her neck, and shakes her back and forth.

Through her insane laughter, she gasps, "The steak! I'm the steak!" She turns in Deo's arms and kisses him, the slaps at his chest. "And you," she turns to point at me, "need to find your mashed potatoes."

"I thought you were going out for Mexican tonight?" Deo asks, kissing Whit behind the ear.

"I'll explain later," Whit whispers, clearly meaning later

when they're locked in the bedroom for hours on end.

As much as I totally love my friends, eavesdropping on their sexy-time plans is not my bag. "Hey, I better get going. Thank you for messing up my hair, Whit."

"Trust her." Deo says, clapping his hand against mine. "She knows what looks good. Obviously. She picked me."

"Ass!" she cries, biting his jaw with little nips as I head out the door.

"And Cohen!" Deo yells as he throws Whit over his shoulder and she pounds her fists on his back. "No worries, man. You got this. Just be cool. Be yourself."

"Right. Okay." I leave them, crazy laughing and so damn in love it hurts to watch, and head to my car, a responsible gray Honda that gets amazing gas mileage.

I pause, my key in the lock. Maybe I am totally not spontaneous enough. Maybe I am no fun. Maybe I need to break out a little.

And Claire may just do that for me. I drive to the restaurant we planned to meet at, a little open-air Mexican place on the beach that serves the best pozole. It might even be better than my abuela's, though just thinking the thought makes me nervous that lightning will strike me down where I stand.

Claire is next to her car, a little yellow Beetle with a

crushed-in headlight. She's leaned back, her hands splayed over the scratched hood, a big, sexy smile on her face.

"Hey. How are you?" She pushes back off the car and makes her way to me, kissing me softly on the lips as a 'hello.'

"Uh, I'm, uh, I'm good. I'm really good now that I'm finally here with you." She has her arms around my waist and is running her fingers over my back in a way that's more intimate than that kiss.

I feel like our wires got crossed in a huge way. Like maybe she thinks we've met before; I know her from Deo dating her, but we never did more than wave across a parking lot on the first of their three disastrous dates. Maybe Deo has some other half-Mexican half-Jewish friend he introduced her to?

When she tilts her head back, I can see her eyes are pretty glassy, and I realize that, like most of the girls Deo dated before Whit, she probably spent the day tanning and getting high. Not that I'm judging. It's just those girls were never really my type. At all.

"So, I'm, like, so totally starving." She pulls the words out so they're a few seconds away from a slur. "Wanna go in?" She bites her lip and grinds her slight hips against my side.

"Sure. After you." I hold my arm out to let her go before me, but when she almost crashes into the statue of St. Francis in the poppies by the walkway, I grab her around the waist.

She loops her arms around me and giggles. "Oh, Calvin, I'm gonna like you!"

"Cohen," I correct, walking her in quickly. I try to ignore the dread that's rushing through me and chalk it up to nerves instead. "Two for dinner, please," I say to the hostess.

"Mmm," Claire sighs. "Can you tell our waiter to bring over some bread?"

I cringe and the hostess rolls her eyes and says in a flat voice, "This is a Mexican restaurant. I can bring you some tortillas and salsa if you want."

"Perfect!" Claire claps. "And hurry."

No 'please.' Maybe it is super dorky of me, but my parents are all about manners, and Claire's brusque behavior is grating.

But I'm supposed to be staying open-minded. I'm supposed to be taking chances. So she came on a date a little toked? It's not something Kensley would have done, but maybe that's a good thing. Kensley ripped my still-beating heart out of my chest and shredded it. I want the anti-Kensley.

I look at Claire's brown curls, her sweet hazel eyes, and soft lips, curved in a flirtatious smile. So she yanks the tortillas out of the hostess's hands? So she eats with her mouth open? So she interrupts me a couple of times and can't seem to remember my name? These are tiny things, and I decide to stop being so damn judgmental.

Then she opens the drink menu. "Jose Cuervos!" she squeals. "Double margarita, frozen, sugar on the rim, and fast," she demands. "And enchiladas. Extra sour cream."

I will not judge her disappointingly generic order. I will not.

"A Negra Modella and the pozole, please." I hand the menus back to the waiter, who was sort of checking Claire out before she opened her mouth. Now he's looking at her with the same feeling of dull horror I'm trying to suppress clear on his face.

"So, Claire. Are you in school?"

She shifts some half-chewed chips and salsa around in her mouth. "Mmm. Yeah. I am."

I wait for her to say more, but the salsa must be pretty damn amazing, because she's scooping it up so fast, she'll be scraping the bottom of the bowl soon.

"Um, what's your major?" I wince at my predictable question. I'm not doing much to stray from the dud Kensley accused me of being so far.

"Undeclared." She's licking some salsa off her thumb. I'm half sure she'll lick the bowl any second now.

"Yeah, I hear that. Sometimes it's hard to know what you want. I started as an engineering major, but eighteen credits a semester along with the pressure of keeping an insanely competitive GPA was pretty intense. Plus, I basically hated every class, so I switched to accounting." The waiter puts our drinks down and she picks her glass up with both hands, sucking on the rim and chugging at least half the liquid in a few long gulps.

When she sets the glass down, she licks some sugar off her fingers and lets out a sigh. "Oh my god, so damn good. Did you say eighteen credits?" I nod, she shudders. "I did twelve when I was a freshman, and I failed three of the classes. No way. I can only do six a semester."

"Six? Credits?" Now it's my turn to chug my drink.

"Yeah. My father said it's way smarter to just go slow, you know? College will be the best years of our life. Tons of my girlfriends are doing six or nine credits. It just lets you focus more, ya know?" She pauses. "So, you're an accounting major."

I'm trying really hard to keep my eyeballs from rolling out of their damn sockets. Six credits? That's, like, eight years of college! "Was. I *was* an accounting major. I graduated."

"Wow." Her mouth forms an adorable little 'o' and her eyebrows go so high, they almost disappear into her brow line. "I thought you graduated with Deo's class? A year ahead of me?"

I nod around another long sip of beer, hoping the alcohol dulls my brain sooner rather than later.

"So, did you keep taking eighteen credits? Cause I thought that was too hard?" She takes another drink, and I decide to blame her misunderstanding on all the pot and booze she's currently full of.

"No, I always just took fifteen a semester after that, like most people do, and that put me on course to graduate last May." I try not to sound like some tightwad prick, but I shouldn't have worried. She's using the stirrers to take a sip so long and deep it sucks her cheeks in.

By the time she comes up for air, her back teeth are definitely floating.

"Most people do *not* take fifteen credits!" She throws her hands up and giggles when she bumps her drink. "Fifteen! You…" She points and me and smiles a smug, loopy smile. "You are smart, Calvin. I like that. I really do. You know that?"

I don't bother to answer. Why should I? She's so far in, she won't recognize a word I say. The food comes, and it's delicious. Or mine is. I would ask Claire what she thinks, but the question might confuse her. Anyway, she's way more interested in sucking down a second enormous margarita.

She doesn't seem to notice that I've stopped trying to make any conversation, and she continues to jabber about brain freeze, some kind of mutant puppy she desperately wants to own that's made when you mix a Chihuahua and a poodle, and how she always tries to get in classes with male professors because, and I quote, "lady professors can be so unfair if they're older and jealous of what they don't have."

Like eight years of college and no medical license to show for it?

I laugh at my own joke-thought, and that's when I realize this date is just a lost ass cause. I call the waiter over and nurse two more beers. I know for a fact the third is a huge mistake and realize I'll probably have to break up Deo and Whit's sex-fest to have one of them pick me up, because I'm in no position to drive. I am officially that loser friend. The uptight, anal-retentive, no-fun asshole who's the perpetual butt of every joke in every comedy.

My life is a cesspit.

By the time I pick up the check, Claire's voice has

reduced itself to fuzzy white noise that I'm totally happy to tune out.

When we walk through the exit, she totters to my car, and I grab her under the elbow.

She laughs and tosses her arms around my neck. "Calvin," she singsongs. "I wanna go somewhere jus' me and you."

"Look, Claire, this was a really great night, but I had more to drink than I should have, and I think you did too. My aunt runs a cab company. I'm going to get one of her drivers to come pick you up." I pull my phone out of my pocket, but she grabs my wrist, her nails digging into the skin.

She stands on tiptoe and whispers in my ear, "But…I'm so horny right now. For you."

"For me? Or for Calvin?" I shake my head and take her by the shoulders while she giggles at what she thinks is a joke. "Look, it was really fun, Claire, but neither one of us needs to be, um, getting horny in our condition tonight. I'll even give you my aunt's number so you can get a cab back to your car tomorrow. Or whenever you're good to drive. It's on me."

She slides one hand down my arm slowly, then grabs my phone, holding it over her head. Even though it has a good cover on it, I'm worried she'll break it.

That thought snaps all the frustrations from the night, and my patience is gone. I'm not ready, I guess. I'm not cool with going out with a girl who comes to a date stoned and is rude and stupid. Maybe some guys would embrace the moment, but I can't. I just can't.

"Give me the phone, Claire." I make a swipe for it, but she jumps out of my reach and runs towards the back of the restaurant, where a large patio borders the beach. I follow her as she ducks under clearly marked 'no trespassing' signs and runs toward the waves.

My phone is going to wind up in the ocean. This date is about to get a hell of a lot shittier and more expensive fast.

Fuck me and my stupid need for adventure!

"Claire! Claire, get over here NOW!" I bellow.

She stops so fast sand kicks up around her feet. I catch up to her and hold my hand out, and she drops the phone in and does this stupid lip-biting bit that's such an obvious fake-out.

"I'm so sorry." She twists her hips and bats her eyelashes, pulling me close to her by my belt. "I've been really bad, haven't I?"

I know some girls think the baby voice thing is sexy, but it seriously creeps me out.

"Super bad," I say dryly. I tap on my aunt's contact and

DEPTHS

ask for a cab. "It will be twenty minutes before she can get all the way out here, but then you can get home and sleep this off."

She plops on the sand and presses her bottom lip out. "We could have had lots of fun," she whines.

"Yeah. It could have been a real ball." I tuck my hands in my pockets and will the crashing waves to drown her whiney voice out.

"It's a little chilly here." She rubs her hands up and down her arms, and, suddenly, she looks very frail and worn-out, like her internal light has gone out.

Or her buzz is wearing off and the beginnings of her hangover are starting to riot in her brain.

"C'mon." I hold a hand out to her. "We can go wait in my car."

"What about the restaurant?" she asks. "We could get one more for the road!"

I haul her to the car and get her in the passenger seat. "You don't need any more, Claire. What you've already had is going to hurt like hell tomorrow."

The sun is setting. I thought, by this point, we'd maybe take a walk on the beach, maybe head somewhere quiet and have coffee, tell stories, laugh. I hoped the night would end with something…not sex. The first date is freaky fast for sex. But maybe just kissing. Holding each other. Just enjoying the kind of romance that had seeped out of my relationship with Kensley in the end.

"Whatchathinkin' about?" Claire asks, turning in her seat. Her shirt pulls up on her back and her skirt is low, but I don't even try to sneak a peek at her bird tattoo. This is beyond sad.

"Nothing. Work. Things I have to do," I lie.

"Work?" She reaches her hand over, pressing on my leg. "That makes me feel kind of depressed. No guy ever thought 'bout work on a date with me." Her fingers slip up my pants and yank at my belt.

I put a hand over hers. "Claire. Don't. Look, your cab will be here soon. And, to be honest, something just didn't click on this date."

"I know," she says, nodding emphatically. "I know it. You think I'm an airhead." I'm about to protest, but she puts a finger to my mouth. "I smoked a tiny bit before I came out, okay? But I was so nervous. And then I tried to loosen up by drinking, but you're kinda intimidating. I never was with an engineer before. And all that credit talk?"

Her fingers are working to unbutton and unzip my pants, and it seems like she's growing multiple arms, because, no matter how I bat her away, she's always got a hand on my

DEPTHS

crotch. And then my pants are open and she's yanking at my boxers.

"No. Listen to me, Claire. No." Claire is surprisingly strong and persistent, and I have no damn clue what to do. I just pray the cab shows up fast, so I can get her out of my car and into it and be done with this hellish night.

"Maybe I don't have the brains you do, Calvin, but I have other things. Things guys like. A lot." After she says those words, she nosedives for my junk, and I scramble to get the car door open.

I'm willing to jump out of this car with my pants half off my ass if that's what it takes to shake this girl.

But my door is stuck and she's wiggling around, trying to pin me, and suddenly she heaves.

The sound is so specific and disgusting, I almost heave too.

"Claire!" I reach down for her shoulders, but she already has her hand at her mouth and is bucking, trying to hold it down.

Before I can sit her up and attempt to get her out, there's a hot, wet torrent on my lap and down my legs.

I finally manage to elbow the fucking door open, which just gives her the opportunity to finish what she started on my driver side seat.

"Calvin?" she gasps. "I'm so sorry. I think I drank too much." Her mouth twists into an ugly shape and she starts to sob.

I may be covered in her vomit and out of patience, but I'm not a total dick. I go around and help her out of the car. I lead her back into the restaurant and explain what happened to the hostess, who's so disgusted, she waves us to the ladies' room and promises to not let anyone in for a while.

I manage to prop Claire on the counter and use wet paper towels to clean her up as best I can. "C'mon," I say, leaning her over the sink. "Take a sip and rinse your mouth."

"Cup," she moans and burps.

I cup my hand and catch some water in it, then hold it to her mouth. She sips and winces as she swishes it around. After she spits, she sticks her tongue out. "Tastes sweet," she mutters.

I brush her sticky, wet hair out of her face and all my aggravation melts.

I don't want a second date, but I feel bad for Claire. She's probably going to be too mortified to ever call me again by tomorrow anyway.

"You're so nice," she says sleepily. "Why am I so drunk?"

"Too much tequila," I explain. She sags against me so

heavily, it's easier to just carry her out.

My cousin Madeline is in the parking lot when I get there, tapping her foot, but her aggravation turns to disgust mixed with hilarity. "Holy shit, cuz! When you have a bad date, you go all the way!"

"Hardy har har." I nod at the door. "Help me get her in."

"Wait." Madeline goes to the trunk and takes out the heavy, plastic-backed blankets my aunt made especially for situations like this. Her company runs taxis just for women who are more comfortable having other women drive them home. And situations like Claire's are common enough that they have puke-resistant seat covers.

My cousin finally waves me over, then rifles through Claire's purse and finds her id.

"Is it far?" I ask.

Madeline laughs. "I hope you've been selling lots of corner units, Cohen. Her place is forty minutes away in Friday night traffic." She jumps in the cab and leans out the window while I close the door on Claire, curled up and moaning on the back seat. "You need a ride?"

"Nah." Madeline would have to drive in the opposite direction for me. "I'm cool."

"I'll send you a bill!" She calls as she pulls out.

I'm left in the middle of the parking lot with puke

dripping down my pants, slightly too buzzed to drive safely, and with a seat full of vomit even if I was sober. I could call Deo and Whit, but I'm not in the mood for his laughter and her pity. I'm way too far from home to walk. But my parents' storage warehouse is twelve blocks from here. It's got a little office in the back that has a tiny shower my father uses on his gym days. If I'm lucky, my over-prepared dad may have left an extra gym bag there. At the very least I can lie down on the couch and sleep my buzz off in peace.

When I get to the storage warehouse, I luck out on every count, though it would be a serious stretch to say I'm feeling lucky after tonight's date.

I shower and change into my dad's too-short gym shorts, then settle back on the couch to catch some sleep, wishing Deo's mom made some kind of potion that could erase the memory of the world's shittiest date along with your hangover.

4 MAREN

Jacinda and the group of a dozen women she invited, who range from her neighbor's obnoxious teenage daughter to Jacinda's half-deaf grandmother, are sitting in her sparse living room, vibrators and anal beads covering every surface, playing a "game." The "game" consists of screaming "dildo" whenever the words man/guy/boyfriend/husband/fiancé come up. The Jell-O shots, which Obnoxious Unsupervised Teen has already partaken of twice, are making the game even more hilarious and fun.

Hardy har har.

I've got a half hour drive home after this shindig, so, as appealing as berry blue flavored vodka is, I'll pass.

The problem is, a bunch of shrieking women going nuts, so to speak, over sex toys wouldn't usually be my scene on my craziest, drunkest night. So being stone cold sober isn't helping me deal with this at all.

I've been playing Scrabble against some random player on my phone and wishing I had earplugs, when an email pings, interrupting my game.

Usually I get irritated that work occasionally interferes with my free time. Now, I'm ecstatic.

I try to wave Jacinda down to let her know I'm going to

use her office to take care of this issue, but there's a knock at the door, and when it opens, a cop with a huge, white smile bursts in. The entire mass of 'dildo'-screaming women hushes when he points a baton at them.

"I'm Officer Miller. I got a report there are some very bad girls in this room. Very bad." He grabs at his shirt and rips it away, revealing a very nice, tanned set of abs and pecs.

"Stripper!" Obnoxious Teen yells, jumping on Jacinda's couch. The ladies go ape shit. Jacinda smiles smugly, winks at the 'officer,' and turns on Jace Everett's "I Want to Do Bad Things to You." He hip-swivels in, and I dart for the office, secure in the knowledge that no one will miss me or care that I'm gone.

Obviously, since my being out of the living room means more 'Officer Miller' for the sex-crazed women out there.

In the safe comfort and quiet of the office, I skim the email from one of our suppliers and decide to leave a message on Mr. Rodriguez's phone. There's no point in trying to email him. I love that man to death, but he's practically Amish about technology. I'm just thankful he uses voicemail…unless of course he has an actual answering machine in his office. The thought of some old push button machine that works off cassette tapes makes me smile through the message I leave.

"Hello Mr. Rodriguez. I hope you get this bright and early Saturday morning so you can get back to your lovely wife and all those sweet kids. Sherman's called and they promised they could get a definite AM delivery on Mrs. Guarez's mirrored hutch. Just use Marty's extension and tell him which location to deliver to. If you have any questions, just call me—"

"Hello?"

The shock of having someone pick up makes my heart skip a beat, but I pull myself together because I can be professional even when I'm holed away at a party full of lusty women screaming sex words and running their hands over a stripper's oiled body.

"Mr. Rodriguez! I thought you'd be home for the night. I could have sworn you were taking your wife to that heist movie?"

The low chuckle on the other end is half sleepy, half sexy. I'm mortified to feel a tingle of heat low down between my legs. I press my lips together to choke back a groan. *Bad Maren!* He's a happily married man with five children! I have no business being turned on by his laugh.

"Maren? It's Cohen."

Relief rockets through me. "Cohen!" I actually squeal,

relieved that I'm not some pervert home-wrecker. "I'm sorry, I didn't expect you to pick up. Honestly, I didn't expect *anyone* to pick up. I was just leaving a message for your father because an email we needed for scheduling came in late."

Oh, and I was also just getting hot and bothered over your sexy-as-hell laugh, but we can totally ignore that little fact.

I smooth my hair like he can see me, then drop my hand quickly because he can't. And I feel stupid worrying about my hair like some high school girl anyway. Anyway this is Cohen. He wouldn't care.

Would he?

Ugh. Maybe all the dildo chanting and male stripping is just pushing my hormones into overdrive.

"I didn't expect to be here, either." I can hear him moving around, like maybe he's just waking up, and the first thing that crosses my mind is that he's there with a girl. He's newly single, and, though I've never seen him, he can't possibly be bad looking. Who could have a laugh that sexy and not be hot? Shitshitshitshit! I interrupted Cohen's rebound sex! "So, do you need me to leave a note for my dad?"

"Um, the message pretty much sums it up, but if you

want I can repeat it. Unless you're, um, with someone." I wait, hoping he'll ask me to repeat the message so we can stay on the phone for a few more minutes.

Wow, my life really had sunk to new lows, and it gets even worse when he tells me 'no' and my heart flops pitifully in my chest

"I'm alone, but it's okay. You know Dad's pretty OCD about how his work stuff is organized. He'd rather have the message than a note." I wilt in the chair and wait for him to get off the phone. "So, that sucks that you're working this late on a Friday night. You should have just let it go til Monday."

"Are you kidding me?" I settle into Jacinda's rolly office chair. "Mrs. Guarez has been a pain in the ass for weeks, stressing your poor father out like crazy. Now she's going to be taken care of, and then he'll be free of her and her constant bitching."

I sink my teeth into my bottom lip. Damn! Mrs. Guarez *is* a pain in the ass, but she's also a customer at his family's business, and I definitely stepped over the professional line even more than Cohen and I usually do.

"Ah, Mrs. Guarez. Trust me, she'll be back," Cohen says, that great, gravelly voice a low rumble in my ears. "The pain in the ass ones never go away. But thanks for going the extra mile for my dad, Maren. That was really sweet of you."

"No problem." I pause, totally debating if I should fish for some personal Cohen life details. "Are you working late?" Fish it is.

His chuckle becomes a full-on laugh. "Tonight was one of those nights I *wish* I'd pulled an extra shift at work. Have you ever had a date so bad, it makes you contemplate a lobotomy?"

I cradle the phone close to my ear "Brain annihilation, huh? Sorry, but you have to spill now. I'm intrigued. And definitely wondering if I can one-up your story."

"I doubt it." I imagine what his smile looks like, because I can hear it netted over his words. "Unless you have a story where you end up covered in your date's vomit?"

"No!" I cry, pressing my fingers to my lips so I don't laugh. "Really? Was it food poisoning? Oh, poor girl. She must have been so embarrassed."

"Well, maybe she ate something bad. But the half bottle of Tequila she sucked down across a couple double margaritas probably didn't help." He pauses like he's wondering whether or not he should say the next words. "And the, uh, position she was in didn't help."

I feel a blush run over my cheeks and wonder if this conversation is about to go the way of the raucous party I

DEPTHS

can hear through the closed office door. "So, um, she was…"

"She was eager to take the date to the next level in my car. Which is weird, since she didn't make any actual attempt to talk to me while we were together and seemed to think my name was Calvin."

I giggle. "Uh oh. So her last ditch effort to salvage the date wound up a little less romantic than she expected?"

"Unless a puddle of vomit on my lap is what she was going for. I've been told I'm that kind of boring. Is that what the kids are into nowadays?" I love that he had this mad, crazy night, but is still laughing about it.

"Ugh. I don't think I can beat that story. My worst was going on a date with a guy who left me at a party one of his friends' friends threw. I wasn't even that upset about him ditching me, because, frankly? He was a complete dickhole, pardon my French. But I'd driven us to the party, so when he wanted to leave and didn't feel like coming to get me, he stole my keys and took my car home." I grimace at the memory.

Cohen is very quiet on the other end. "He just left you there?"

He sounds pissed. Furious, even. I've never really heard Cohen's voice like that, and we've been in some pretty infuriating situations. Missed orders with customers

61

screaming in his face, employees not showing up leaving departments understaffed at Christmas, deliveries getting sent across towns…all kind of things that would test a saint's patience, and I've never heard him use the tone he's using now.

"Yep. And his friends were all talking about Danish cinema and how the climate changes are actually part of this big multi-layered government conspiracy and tortes are going to be the new 'it' food after people rebel against cupcakes. It was freaking ridiculous." I wait for him to laugh, but the other end of the line is weirdly silent, so I rush to finish, "Thankfully my sister was right around the corner, and she offered to pick me up."

"So he just left you there?" Cohen clarifies, his voice steely.

I feel embarrassed.

I feel like such a fool all over again. Ricky made me feel like a jerk the entire time I dated him, and I wanted the story of that awful night to be…funny or something. But, instead, Cohen makes me feel like an idiot, and I wish I could get off the phone.

"Yep. It wasn't even the first time, either. Look, I'm at this thing for a coworker of mine." I try to make my voice cool and breezy. Not the voice of a girl who gets left places by guys whose interest she can't hold.

"Yeah, of course. I'll let you go. Just, Maren?"

I can hear him hesitate, and I don't want that. I don't want him to stop saying what he needs to say.

"Yeah?" The artificial brightness in my voice makes me squint.

"I don't know about the guy you were with that night, but I hope he was just some random asshole and not someone you dated long-term. I might be sticking my nose in where it doesn't belong and all, but no guy should ever leave a girl alone anywhere. Ever. Even if she vomits on his lap. He should still get her home and make sure she's safe. That's, you know…that's just my opinion."

There are a few beats of silence while I collect my thoughts, and, finally, allow a smile to break across my face.

"You know what, Cohen? You're a stand-up guy. And you deserve way better than a lapful of vomit."

His laugh is the best sound I've heard in a long time. Deep and throaty, and disturbingly sexy. But so genuine and kind. "Thanks, Maren. Now, go enjoy your night off. I won't hog your time anymore."

"Goodnight, Cohen."

"Goodnight, Maren."

I click off and hold the phone hard in my hand for a few

minutes.

Cohen. I wonder what he's like when he's not just a voice on the phone. I wonder what he's like in person.

The screeches from the other room interrupt my Cohen Rodriguez daydreams and send me creeping into the living room. There are several bras piled on the table Officer Miller's dry-humping, his navy blue man-thong practically falling off under the weight of so many dollar bills.

"Where have you been?" Jacinda shouts over the music.

"Just talking to a guy I work—"

"Dildo!" the entire room screams, stopping me in my tracks for a few seconds.

"It's times like these that make a lap full of vomit seem almost appealing," I mutter before heading back out into the throng.

I so need a Jell-O shot or five to get through this night.

***

Two hours later, I'm finally home. My sister texted me twice, just to check in, but I don't text back. I haven't broken the news to her about dropping out of my classes again. She'll blame Dad like she always does. And I get it. It's his fault, partially. And mine, of course. But it's too much to think about right now in the dingy dimness of our apartment, especially since I never did those Jell-O shots after all.

DEPTHS

The daughter of an alcoholic with a string of intoxication-related failures and arrests does *not* tempt fate by drinking even a little and driving.

Dad is snoring on the recliner, his arm hanging over the side, his fingers curled around the glass neck of his Evan Williams bottle like a child clinging to his cherished lovey. I pull it out of his hand and screw the cap on, making sure to tilt it away from me so I don't catch a whiff. It's not that I don't drink, but I loathe the smell of whiskey. Just one whiff will make my stomach roll and churn. Smelling the thing that turns the person you love and respect into a blubbering mess will do that to you.

I throw a blanket over him, one of the dozens my mom knitted before she left. He won't get rid of any of them, even though the weather in our area doesn't really call for blankets most of the year. Also, they make him even more pathetically depressed.

But I guess he likes being a sad sack.

I tuck the fringed end under his chin, the chin that used to be so strong and handsome. It's lost in the extra weight all the drinking added to his body. His skin is pale with smatterings of broken blood vessels and a greasy sheen that always makes him look sweaty and unwashed. He looks old. Pitiful. But still like the dad who used to lie on the floor with me, reading from piles of books until I fell asleep pillowed on his arm.

I blink hard. I want *that* dad back. I want him so badly, I've let dreams slip away left and right on the off chance that maybe he's there, deep down. Maybe he just needs one more night to drink, one more day to mope before he'll stand up and say, "Alright, Pumpkin Pie, let's get the yard cleaned up. Get the lead out." And I'll be here to help him when he does.

Except that fantasy is pretty hard to imagine now that the yard he loved was sold long ago because he couldn't handle the mortgage on his own after the divorce. And all his yard work was done with Mom's complicated diagrams tucked in his back pocket back then anyway. She'd come lean off the deck and say, "Thomas, it looks amazing. I wish I had your green thumb, babe."

And he'd say, "But you got the sugar palm. You married the green thumb, smart girl."

He'd wink and she'd blush and go make some delicious baked thing that would knock us all out. It's weird, that their inside joke would become her business, Sugar Palm Baked Goods, and her business would lead to the end of their marriage.

I tiptoe to the dimly lit galley kitchen, where nothing sweet has ever been cooked, at least as long as Dad and I have lived here. I didn't inherit my mother's sugar palm or my father's green thumb. Did I inherit anything useful or good?

Some days I feel like I'm just the outline of a person, with no real shape or substance.

My sister, Rowan, would tell me to let go of the past. Quit being a martyr. Let Dad face his responsibilities. But she's tough and strong, like our mother. To the point where they both tend to trample other people if it serves their needs.

I'm not like that. Dad and I are softer. Givers. We get bumped and smashed by life, and, while Mom and Rowan could build a ship during a storm and then navigate a steady course home, Dad and I would cling to driftwood for dear life, constantly in danger of drowning.

I grab a bottle of water and some Ritz crackers and head to my room, closing the door tight and dropping my bag on the bed.

My party favors spill out.

Including a tiny silver vibrator and small tube of lube in a Ziploc baggie with Jacinda's card.

I sit on the far end of my bed, munching on crackers and eyeing the sex toys. I've never used one, but I've usually had a boyfriend.

Tonight, I don't have anyone.

I push my crackers away and pick up my phone, flipping to Jason's contact. My thumb hovers over the 'call' button, but I never press it. I go into my photos and run through them until I find the hottest picture of Jason, which is impressively incredible. He's at the beach, his shirt rolled and tossed over one shoulder, his smile so cocky it's a hair away from arrogant jackass. Each glistening, gorgeous muscle shows in high definition as the sun glints off his wet skin.

Every single time I've ever looked at this picture, I've gotten instantly horny, even when I'm enraged at my own traitorous body for that. I focus on the picture and pick up the vibrator, but I don't have any urge at this point to use it, and the weight of that depressing feeling makes me fall back in the bed with a thump.

When did life get so boring and sucky and…lifeless?

I grip the phone tighter in my hand, as an idea suddenly, crazily, presses against my brain and won't shut the hell up.

I go into my messages and push the one I've saved a few times already, secretly.

"Hey, Maren. I hate to bug you, but you know that sheet you sent me? Well, I'm looking at it…"

Cohen's voice is going on and on about columns lining

up and dividends and taxable expenses, but I ignore the words. I just listen to that perfect, sexy, velvet voice.

And press my thighs together. This is faster and wetter than it ever was with Jason's picture. I lie back on my bed and slide my hand down under the waistband of my sensible cotton underwear.

Damn.

I'm more turned on by the sound of Cohen's voice talking about one of the most boring topics on earth than I ever was by Jason in person, even at his sexiest.

"...with the bar graph. That one looks, um, like it's about sofas? I think. I'm reading this wrong, aren't I? I'm sorry to ramble like this on your voicemail, but I need to receive this by tomorrow morning..."

I hold the little silver vibrator up. It glints from the low light of my alarm clock. I put my phone down on the pillow, his voice slipping into my ear like a lover's whisper. I click the vibrator on, move it down, and jump when it buzzes against the skin under my bellybutton. I feel the vibrations low and hard in the center of my body.

I pull all the air in my stale little bedroom into my lungs. His voice is indistinct enough that the words are just a rumble, but their tenor is clear and so damn hot. I press down one inch, another, one more, before I let out a single, tiny whimper.

A tremor bolts through my body. My free hand fists the sheets, my toes curl, and I tilt my head back. Normal breathing has been replaced with a pattern of pants and whimpers. I press that little bit of vibrating silver against my clit so gently, I don't expect to feel anything, but something springs alive in me like a wild animal freed from a cage. My spine lifts off the mattress and bridges under me, and I press harder, the hum rippling out until I can feel the vibrations up my arms, along my neck, on my lips.

I unknot my free hand from the sheet and brush my fingers over my lips to see if they could possibly be shaking the way I think they are. But it's all inside me, all bursting and tearing to explode out.

I turn my head to the side, my whimpers hard and quick and hear his voice, soft, sweet, real, and right in its own secret way.

Cohen.

My secret.

I squeeze my eyelids shut, slide my heels against the blankets and shudder three, four times as a deep, solid orgasm rocks through me. It's over faster than I want it to be, and I'm left feeling slightly hollow. Next to my ear, I can still hear Cohen's voice, and the plan that sounded so sexy

DEPTHS

and daring a few minutes ago now feels kind of dirty. The only other sound is the hypnotic hum of the vibrator, which I flick off and toss aside. I click my phone off, embarrassed.

I should have just called Jason. I flop back on the bed and wonder when life is finally going to right itself. I feel like I've been in a tailspin since my mom finally bailed, and that was freshman year of high school.

I'm getting too old to waste time with people like Jason and jobs like the one I have now. When is life going to start?

I punch and prod my pillow, desperate to get it to a point where I can relax comfortably, but nothing is working the way I want it to. I settle with my neck at a strange angle and reach out to finger the old Polaroid of my family, camping. Rowan has a new fishing pole. I'm pouting, arms crossed over my puffy red vest, because she wouldn't share. Dad's arms are around me, to make me feel better, and Mom, because he could never keep his hands off of her. They seemed so in love.

That's what Mom said in the end to Dad. I remember her standing in the doorway while he cried. She was crying. So was I. Rowan was the only one who wasn't, and even she looked pale and droopy. "I love you, Thomas. I'll always love you. But you can't ask me to choose, because this is part of who I am now. I can't be who I was, and I think

71

that's who you still love."

"Bullshit," my dad sobbed. "You made me choose. You or the band. I chose you. I chose this."

It's painful, even in memory, to picture my dad sobbing. Standing in front of him cored my heart. That was the moment I stepped away from mom and dropped my bags in the hallway.

"I'm staying here. With Dad," I declared.

Mom didn't argue. I think she was relieved. She knew he was in a bad place. We all did. I guess no one knew just how bad. Or maybe no one *knows* just how bad. I've been doing a pretty fair job of keeping my father's secrets, and Mom and Rowan have been busy expanding the business. Which is why I can't ask them for help or money right now. They're under tremendous pressure, and they don't need all this extra worry piled on top.

I want someone in this family to make it, to have it good. I guess my turn will come. Just not yet. Not right now.

Right now I'll take the few simple, secret pleasures I get and deal with the rest.

With that in mind, I click my phone back on and listen to Cohen's message, sinking into the silky softness of his tone as sleep takes over.

DEPTHS

5 COHEN

"You're going to *love* Tracey." Marigold pulls all her long, dark hair into a sloppy bun and drizzles a little bit of oil into a jar.

"Thanks for setting this up, Mrs. Beck—er, Marigold." Deo's mom has been asking me to call her by her first name since Deo and I were out of high school, and I almost always remember.

It's not all that hard, since Marigold is cool and funny and so down-to-earth, it's easy to see her as a friend. But I imagine how hard my mom would slap me upside the head if she ever heard me do it; my parents are old-school, manners-wise. I don't think Deo even knows what their first names are.

"Forget about it. I love getting awesome people together. And here is your scent." She holds a small blue vial under my nose, and I breathe in deep.

There's sandalwood, a tiny hint of something sweet…maybe vanilla, and a last burst of mint. "This is great. What do I owe you?" I reach for my wallet, but Marigold smacks at my hand and shakes her head.

"Don't you dare. Have fun and be careful tonight, sweetie." She hands me the paper bag and kisses my cheek just as Deo trips the bells on the front door.

"Hey, hey, hey!" He runs over and half-tackles me away from his mom. "Geez, kid! You break up with your woman, and I can't turn my back without you trying to scoop up all the ladies in my life."

"Deo!" Marigold rolls her eyes and pulls him in for a hug. "Don't be greedy. You were always such a greedy kid, and it was bad enough when you were an adorable little boy. It's terrible now." She licks a thumb and moves to press it on his cowlick, but he jumps back.

"Woman! That's crossing the line. No more spitting on my hair." He rubs his hands down on his head, flattening his hair for a second before it springs back up.

"Learn to share," she singsongs with a grin. "Cohen was here because he wanted a special mix for his date with Tracey."

"Tracey, huh?" Deo unscrews the lid of a random bottle of oil, takes a whiff, and gags. "I hope you didn't mix any of that crap in. He's already batting out of his league with sexy Tracey. He doesn't need to smell like a damn skunk to top it all off."

"Don't be an idiot all your life, sweetie," his mom says, swiping the vial out of his hand and smiling my way like she can sense my gut-gnawing nervousness. "Cohen, you are

DEPTHS

exactly the kind of sweet, grounded, sexy—"

"Ugh, Mom! Stop!" Deo groans.

"—man she needs in her life." Marigold's smile makes my heart slow down a little.

"What's time's the date, lover boy?" Deo asks.

"Dinner at six. She needs to be home by one for her babysitter."

"Come again?" Deo squints from me to Marigold. "Sexy Tracey has kids?"

"Kid. Just one." I try to keep my voice even, like it makes any difference that it's just one kid. Like one kid doesn't scare the shit out of me and make me feel like I'm in over my head before I even started.

"Sage is an amazing child." Marigold puts her hand over her heart. "A true old soul. I love them, I love you, and I love you." She gets misty eyed and kisses Deo's forehead. "I feel like love is out there, just waiting for you to scoop it up. And, if in the middle of all that love scooping, you wind up doing the blanket hornpipe—"

"Mom!" Deo bellows, sticking his fingers in his ears like a little kid. "Enough. Goddamn, woman! Just when I think a conversation is as awkward as it's going to get, blam! You bring out the extra awkward."

"Well, I have no idea why you're being such a prude,

Deo. It's perfectly natural. Oh! And speaking of natural, I just got this shipment of vegan condoms. Rocko and I haven't had a chance to give them a try—"

Deo just shakes his head and groans.

"—but the customer reviews say they're amazing! Take some on the house. And don't thank me! Just tell me how they worked out so I can pass the info on to my customers."

Marigold holds the small packets out, and I grab them and shove them in my pocket, embarrassed that this is so embarrassing. I'm an adult and safe sex is not something I get all weird about.

But taking condoms from my best friend's mother so I can maybe use them on a date with her friend? I can't pretend to be cool. This is weird.

"Thanks, Marigold. I'll, uh, be sure to let you know. How they work." *I love you like a second mother, but I will never discuss condoms with you. Ever.*

Deo kisses his mom's cheek and drags me out the door.

"Holy shit. I will never be able to apologize enough for her, man. Mom's always been a little nutso, but she's gone off the deep end lately." He walks to my car with me. "So? You're going on a date with a mom?"

"Don't make it weirder than it is for me, Deo. It's not like I hate kids or anything." I actually would love to have a big family someday. Of course, I wasn't planning on it right away. But I also wasn't planning on getting my ass dumped by the girl I'd been with since I was in freaking high school.

"I know it. You'd make an awesome dad and all that. It's just kind of heavy, right?" He leans against my car.

"I guess. But maybe I need someone a little more mature." I think back to the awful mess of my date with Claire.

A huge grin cracks across Deo's face. "Sorry, but I accept zero responsibility for that one, man. You were warned to stay far away. I begged, even. I mean, I feel for you. No guy deserves a lap full of vomit. But she was always a loose cannon, and I knew that even back when I had no standards."

"Yeah." I close my eyes and try to blank on the details of that crazy night. "I guess I got what was coming. If nothing else, I'm excited about meeting Tracey because, seriously, your mom is awesome, and she picks awesome people to surround herself with. So what do I have to lose?"

Deo claps a hand on my shoulder. "Nothing, man. Nothing to lose. I wish you luck. May you use many vegan condoms and not get vomited on."

I can't help laughing as I get in my car and pull out of Marigold's lot. "Thanks. I appreciate it."

"No worries! Being my best friend means you get the

Deo deluxe deal, wisdom and blessings included for free!"

Deo's an ass, but he manages to lighten my mood to the point where I'm not even nervous when I pull up to Tracey's place. Before I can get out of the car, the door opens and a woman backs out, kissing a frowning little girl with a head full of braids.

And then I feel like a total pervert because the first thing I notice is the way this mom's tight jeans hug the most gorgeous ass I've ever laid eyes on. And her legs? Ten miles long and made to look even longer because she's wearing heels at least five inches high. When she turns to come down the walk, my mouth dries up. She's wearing what pretty much amounts to a leather vest, and I can see a little black lace from her bra peeping out...along with some seriously perfect cleavage.

Holy mother...

Tracey is a *mom*. And a friend of Marigold's. I guess I was expecting a sweet-faced woman in a long, flowery dress. Not cheekbones and full, pouty lips poured into leather and tight denim.

Damn.

"Um, hi. Tracey. You must be Tracey. I'm Cohen. It's nice to meet you."

She skips my hand and wraps her arms around me. She

smells sweet with a hint of musk. It's so sexy my knees knock.

"Cohen." She pulls back and her smile is warm and real. "It's amazing to meet you. I'm so glad Marigold set this all up." She glances at my car. "Would it be okay if we took my bike? I hardly ever get to ride anymore. It makes Sage a little nervous. Plus, I'll be honest, I like to take my own vehicle on a first date. I know I have a spare helmet in the garage."

I swallow hard. "Sure." Maybe my voice squeaks. Maybe.

I follow the sway of her hips to the little garage, and, before I can jump in and open the door for her, she's already yanked it open and is purring over a little red Ducati.

"It's beautiful," I manage to get out.

She swings a leg over the seat and presses against it in a way that makes my mind fritz. She strokes up and over the handlebars and rolls her neck. "Mmm. Love this bike." When she turns her smile my way, I'm half sure I'm going to seizure. "Grab that helmet, and we'll get going."

I do what she asks. Does anyone ever tell this gorgeous woman 'no'? I somehow doubt she's ever heard the word.

She secures her helmet and we roll out. I hop off to close her garage door, happy to do her bidding, happy to do anything that makes me useful to her. I hold onto her hips while she buzzes down the streets, the wind whipping through my light shirt, the speed we're racing at making my adrenaline pick up and scream through me.

She takes turns so fast, we dip over to the side, so close to the asphalt, I can smell it. Guys stop at every red light and gawk. Something animalistic in me is proud that she's my date, that I'm the guy on the back of her bike.

We pull into a little bar right by the ocean, and my disastrous date with Claire clicks into high resolution in my mind, making me all kinds of nervous even though this date is nothing at all like that one.

I follow Tracey into the bar and she doesn't even make it to the counter before the bartender has a glass of something dark amber and strong-as-hell slid towards her.

"Make it two, Scotty?" She hands the first shot to me, and her sexy smile does a lot to pedal back Scotty's scowl as he looks my way.

She holds the glass up. "To a night of being free and just a little crazy. Just a little."

We clink and the shot burns down my throat. She closes her eyes and bites her bottom lip as she sighs. "That hit the spot. It's been a long week."

I follow her to a small, private table in the back, and a teenage girl with pink hair rushes over.

DEPTHS

"No way. No way! Tracey Bellington? Scotty said you'd come in when you got back from your Tokyo tour! I am such a huge fan. I love you. Okay, okay." She takes a deep breath and calms down as I look at Tracey and wonder what I'm missing. "I know this is, like, so unprofessional, but..." She holds out her waitressing pad.

Tracey laughs and takes it. "Forget professional. I got fired once for kissing the very handsome drummer of a very amazing folk band that I maybe happened to open for five years later."

"You mean..." The girl fans herself and Tracey hands her the pad back with her autograph, surrounded by little hearts, and winks. "This is...this is so amazing. Can I...do you need...is there anything..."

"Does Roxy still make those amazing mussels? With the white wine sauce and the shallots?"

"Of course. Of course. And I will get those for you right away." The girl turns and runs, and Tracey smiles as her cheeks go bright pink, her big brown eyes on the scratched table top.

"I'm so sorry," I say, feeling like the biggest asshole in the world. "Clearly our waitress is way cooler than I am. What exactly is it that you do?"

"I play violin and do some back-up vocals for The Season

of Release. Don't. I can see you trying to pretend you know who we are." She lifts her eyes and bats her long lashes in my direction. "We are only very marginally successful, and our fan base is mostly…" She glances at our waitress, wiping down the counter with her head turned back like an owl until she sees Tracey look and whips it back around. "Well, you get the idea. I just got back from a very limited world tour."

"That's…that's incredible. That's amazing." I mean it.

This woman is *it*. She's the whole package: confident, passionate, sexy, kind. I'm hands-down amazed to be sitting across the table from her.

She twists her hands together and sighs. "It is and it isn't? It's a mixed bag, if you want to know the truth. I always wanted my career to break out this way, but I never thought about what it would *really* mean. I mean, it's awesome to be on a stage with screaming fans, getting paid to travel."

She spreads her hands flat on the table top. "But leaving Sage for months on end? Having, private pictures of me pop up on the internet? Being hounded by photographers and fans?" She glances up at our waitress, who's rushed over with glasses of ice water and two more shots before she darts away. Tracey's smile is wistful. "Not fans like her. She reminds me of *me* when I was a teenager, so excited and awed by everything. It's the groupies, the fame whores who make me rethink everything."

She shudders, just a slight tremble of her shoulders. "Enough depressing talk." She holds up her shot. "Last one. I'm not about to crash when I have someone as sexy as you on my bike. I need you to make it to my place in one piece."

The shot rolls down the wrong way, and I choke and cough like a madman. Tracey's throaty laugh is sweet and helps dissolve some of my piercing humiliation.

Our waitress brings us the tray of mussels, and watching Tracey eat forces me to lean back and enjoy. There's something so sensual about the way she savors each mouthful, the noises she makes while she's enjoying her food. And when we're done, the band starts up and she grabs my hand.

"Dance with me, Cohen!"

Like I said before, I doubt many people tell this woman 'no,' and I'm not about to start that idiotic trend. I follow her to the dance floor and thank whatever gods allowed me to inherit my parents' decent sense of rhythm.

The band is playing a fast song, and the beat kicks in, deep and frenzied. Tracey puts her hands over her head then pulls them back down her face, her neck, lower, letting them trail along every curve with excruciating slowness. She moves closer, rubbing against me the way she rubbed against the Ducati before we went roaring down the street.

Sweat glistens on her skin, her eyes are closed, her mouth is parted, and her body drags over mine like she has plans that she's going to carry out, no questions. I rub my hands along her shoulders, down to her elbows, then get bolder. Touch her hip. Drag her closer. Tilt her back on my arm and watch the slow, smooth dip of her neck.

Suddenly the music changes. I don't think I would have noticed except for the fact that Tracey has snapped to attention and is staring at the stage. My arms are still loose around her waist, and I follow her line of site.

A guy with a shaved head and a lot of piercings and tattoos looks at her with possessive eyes, nods once, and straps his guitar on.

Tracey presses one hand to her breastplate and shakes her head. "Um, can we go? I'm so sorry. Do you mind? Is it okay?"

"Sure. If you're ready, I'm ready." I get to pay the tab, only because Tracey is so shaken, she's not really paying attention anymore.

Before we get on the bike, she stands up on her tiptoes and presses her mouth to mine, long and sweet and hard all at once. She pulls back, panting, and gasps, "Your place?

Can we go to your place? Please."

I know the answer should be 'no,' but I'm in no position to tell her 'no.' Again, I wonder if she's ever heard it. I can't imagine a guy who could resist her.

So I give her my address. We fly through the cool night and, when we get to my place, she drags me to the front door by my wrist like it's her place.

"Tracey," I say as we get to the door. I have the key in, she turns the knob and presses us into the foyer, kicking the door shut with one heel.

Her mouth covers mine before I can say what I need to say. A few incredible minutes later we stop for a split second so she can tug me back to the bedrooms.

"Tracey," I try again. It's hard to pull away from her.

"Cohen?" She smiles, tries to sound coy, but something about this isn't quite right, isn't the way I want this to happen with her.

Though I do want something to happen with her. Badly.

"That guy at the bar? On stage?"

She blows a short breath out and pulls at my shirt with her fists.

"That obvious, huh?" Her lips curve into a half smile that's got way too much frown peppered in.

"Who is he?" I don't really want to know. I just want to

85

enjoy her in my arms for a few more minutes before this night ends worse than I had hoped.

"A boyfriend. A fiancé. For a few weeks. Almost my husband. But I got cold feet." She presses her lips together. "And I got cold feet for a good reason. But it still hurts to see him and remember all the good stuff." She puts her hands on my face. "Cohen? Sexy, sweet Cohen? Please let me forget Tanner. Just for tonight. Please."

She's definitely never heard 'no,' and it doesn't occur to her that I may be thinking 'no.'

Because, even though I know we shouldn't, I let her lead me to the bedroom. When she kicks off her heels and strips off her leather and denim, I know I should tell her that she probably needs time, that things are obviously unresolved between her and Tanner.

But then she undoes the buttons on my shirt and unzips my jeans. With a flick and a push, we're standing close, almost naked. Her skin is smooth and warm against mine, her hands small and gentle on my back. I kiss her and she moans into my mouth, letting me know how much she wants this, wants me.

My hands go to work and we move from being almost naked to completely naked in short order. She walks me back to the bed, our hands and mouths moving hungrily, our bodies twined together. It's hot, it's sweet, and neither one of us is very patient about it. I reach for my jeans and find one of the damn weird vegan condoms.

Tracey smells so good. She feels so good in my arms, wrapped around me, rubbed against me. And she's whispering things, pleading in a way that makes everything rush too fast. I press deep into her, and it's so freaking good. She feels amazing.

She doesn't look into my eyes, there's nothing sweet or gentle about what we're doing, but if feels so fantastic. I pump into her and think of how she's *not* Kensley; how it's official that there is someone else, and I'm glad it's her.

It's incredible. We fall asleep, she wakes me up kissing my neck, her hand roving down between our bodies, and it starts all over again. By the third time, I'm half-nervous I won't be able to get the job done, but my recent hiatus doesn't seem to have done any permanent damage to my sex drive. When she's finally tucked by my side, warm and satiated, I notice the sun shining warm, rosy dawn light and fall fast asleep, ready to make her breakfast. Ready to meet her little girl. Ready to help her forget the guy she left at the altar. Ready to listen to her music and make her part of my new life.

***

"No more!" Deo begs. "No more of this music! I feel like I should be watching an animal cruelty commercial. This is sad. This is so sad. Whit, my angel, make this madness stop."

Whit plops between us on the couch and hands me a fresh beer. She ropes an arm around my neck and rumples my hair as she answers Deo. "He's sad. Let him be sad."

"I'm so cool with him being sad. Right there. Quietly. So I can ignore him. Explain why I have to listen to all of these whining girls and their fiddles?" He pulls Whit on his lap and kisses her shoulders.

"This music is fucking genius." I would say I'm arguing, but you'd have to put some real effort into presenting your point to make an argument, and I have no energy for that. What I do put effort into is drinking this beer so I can deaden some of my depression.

"It's alright," Deo gripes. "*She* was alright. Take her off the damn pedestal, man. It was one night. One date. I know you never really wanted one, but you had a pretty decent one night stand. Appreciate what you had for what it was and stop acting like you lost the love of your life."

"A one night stand with the perfect girl is like…it's like getting to the airport in Hawaii, then getting right back on the plane and flying home. It's depressing to have been that

DEPTHS

close to paradise without actually getting there." I tip the bottle again.

"Jesus, Cohen. It wasn't that freaking bad. It's more like you landed in Hawaii and spent one incredible night in a pretty nice four star hotel—"

"Definitely a five star hotel," I growl.

"Calm down, man. It's just a metaphor. Anyway, you stayed the night. But you know what? Maybe in the light of day, you would have realized that the hotel wasn't as swank as you thought. Maybe you would have realized that five star hotels aren't your thing. That you'd rather sleep on the beach, you know?" He sits forward, all into this lame metaphor we've got going on.

"So you think I'm more a homeless beach bum than a swank hotel stayer?" I clarify.

Deo throws up his hands. "Yes! You're finally listening! In real life and metaphor. Holy fucking hell, I'm tapped. I'm done. Whit, doll face, help me out here. What do I do with this sad sack?"

Whit tilts her head to the side and considers, her dark eyes squinted. "You need to have a fun date with an escape hatch. You need a double date."

Deo and I both groan and Whit slaps Deo's arm. "Stop it. Both of you. Stop being man-babies. You need to go out with other people so if it's not going well, there's a whole group to pick up the heat. And if it's amazing? There will still be other people to balance it out. It can't get too insane, but it also can't get too intense. Perfect."

"I'm not going on a double date with this whiny asshole," Deo declares, which is fine, because I'm not about to find a nice girl to date only to have Deo's big mouth and lousy sense of humor fuck it all up.

Just when I'm about to say that all to his stupid face, my phone rings.

"I gotta take this." I jump up and head to the back deck.

"Who is it?" Deo calls.

"Maren! From work." I start to close the sliding door behind me.

"Hook her, man." I look back at him as I accept her call. "The way you looked when you saw it was her on the line? I've only ever seen you look that way before a major swell. That's love, dude. That's beach-bum, perfect-for-Cohen love."

Maren says 'hello' for the second time, and I do my best to slam the sliding door on Deo and his endless stupidity.

"Hey, Maren. I'm sorry. I'm at my idiot friend's house. You doing okay?"

"I am. And I did have to tell you that the Reyes account

needs to be looked over tomorrow morning. Unless they want three sectionals, there's an input error on their order, and it's going to production tomorrow morning, so we still have a window to catch it."

"You're a damn angel, Maren, you know that? Seriously. I'm calling Maurice and having him give you a raise. You're a lifesaver." I lean against the deck railing and look into the clear blue sky, relieved that Maren caught the slip-up before the Mrs. Reyes came in and gave me an ass-chewing I'd never forget.

She clears her throat. "Also. Um. This is a little weird. Uh. I know things didn't go the way you…the way you planned. On your last date. And this may be too weird and too soon, so please feel free to say no—"

And it hits me.

Maren is going to ask me out.

Maren.

Sweet, perfect Maren who fixes problems and has this voice that can flip from bedroom-sexy to furniture-ordering-fierce like a switch.

No. No, no, no, no. I want one dream girl, unruined by a clusterfuck of a bad date. Just one. I need her stability in my crazy, drowning world.

She clears her throat a second time. "My

boyfriend…well, he's kind of my boyfriend. It's on and off. It doesn't matter. God, I'm rambling! Okay, my boyfriend got four tickets to the Angel's game, and our friend's ditched last minute. They're *really* good seats, and Jason knows this girl from work who wants to go, but she's single and, um—"

Maren has a boyfriend? An off and on boyfriend? What kind of idiot wouldn't commit to a girl like Maren? And what kind of idiot takes his girl to an Angels' game, rather than a Dodgers'?

Granted, what I know about her is based on months of work phone calls, but I feel like I know her well enough to be sure she's the kind of girl who's a keeper.

Not for me. Obviously. I just want to know that good people, like Maren, are dating other good people. It gives me hope.

Not that I'm feeling all that hopeful right now.

I rake a hand through my hair. I'm not ready for this again. I'm not ready to put myself out there and get my heart trampled on again. I'm not ready for more disappointment.

I glance up and see Whit and Deo through the reflections on the sliding door. I can see his face, watching her while she tells him a story. I see the way his eyes never leave her, the way she gets him to smile no matter what's going on. He kisses her, and I stop watching, 'cause I'm not a perv like

DEPTHS

that.

But I want what they have. I want it bad. And I'll never get it drinking my sadness away in their living room.

Isn't this exactly what Whit just told me I needed? Isn't this kind of like fate slapping me upside the head?

I take a deep breath and just go for it.

"Sure. I'd love to go."

I hope to God this isn't another huge mistake.

6 COHEN

The stadium is crazy crowded, and the fans are already getting rowdy as the sun dims behind billows of dark clouds. It looks like rain.

I wonder if this date will suck for reasons that have nothing to do with me and everything to do with the weather. And I wonder if I can stop thinking about the weather long enough to beat down my nervousness at finally meeting Maren.

And Ally, of course. I'm obviously nervous to meet the girl I'm going on a date with.

I admit, I tried looking Maren up on Facebook, just to have a reference. Asking for her picture straight-out seemed creepy, but I was willing to do some cyber stalking, just so I'd at least be able to recognize her. Unfortunately, there were a million girls with her name, and a ton of them lived in California. There were so many girls who could have been my Maren, I just gave up looking and accepted the fact that I'd have to live with watching for her under the giant red Angels' hat on the left, like she'd told me to.

She told me she's going to be in head to toe Angels' gear, which isn't remotely weird for this insane crew. She'll also be holding a sign like one of those guys who pick you up at the airport.

I head to the hat, my guts clenching tight, and wish I could rewind time. As sucky as things may have been with Kensley in the end, there was this sense of safety, of belonging, and I took that for granted. I had no idea what it meant to have that ripped out from under me, but I know now. And it fucking sucks.

I scan the crowd, but people are moving fast, and I'm not exactly sure what I'm looking for. I didn't want to ask for the details on her appearance, because I didn't want to sound like a dick, like I cared either way, but it was making finding her difficult.

Is she tall? Short? Curvy? Willowy? Blond? Brunette? I can't help smiling a little when it occurs to me just how many ways a girl can look damn good. Deo would be proud of this thought process.

"Cohen?"

It's the voice I know, right away, no questions.

Damn.

Maren.

She's a short little thing, curved in all the right places, dark hair twisted in two shiny braids. Her eyes are wide and a clear, light blue. She smiles like she's thinking something she shouldn't, and for a stupid blip of a moment, I hope she's thinking whatever she's thinking about me. Something about her is…familiar. Like I know her from somewhere. Like I've seen her before. But I wrack my brain and can't think where it might have been.

I'm probably just being a lunatic.

"So you weren't kidding about being all A'ed out." I smile at her jersey, hat, red sneakers, and A's jacket.

"I'm dead serious when it comes to baseball." That smile. It's all over her face, it's making my own lips curl up. It's contagious. "And Ally is going to have a hard time keeping her hands off of you. You are *hot*."

I wish it were weirder than it is that she says that. I wish it felt like she crossed a line.

But it sounds like a girl who has a boyfriend being excited for a girl who needs one.

Maybe Maren's sometimes-boyfriend's friend will be amazing. Too bad I'm having trouble remembering the girl's name already.

"Thank you." I want to tell her that I haven't felt so attracted to a girl in…*ever* maybe. Damn. She's not as movie-star beautiful as Claire. She's not as sexy as Tracey. She's not as polished as Kensley. She just looks…so good. Really damn good.

But you don't say shit like that to a girl with a boyfriend.

"It's so cool to finally meet you-meet you. Even though I

DEPTHS

sort of feel like we already do know each other, you know?" She rocks on the balls of her feet, and I nod but feel like a douche for not saying more.

"It really is. Thank you for using your extra ticket on me."

She stands on her toes so she can stretch enough to fish the tickets from the front pocket of her tiny shorts. I reach out for the one she holds in my direction. "I'm so glad you made it. Ally and Jason get along really well, but I feel like it might have felt awkward for her, you know?"

"Mmmhmm." I follow her into the stadium and try not to stare at her ass.

Funny how many times we've talked on the phone and I never had any idea how she looked. But now it's been ten minutes since I met her, and I feel like I can't remember what it was like to not know the long line of her neck or the fact that she has freckles across her nose and next to her ears.

When she comes to our row, I nearly knock her over because she stops short and just stares. It's always a little strange to meet new people, but, right now, there's a pointed awkwardness in the air that has nothing to do with a lack of introductions.

The asshole I assume is her sometimes-boyfriend is getting pretty snugly with the girl I assume is the co-worker.

The girl at least has enough shame to look guilty. The guy stares up at Maren almost like he's daring her to say something about how his arm is around some other girl's waist.

I'm a fairly laid-back guy, but my fucking hackles are up. Maren goes all pink and looks painfully embarrassed, which makes my temper spark big time.

"So, um, Jason, Ally, this is Cohen."

Ally jumps up, and Jason doesn't bother to hide the way his hand lingers on her hip as she moves away from him.

"So nice to meet you. Are you a baseball freak like Maren?" She tosses a look over her shoulder at Jason, like they're sharing a joke.

At Maren's expense.

"I am a baseball freak," I admit coolly. "But I think Maren has me beat by a mile." I look right at Maren, not giving a shit if I'm making things even more awkward. "And I think girls who get all into baseball are sexy as hell."

If she was pink before, she's a shade away from boiled lobster now. "Um, anyone want drinks? Food?"

"Sit," Jason barks, the same time I say, "Sure."

She looks between us and takes a deep breath. "Get stuff later," Jason says.

I ball both my hands into fists and beat the fury back. I

DEPTHS

can't go ape shit because a girl I just met in real life and her sometimes-boyfriend agree to not get snacks at a ball game.

Because that's what this is.

It's not that I feel a way I never expected to the minute I saw Maren. It's not that I think her sleazy sort-of boyfriend is probably screwing around with this Ally brat. It's not that I'm going fucking rage-blind with jealousy. Nope. Couldn't be that at all.

"So, what do you do?" Ally asks, trying to make it look like she's not glancing over at Jason every other second.

"My parents own a furniture store. I help manage it." I can tell from the way she raises her eyebrows just slightly that she isn't impressed. "What do you do?"

"I'm in college right now. I do part time work as a secretary at Bingham and Walters." She twirls a little piece of her hair like she's sending an SOS Jason's way. He's too busy hissing something low and quick in Maren's ear. What the fuck is he saying to her? "Jason is the corporate finance manager of the entire department. The youngest one they've ever hired in that position, you know."

I don't know. And I don't give a shit what this prick's position is or how young he was when he got it. What I do care about is the way he's shaking his head at Maren, like he's disgusted with her.

That I care about way fucking more than I should.

"Are you okay?" Ally asks, her face blocking my view of Maren and Jason. "You look kind of pissed. Is it the game? Jason was getting all bent out of shape because the Tigers managed to steal second, but the Angels will bounce back. They always do."

She's trying to be cheerful. She's trying to make this less of a clusterfuck than it is, but, for once, I'm not interested in being the nice guy. I have no clue where this insane overprotective vibe came from, but once it rips out, there's nothing I can do to shut it back down.

"I'm actually a Dodgers fan," I say a little too curtly, and watch Ally's face fall.

It's so not me. I'm usually a peace keeper. A good guy. Not a raging lunatic about to jump over some chatty ditz to throttle a guy I hardly know for looking at girl I just met the wrong way.

Just when I'm about to stand, Maren beats me to it. She's clamping her jaw and breathing hard and fast.

"Don't get mustard on my hotdog. I hate that." Jason's eyes are small and mean, like he knows exactly what a dickhead he's being to her and enjoys every second of it.

"Should I go with Maren?" Ally asks, moving to get out of the way as Maren rushes by, knocking her in the shoulder.

DEPTHS

"Nah. I told her what you wanted." He pats the seat Maren just left and Ally slides over. "Hey, where are you going?" he calls to me.

Fuck this guy.

I don't bother to answer, and it takes me a few minutes of weaving through the bottlenecked crowds before I reach Maren, trembling in the concession line.

"Hey." Now that I'm standing in front of her, I have no idea what to say. She's staring at the toe of her bright red Chuck, her eyelashes fluttering rapidly. I reach one hand out and move a finger along her knuckles. That tiny brush of a touch seems to jolt her out of her thoughts.

"Cohen." My name from her mouth is sweet. "What a freaking mess. I'm so sorry. This was a bad idea."

I shake my head. "It's alright."

"You're just being nice." She yanks her ball cap off, rolls it up, and stuffs it in her back pocket. "Jason can be—" She pauses like she's trying to find a nice way to say that her sometimes-boyfriend is an asshole. "—an asshole," she finally says.

I can't help laughing. "I've dealt with lots of assholes. Remember the Rickmans?"

Her eyes have a lot of green in them. And she has nice, plump lips. I love how they look when she smiles. "Ugh!

Yes! Remember he ordered that hideous orange sectional, and then they needed it moved *seven* times in a month? I think his wife must have had a thing for one of the moving guys."

"Yep. He wasn't even the worst. So, I'm alright with assholes." I watch her twine her hands around one another, nervously. "Strike that." Her eyes fly up to my face. "I'm fine with assholes when they're being assholes to me. I'm not all that cool with assholes who upset the coolest girl I know."

She inches toward the concession window and chews on her lip. "Thank you. Really, thank you. But don't do that."

"Do what?" I love how much smaller she is than me. How I could tuck her head against my chest and rest my chin on the crown.

"Do that thing where you come riding up like some awesome knight-in-shining-armor because I'm being all damsel-in-distress." She tugs the elastics out of her braids and pulls her hair loose. It falls down around her shoulders in shiny waves, and the air suddenly smells like coconut and salt...like the beach. "You did it that time on the phone, too."

I try to remember the phone call she's talking about, but, instead, my mind flips to Maren in a bikini on the beach and short-circuits for a few quick seconds.

"I just hate seeing someone as rad as you are with someone…who's an asshole. Your words, not mine." I hold my hands up and grin.

She tries to grin back, but it falls flat. Suddenly she squares her shoulders and looks me right in the eye. "You know what? I sometimes hate being with him."

I'm not sure how to respond, but it winds up that I don't need to, because she's plowing ahead.

"I sometimes hate him. I hate how arrogant he is. A year and a half ago, we had a good thing going, and then he got promoted, and he became this monster. I broke up with him, and promised myself I wouldn't go back to him…I should have followed through with that."

"Yeah?" I lean closer to her. "You think so?"

Her eyes crackle with a fire that makes her even more gorgeous, and, instead of answering me, she turns to the concession attendant. "I'll take a hotdog, extra mustard and a beer. Lots of ice." She must sense the horror on my face, because she turns towards me and puts a reassuring hand on my arm. "Don't judge, okay? I'm not going to drink a beer with ice. It's for… Well, you'll see."

And she winks. That wink tips everything to the side. I don't give a shit if she has an almost boyfriend. I don't give a shit if I was supposed to be here for a date with another girl. And I don't give a shit if this is Maren, the cool girl I talk to on the phone at work and don't want to mess things up with. That wink means trouble, and I intend to follow it wherever it may lead.

Especially if Maren's hot little self is doing the leading with a stomp of her sneakers. I follow all the way to the bleachers where Jason has his mouth too close to Ally's neck while her hand is on his knee.

Maren continues down the aisle and catches Jason and Ally off guard. She shoves the hot dog at him and I clench my fist, waiting for him to go off on her so I have an excuse to pummel this douche once and for all. But he doesn't. He tosses the hot dog onto the cement and stands up, but not before grabbing the cup of iced beer and downing it in two gulps. The fire extinguishes from Maren's eyes, and she seems to shrink a little.

Just when I thought my hatred for Jason couldn't get any more intense, a whole new slew of justifications for kicking his ass erupt in my brain.

"This game blows. I can't believe how bad the Angels suck tonight. We wanna go have some drinks and appetizers over at O'Briens."

Maren's top lip twitches upward in an obvious snarl.

She's seriously adorable, but has zero game face. "You guys want to leave?"

"Appetizers!" Ally yips and jumps up and down like a lap dog excited for its afternoon treat.

"Well, yeah, all of us. Let's go chill and give Ally and Carlo a chance to get to know each other." Jason stands up and rubs his hand along the small of Maren's back. She doesn't shrug away from his touch, and I don't really understand why, but it's not really my place to, I guess.

"It's Cohen," I say. For the love of fried cheese why is my name so hard for everyone to remember? "And, O'Brien's shut down a few months ago."

"What else is nearby?" Maren asks, her eyes trained on mine.

"They had the best potato skins," Ally says. This girl really wants an appetizer something serious.

"My place isn't far," I say. "And, I have a house full of junk food."

It's a side effect of the breakup. I tossed all of Kensley's wheat germ and tempeh, and, instead, stocked up on corn dogs and frozen pizzas topped with bacon. I've never eaten like this in my life, and I feel sort of gross doing it, but if it'll get Maren over to my house—even with her asshole boyfriend—I'll offer it up.

"Your place? Yeah. That'd be cool, right Jason?" Maren is slouched against Jason, his arms wrapped around her waist. It's like she's forgotten every ounce of anger she had for him just a few minutes ago.

This could be a problem.

When she looks up at him, though, his eyes are fixed on Ally's rack.

"My place it is," I say, reaching over and clutching Maren's tiny wrist. Because I may be reserved, and not take chances, but Jason is an asshole and Maren is my friend, and now that I've met her, something about her tells me that she's worth risking a little drama.

7 COHEN

"Holy shit, Cohen, you live here?" Maren kicks her shoes off and holds them the rest of the way. "Like, you told me that you lived near the beach, you didn't say *on* the beach. This is incredible."

She sinks into the sand a little with each step and looks even tinier than she did at the ballpark.

"Yeah, man, this is pretty impressive," Jason says. He's the last person on earth I give two shits about impressing. "I bet you get a ton of play having a place like this." He laughs, proud of his stupid joke.

I pause with my key in the door. Jason's wrong, of course. Kensley was the only woman I've ever had here. Well, other than my sisters or Whit, but none of them count for obvious reasons. I bought this place with the money I made from last year's expedition with Deo. Deo's dad does that sort of thing for a living and had a good tip, so Deo and I sailed up the Coast to Northern California in our crappy boat and dove for treasure like a couple of pirates. We didn't expect to make out as well as we did, but it ended up setting us both up pretty well. Whit and Deo are spending a fortune on their upcoming wedding, and I bought this place and socked a good bit away. It feels awesome to be able to do it, even if financial security is boring according to Kensley.

"So, this is home," I say as I push the door open.

It immediately feels strange to have other people here. Jason marches over to the shelves of alphabetized DVDs and starts pulling them from the shelves and cramming them back in wherever there's an open space. Those spaces allow for more DVDs to be filtered in when I buy them *without* having to reorganize them all. He's just made several hours of work for me in the two minutes he's been here.

I hate him more and more with each second that passes.

Ally hunches awkwardly in the corner near the ship's wheel that's mounted to the wall. Her expression might pass off as bored, but I can see the daggers she's shooting in Maren's direction.

Maren.

She's sitting at the island in the kitchen, hair mussed from the braids she'd pulled out earlier and the humidity in the air.

"Can I get you a drink?" I ask her.

She's the only thing that doesn't feel out of place right now. I had figured it'd feel weird as hell having another attractive girl here for the first time. But Maren, she fits right in. Probably because we're friends. Longtime friends, technically, if you count all the time we've logged on the

DEPTHS

phone.

Yep. Just friends.

"I'll have a shot of Jager if you have it," Jason pipes in from across the room as he crams the *Godfather* boxed set in between *Pineapple Express* and *Pulp Fiction*. I cringe.

"Sorry, dude, haven't kept that around since I was in college," I say without a twinge of actual sincerity. Jason is one hundred percent predictable. What grown man shoots Jager at home with his girl around? I'd never have to have a drop of alcohol in me to appreciate Maren.

Fuck, I need to stop thinking like that.

"Wine? White?" Maren finally says. Her voice is soft, uncomfortable, and I hate that for her.
I nod, grab a chilled bottle of Pinot Grigio, and pass her a heavily poured glass.

"You okay?" I ask.

She runs her palm across the zebrawood counter top. "This is incredible. All of this, Cohen. You should be really proud of your home."

I shrug. "Thanks. Though it was a lot of luck that Deo and I made out the way we did on that dive last summer. Otherwise, I'd still be squatting at Mama Rodriguez's place."

Maren lets out a tiny laugh around the gulp of wine she

just drank. "Please. We all know you're only working for your folks to help them out of a bind. If it weren't for the economy tanking, you'd be off doing something you love."

"I love my family," I say before I can stop myself, because it sounds douchey and weak, but it's true.

Her eyes are wide and this soft blue, like the ocean in the spring, right when the bite is gone from the water, and they flick to my face over the rim of the wineglass. Her words are half muffled behind it. "I know you do. It's one of the things I like best about you."

Something. I need to say something to that, but all I do is nod like an asshole while she puts the glass down and runs one finger around the rim in quick, nervous circles.

"Ahoy?" Ally says from across the room, pointing to the ship's wheel. "What is this thing for?"

"Yeah, man, what are you, a pirate or something?" Jason makes a hook with his finger and squeezes one eye shut, and he and Ally explode into laughter that I don't fully understand.

Which is a relief. Something tells me not quite grasping their humor is a good thing.

Maren rolls her eyes, and I just smile at her, loving that there's this feeling when she's in the room, like she belongs and always has. Like I never want her out of this room again.

DEPTHS

Her boyfriend is sitting right across from me. I gotta turn that kind of thinking off and fast.

"It's like a talisman," I explain, and leave it at that.

Or I intend to leave it at that. Except Ally and Jason stare back at me, blinking. Stumped.

"It's, you know, for good luck, or hope. It's supposed to bring good fortune," I say, hoping they'll understand at least one explanation.

"Right, and he lives at the beach, so you know, it sort of goes," Maren says, her voice dripping with annoyance.

"If you say so." Jason shrugs and raises his eyebrows. "Hey, if it's supposed to be a good luck charm, maybe it'll bring you a babe like Maren." I cringe as he reaches over and squeezes her ass. "How about that drink?"

I hand him a glass of Maker's Mark. There's no way I'm wasting the Pappy's on him.

"I think it's beautiful," Maren says, cupping her glass close to her chest and looking at the ship's wheel like she's feeling exactly what I'm feeling: that she wishes we could hop a boat and sail away from these assholes.

"You're beautiful, doll." Jason crosses the room and sets his already empty glass down on the counter next to her.

"Hit me with another, bro," Jason says without looking my way as he taps his glass with his knuckle. My fist curls around the neck of the bottle tight enough that I have to force myself to loosen it.

If I need to kick this prick's ass later, it'll be easier to do without a bloody palm.

"You don't want to slow down?" Maren says under her breath, her lashes shadowing her eyes.

Jason ignores her.

"Sure thing," I growl as I hand him his drink and offer one to Ally, who declines. I hand her a bottle of water anyway.

I fill my own glass with bourbon and toss it back quickly while I watch Jason trace circles on Maren's back. Ally is on the couch looking somewhere between bored and pissed. What am I doing?

"You guys want to go out back?" I ask, but Jason's already walking across the room and picking up one of my gaming controllers.

"You got the new *Call of Duty*?" he asks, and Ally perks up. Maren groans.

"Yeah." Deo and I play. Not obsessively. Sometimes obsessively. It's not necessarily something I drag out when I have a girl over. For one thing, there's only two controllers. I point that out.

"That's alright. Maren hates this kind of stuff anyway,"

DEPTHS

Jason says, flicking on the TV and grabbing a controller. "You wanna play, man?" he asks reluctantly, eyeing Ally.

How kind of him. To offer to let me play my own game at my own house.

"Uh, no thanks. Help yourself though." I glance at Maren, but she's looking like she might be making a wish that involves huge holes and getting sucked into them.

Weird, but the thing I hate the most about Jason is the way Maren seems to feel like she has to apologize for him.

"Get over here, Al," Jason orders, and Ally giggles, plops too close to him on the couch, and takes the controller he holds her way, bumping his shoulder as the game loads up, the volume turned on high.

She's not my girlfriend, so the whole scenario doesn't bother me. Or shouldn't. The thing is, Jason is Maren's boyfriend, no matter how much I wish he wasn't, and it's just dick the way he's cozied up to Ally right in front of Maren's face.

We watch in silence for a few minutes. Jason was wise enough to drag the Maker's Mark over to the couch, so, with a cheap girl at his side and some cheap liquor in his glass, the douche seems like he's content to make a night of it in front of my video game console.

I look over at Maren, her face a perfect blank.

"Hey, you want some fresh air? My head's pounding," I say.

She glances at Jason and narrows her eyes, then smiles at me. I usually love seeing her smiles, but this one reeks of revenge, and there's no way I'm cool with being her ammo against Jason.

"I'd love to go walk," she says loudly, but Jason is too busy screaming with triumph as he and Ally score a helicopter and blast through the CG landscape.

"C'mon." I grab an extra hoodie on my way out, and, sure enough, Maren shivers the second we step onto the sand and feel the first whip of ocean breeze. I hold it out to her wordlessly.

"What's that?" she asks, staring like she's never seen outerwear before in her life.

"That is a hoodie, which I guessed you'd need because that Angels shirt, besides hurting my soul, is not going to keep you warm." I press it closer to her. "The Angels find so many ways to suck, don't they?"

She yanks the jacket away and inspects it. "I was afraid for a second it might be a Dodgers jacket, in which case, I'd have to freeze to death, because I'd never let it touch my body." She slides her arms in the over-long sleeves and flips the hood up over her tousled hair, grinning at me. "Thank you."

"For not grabbing the awesome blue hoodie that was right next to that one?" I ask.

She's still smiling, but it looks like it might slide off her face at any second. "Thank you for thinking to grab me a jacket. That was sweet." When I shrug, she pokes me with her elbow. "I guess you're pretty nice. For a Dodgers fan, of course."

We walk along the wave line, jumping to the side to avoid getting too soaked.

She presses her hands deep into the jacket pockets and says, "So, about Jason—"

"Hey," I interrupt. "Let's not talk about Jason right now, okay?"

"That bad, huh?" She shakes her head. "I'm so sorry—"

I'm not usually a big interrupter, but I have to cut her off here. "Don't."

"What?" I can't see the exact color of her eyes in the near darkness, but I can tell they're wild and desperate.

"Don't ever feel like you have to apologize for Jason. You're not him, you're not his keeper. If I'm pissed that he's acting like an asshole, that has zero to do with you." I let my feet sink into the damp, receding sand as a fresh wave gets ready to break in.

I wonder if she's going to argue on his behalf, maybe say something about them being a couple or whatever, but she doesn't. "I didn't realize you had a sister who was a lawyer," she says instead.

It's way out of left field, but it's not talking about Jason Though, speaking of assholes...

"Yeah. Lydia. What made you think of her?" I ask, trying to see her face around the hood.

She pushes the cloth back, and I think her face might be even more gorgeous in the moonlight, if that's possible. "You told me your dad said I remind him of Lydia."

I groan. Awful comparison. "You are nothing like my sister," I say. *You are nothing like any sister of mine, thank God,* I think, *Because otherwise, all the dirty things I've been thinking about you tonight would be pretty damn horrible.* "My dad just meant that you're super smart and driven."

Maren snorts. "Hardly. Funny thing is, actually, Lydia sounds a lot like my sister, Rowan. Super smart, super driven. She has a masters in business already, top of her class. She runs my mother's bakery."

"I had no idea your mom had a bakery." I try to think if Maren ever mentioned her mother before, but I don't remember it if she did. "Lydia's a lawyer, and my parent's kind of act like she walks on water."

Her smile is very real this time, and very proud, in a way. "Can you blame them? You guys are all so amazing. You especially. Your parents must be so damn proud of you."

I shrug, pretty much loving hearing Maren's high opinion of me from her own mouth. "I don't keep them up at night, you know. But it was more like they expected me to do what I'm doing. They just want me to live and die for the business. They wanted that for my brother, Enzo, too, but he basically told them it was never happening and took off."

"They're lucky they have you." Her hand brushes against mine, but she pulls back fast.

"I guess." I stick my hands in my pockets. "Enzo is kind of drifting right now, so it's not like I want to have his life. But he never had a girl dump him because he's boring. My brother is one of those people who could start a cult or run for president. He's just...it's hard to explain. He's got, like, this weird charisma."

"You have charisma," Maren protests, but she's just being sweet. "So, you have four siblings?"

"Yep. Lydia, the brain. Enzo, the fucking prophet." We both laugh. "Gen is the family basket case. And Cece, my favorite sister, is in a PhD program for her women's studies degree. She's actually home for a break now. I gotta get home to see her."

Maren's shoulders seem to slump a little. "It sounds great. You guys sound super tight."

"You don't see your sister so much?" I ask. I get that. Lydia flits in and out, breaking Mom's heart on half the holidays because she's too busy skiing in Vail to come home for Chanukah or off on another Caribbean getaway with her girlfriends over Passover. Even Enzo is better about showing up for the big stuff.

"Hardly ever in the last few years." Maren wades out a little farther than is comfortable. She's going to freeze if she doesn't come back.

She doesn't say anything else about her sister, and, when a rough swell comes in, it looks like she's going to fall over. I dart into the water and grab her.

We stand in the middle of the cold ocean, lapping with more dangerous intensity as the tide rushes, my arms around her, her face tilted up to look into mine, the hood knocked back when I pulled her close.

"Your pants," she says, her lip shaking, from cold or fear or what I don't know.

"Forget them. Are you okay?"

She nods, but the waves suck back, and she almost loses her footing again, grabbing onto my jacket with her small hands. "I'm sorry."

"Don't apologize," I tell her for the second time tonight.

We walk back out of the waves, and takes my hands in hers, her fingers so cold, they have to be numb. "We need to go in. You need to change or you'll freeze."

I want to tell her that I don't give a fuck how cold I am, because I want to be alone with her, so I'll put up with any amount of discomfort. I want to tell her that I am thinking of taking off my pants, but that's because I want to get naked with her, right here if I thought she'd agree. I want to tell her that she has a mouth that makes me think of sex every time she smiles or purses her lips or sips wine.

But I say, "I'm cool."

She licks those lips, the ones I've been imagining licking, nipping, feeling pressed all over my body. Good thing I'm half soaked with frigid ocean water, because otherwise, I'd have an uncontrollable hard-on.

"I should get back to Jason."

Her eyes are apologizing, but the words piss me off anyway. Go back to what? Watch him flirt with Ally? Feel some twisted sense of shame every time he opens his stupid mouth and something idiotic comes out? Back to some asshole?

Back to Jason instead of here with me.

Pissed off as I might be, I'm glad she has the good sense to suggest it. It's the right thing to do.

"Let's head back," I say.

When we get back in, the game is on the home screen, blaring through the weirdly quiet house.

Ally is balled up on the couch, snoring lightly, but I don't see him. I make my way upstairs and almost trip over his sprawled body. At first I assume he's dead, but I look close and see that he's breathing.

Jason's passed out. Unbelievable. I mean, what did I expect after those four generous glasses of booze, but shit. I head back down and tell Maren, who starts pacing at the foot of the stairs, her fingers linked together nervously.

"What am I supposed to do?" she finally says. "I mean, what is he? *Fifteen?* Passing out. I'm so sorry about this, Cohen, I feel like such a complete jerk."

"It's fine. No sweat at all."

"But, Jason drove. Even if I could get him into it, there's no way he'd let me drive his car home. Ever."

I seriously hate this guy.

"Just stay here," I say.

"Cohen, I can't. It's too weird. Right?" Maren says.

"Nope, it's fine." Okay, so it's a little weird. But there's no way in hell he's going to be able to walk to the car, let

DEPTHS

alone drive. And there's no way I'm hauling him downstairs. Jason stumbled upstairs like a drunken fool to do who knows the fuck what and passed out on the sofa in the loft. Maybe he and Ally had an argument? I don't even want to know. I head back to the living room and toss a throw blanket over Ally. She may be a sneaky little brat, but I'm nothing if not hospitable.

Damn my parents and all those manners they drilled into my head.

"Where should I... Where should I sleep?" Maren licks her lips, and I try to read on her face what she's feeling, but it's a thousand different things: regret, embarrassment, exhaustion. I hate that this is the way she's reacting to the first time she came to my house.

Honestly, before tonight, I never pictured Maren at my house at all. Now? I hate that she's not happy here, even if it has nothing to do with me. And I hate the thought of the house empty of her, but that's probably the bourbon and my general loneliness taking over my brain.

"You can take my room. Um, the mattress is the best, and I can hook you up with clean sheets, of course. I'll crash in the spare room."

"No. No way. There's nice and then there's just crazy. I will be *more than* happy to take the spare room. You should

121

sleep in your own bed. Of course." She leans so close to me, I catch that coconut smell and have to reach one hand out to steady myself on the wall.

"Nope." I shake my head and my voice drops. "You're my guest, and I'm not letting you sleep in the guest room. I won't be able to get any sleep leaving you on that mattress." She slides her hand along the smooth wood of the banister, but she's looking at my arm. I want her to touch me so badly, I know I need to end this and get to the damn guest room now.

"You're sure?" Her voice is barely a whisper.

"The guest room is better than fine," I assure her.

I leave out the part about how the spare room only has a blow-up mattress crammed in the closet because it's the one room in the house that isn't put together yet. I usually crash at my parents' or Deo and Whit's. I don't have guests...or didn't until now.

And now that I've had her here as a guest, I'm feeling all beast in the castle. I hate the idea of her going tomorrow and tonight's not even over.

She takes her hand off the banister and reaches out, her fingers hot on my skin, her eyes dark and sexy as hell. "Okay. But don't worry. About the sheets, I mean. We're all tired, and I'm not a germaphobe or anything. I really appreciate this, Cohen. I didn't expect things to turn out this way. I feel really bad about everything." Maren motions to Ally with her chin, but her eyes don't break contact with mine.

I clear my throat, rub my neck, look away before she and I lock more than eyes and I'm in deeper than I need to be.

"No sweat. Room's up at the top of the stairs to the left. Get some sleep," I say, managing to keep my voice steady. Maren nods and avoids my eyes like she agrees that we should stop before…whatever might happen happens.

Damnit.

She turns away from me, and I watch that sweet little ass twitch its way up the small staircase. "Oh, Maren?"

She stops and turns to me with a hopeful look in her eye that shouldn't be there. Not when her boyfriend is sleeping twenty feet away.

Regret chews through me, and, for a single second, I consider throwing caution to the wind and scooping her into my arms so I can join her in my king sized bed.

But I don't. I can't. She's worth more a cheap toss while her dickhead boyfriend sleeps in drunk oblivion. If this ever goes anywhere, it will because it's right: right time, right intentions, right everything.

Because, if this is going to happen, I want it to last.

If it's going to happen.

I know it's probably the bourbon talking, but, damn, I want it to happen more than I've ever wanted anything before.

But it can't. Not yet. I hope she can read the regret in my eyes when I tell her, "There's some shirts and stuff hanging in the closet. Help yourself to something to sleep in."

She presses her lips together and nods. "Thank you."

I stand on the stair long after she shuts the door quietly behind her, gripping the banister like I'm planning to tear it out of the fucking wall, Jason's snores rubbing my nerves raw. Finally I head to the guest room where the insistent whine of the air mattress motor is the only sound in the room. Which is fine by me, because I need something to dull the thoughts of Maren that run through my head in a way they really shouldn't.

8 MAREN

I'm wearing his shirt. It's a plain white tee with a V-neck, and it hangs loose over my curves and just grazes the bottom of my underwear. It's comfy and stretchy, like a warm, enveloping second skin. And it smells like him. Just like him.

Also the sheets smell like him.

Clean and crisp with a tiny hint of salt. Exactly the way your skin smells after a day in the ocean waves. I pull the sheets up to my chin and breathe deep, letting the scent of Cohen slide into my nostrils and down to my lungs.

I should be curled up next to Jason. I didn't even check to make sure he was covered or that he had a pillow before I climbed into this big king bed, ten thousand times more comfortable than my tiny twin. Cohen went ahead and checked on Ally, and she's a perfect stranger to him. What kind of girlfriend does it make me if I didn't take basic care of my boyfriend? Because, if I'm being honest, I don't really care.

I don't.

Why am I even with him? At this point it's more a bad habit I'm too far in to break. Jason has been around through so much change in my life, and I guess I've been addicted to the fact that he's the one stable aspect I've been able to count on. Not that Jason's the paradigm of accountability...but he's there when I call, when I need someone to make me forget the rest of my life, spiraling down the drain so fast, I don't know what to do about it.

Lord knows my drunk ass father with his shakes and bourbon-laced sweats hasn't been any kind of anchor. Neither have my tight-ass mother and tighter-assed sister, who spend too much time worrying about the drape of their fondant and the ratio of vanilla to alcohol in their authentic Colombian vanilla extract to spare a second to ask me how I'm doing.

Nope.

I have no anchor at all, and I'd pretty much convinced myself that I liked being adrift. That it was fine to be nowhere and have no one. That traveling from port to port was the way I preferred it, thank you very much.

I could have kept the entire ruse up for a long time if I hadn't docked in Cohen's cozy little house, where, suddenly, for no explainable reason, I felt like I belong. I belong, and I never want to leave, goddamnit.

"I belong," I whisper to the light green walls of his bedroom, the color hidden by shadows but bright in my memory. "I belong here."

Who cares if it's crazy talk? Who cares if he hears me?

DEPTHS

I'm so happy to be telling the truth for the first time in I can't remember how long, I just don't give a shit how crazy my words are.

The problem with thinking out loud is that it's messy. It's gets your brain all jumbled and hungry. And a hungry brain, at least in my case, always leads to a hungry stomach.

I thought I'd eat a nice hot dog with sauerkraut and mustard at the game, but that never happened. And I'd drunk plenty at Cohen's house, but there was no eating, so my head is swimmy with hunger, and my stomach growls and twists in knots.

I slide out of his bed, tug down on his shirt so it covers more of my red and pink lace underwear, and pad to the kitchen quietly. Cohen's kitchen is organized in a masterful way, each thing put in the place where you'd be most likely to look for it. I find what I'm looking for in a few seconds, and there are eggs sizzling on the blue flame of his stove in minutes.

I almost whip the frying pan off the stove to use as a weapon when I hear a throat clear behind me.

But my killer instinct quiets down because it's just Cohen.

Cohen. The guy who owns this house, this cozy, put-together kitchen, and these eggs sizzling in this pan.

127

"Cohen." I put one hand against the white cotton of his shirt and feel his heart leaping under my palm.

"Maren."

It's just my name, nothing special, but the word falling from him mouth makes my breath hitch. *Say it again*, my brain screams. *Say it after you kiss me, say it while you're holding me.*

I didn't think I'd get a second chance to be alone with him after he jumped into the ocean to keep me from going under, and I'd acted like an ass.

Why hadn't I kissed him when his arms were around me, making me feel safe and warm even in the middle of the dark, crashing ocean waves?

Maybe because the attraction I feel for him is so strong, it's almost harsh, like heavy grit sandpaper. It grates against my already frayed nerves and makes me feel overexposed.

"I'm sorry." I use the spatula to point to the eggs, hissing merrily in the pan. "I was so damn hungry. And you had a full dozen. I only cooked..." I look down in the pan and my voice drops to an embarrassed whisper. "Four."

He leans against the doorframe, arms crossed, muscles bulging, smile a mile and a half wide. "Four, huh? You bulking up?"

I let my lips curl into a return smile. "Maybe. You don't

know my life, Cohen."

"Are you a secret cage fighter?" His voice slides up and down my spine like a cube of ice, and I shiver and want more. Now.

"Maybe." Maybe I press the shirt down at my hips so it's tight against my breasts and my nipples strain against the thin white fabric, just to see how he'll react.

Do I imagine the way his pupils grow huge and dark? Well, even if that's just my imagination running wild, there's nothing imaginative about the way he rakes his eyes up and down my body.

Usually a hungry look like that would make me uncomfortable, but Cohen's makes me feel the opposite. I feel like showing off. I turn so my ass is in full view, and I know damn well how good the little bits of lace that barely cover my curves look. I take back every nasty threat I ever hurled Jacinda's way. I can feel Cohen's eyes burning on my skin, and that makes the quarter of a paycheck I handed over to Jacinda in return for lots of lacy, sexy lingerie well worth it.

So worth it.

I should be feeling much worse. If we both listen over the sound of the frying eggs, we'd be able to hear Jason snoring. The sound of my boyfriend, no matter how annoying it is, should be enough to shame me into not showing off my ass for Cohen.

But then I think about Ally sprawled on the couch and how she and Jason didn't even bother to hide their attraction this entire exhausting day.

Well, I'm sick of hiding mine. And I'm more attracted to Cohen than I've ever been to anyone before.

"Cage fighting doesn't seem tough enough for you." Cohen heads to the fridge, pulls out a loaf of bread, and pops four pieces in the toaster. He comes to my side, standing so he's just over my shoulder, his body close enough to mine that I feel the heat of his skin at my back.

My breath comes out in quick, heady pants. "So what would be tough enough then?" I ask, turning my head. My hair brushes his jaw, a few pieces getting caught in the scratchy scruff of his five o'clock shadow.

He should take a step back. Social conventions demand that. But he doesn't. And I'm very, very happy that he doesn't.

"Tough enough for you?" he asks, wrapping one arm around me and tugging the spatula out of my hand. He loosens the eggs, grabs the pepper mill and wraps both arms around me so he can crush some pepper on the golden yolks, then presses against me as he leans forward and lowers the heat slightly. "Maybe alligator wrestling?" he suggests, his voice low in my ear. "Maybe tightrope walking in the Grand Canyon?"

I laugh and lean back into him, not giving a damn how stupid that might be. He doesn't back away.

"I think I like the way you picture me," I say, not moving my hand when his comes around to cup mine.

"If you knew what I was picturing right now," he says, his voice low and rough, "I guarantee you'd kick me out."

My heart beats hard and wild in my chest. We're too close to the stove, to close to the truth, to close to an edge we may fall over and never come back from. I turn slowly, and when he backs away my heart falls.

Until he grabs my hip and pulls me to him.

"I can't kick you out," I whisper, my lips shaking and my voice trembling as I walk back out of his grasp. He shadows my every move. "It's your house. It's your kitchen."

He shakes his head, his dark eyes pinning me against the counter as sure as if his hands were still on me. "You can do whatever you want here."

"Why would you say that?" I ask, and untangle my eyes from his long enough to look down at my curled toes.

"Because something about you makes me want to make you want to stay here. Even if that requires me leaving." His voice has the slightest lazy slur to it, which is a direct contrast to the steady look in his eyes.

"You're crazy." I laugh to make it a joke, but we both know no one's joking.

His eyes stay locked in my direction, and, just when I'm positive I can't stand one more second, he paces to the stove, flips the eggs, grabs two plates, slides the toast out of the toaster oven, butters it, and drops the perfectly cooked eggs on top.

"Eat," he instructs, his voice low and hot, holding the plate toward me.

I take the plate and try not to let him see how much effort I have to put into holding it still as he goes to the other side of the counter.

"Do you know what's so weird?" I ask as I cut into the firm yellow of my yolk. The first bite is creamy, delicious heaven in my mouth.

The only thing I can imagine wanting in my mouth more is his tongue, and my brain skips and sputters just thinking that thought.

"What's that?" He watches me as he eats, his eyes hot and focused.

I try not to get sucked into those eyes, but there's no safe place on him to place my focus. What else can I look at? His broadly muscled shoulders? The bulge of his biceps? His strong hands, deeply tanned and long-fingered? Every new thing I notice about him drives my poor hormones into a serious frenzy.

"You were just a voice on the phone a few hours ago. And now I'm eating eggs in your kitchen and wearing your shirt to bed."

And imagining doing very, very bad things with you all over your gorgeous house.

I would blame that train of thought on the drinking, but I'm sobering up more and more by the second, and I know this has nothing to do with alcohol and everything to do with finally meeting that certain person you never even realized you'd been waiting for.

He shrugs, and I feel a little prickle of…irritation. It makes no sense, but that doesn't stop the feeling from surging through me. Why is he shrugging those damn gorgeous shoulders of his?

"What's the shrug about?" I ask, cutting my eggs with more force than is strictly necessary.

"I guess I don't think it's all that weird." He eats methodically, and I refuse to acknowledge how fantastic his mouth is.

"Really? You don't think it's at all odd that we went from

only talking on the phone at work to having sleepovers in less than twenty-four hours?" I press.

He eats the last bite of his late-night snack and lays his fork and knife on the side of his plate with cautious neatness. When he looks up, his eyes look more than clear; they look a little furious, and it sucker punches the air right out of my lungs.

"I think a lot of things are weird, but not this." He runs a hand through his black hair and gets up, his chair scraping loudly on the stone floor. I watch his back while he puts the plates in the sink, and I feel this stupid, stupid urge to run my fingernails up and down that back.

"So, what's weird according to Cohen Rodriguez then?" I demand.

He turns the water on and squirts dish soap on the plates, then grabs the little blue sponge in his hand. I can see his reflection in the fogging window over the sink, and I notice the way his jaw is set tight before he answers.

"I think it's weird as hell that a girl like you would be with a guy like Jason." His eyebrows are low over his eyes, and his voice is full of sharp fury. "I think it's weird that Ally was supposed to be on this sham double date with me, but spent the whole time ogling that idiot passed out upstairs. I think it's weird that having you in my kitchen feels so damn right, so much more right than it ever felt when Kensley was here, and I thought I wanted to marry her."

I get up as quietly as I can, but he sees my movement in the window, and watches my reflection as I bring my plate to the sink.

When I'm at his side, I put the plate under the water, and his hands cover mine for a second. We're both reflected in the window now, side by side, but I'm too scared to look at us together. So I watch the water pour out of the faucet and foam with the soap in the bottom the sink, washing the memory of our meal together away forever.

"I should go to bed," I say, but the splash of the water is louder than my voice. So much louder, I'm not sure he heard me.

"Go to bed," he answers, pulling the plate away and washing it methodically.

"What if I don't want to?" I venture.

He flips the faucet off and the silence that fills up the room roars in my ears.

He turns to me, and I never want to stop looking at his face. If I could, I'd take a picture of those dark, angry eyes, the hard and soft line of his lips, the wide, strong set of his jaw, but I can't. I shake when I think I'm going to go back to phone calls and nothing else. I can't.

"Do you like Ally at all?" I ask, desperate.

"I haven't thought about her once tonight," he says, his words more growl than coherent language. "Why are you asking about her now?"

"I hoped you'd have another date," I admit, dropping my eyes and fisting my hands in the bottom of the shirt. His shirt.

"Why would you want me to go on another date with her? Look at me." I look, and the deep brown of his eyes is drowning me, and I want it. I would swim away from a lifesaver if anyone bothered to throw me one. "Why would you want that?"

"Because I want to see you again. I want to be with you again," I choke out, turning my head away when he puts his hand on my hip and drags me lopsidedly close.

"Then see me," he dares. "Be with me again."

I shake my head and his hand locks under my jaw.

"I've never done anything with a girl who had a boyfriend," he says, his voice a rasp on my ears. "But that asshole isn't your boyfriend. He's some dumb fuck who's screwing with you, and I don't give a shit what label you two have going on. I wanted you from the second I saw you, and you're right here telling me you want me too."

He jerks me closer, our hips lock, and his hand presses up

my spine and clings to the back of my neck. A tiny whimper escapes out of my mouth.

"Tell me to stop," he begs.

I shake my head.

"Please." His face is close to mine, his voice thick in my ears.

I shake again and push my palms up to the thin fabric of his t-shirt, grabbing desperate handfuls. "I can't. I want it. I want you."

That's all he needs to hear.

Cohen's mouth finds mine and devours it. His lips are strong and entirely in control. He kisses the way he *is*, like he's sure he's going to give me what I want, and he so does. I part my lips and his tongue flicks in, licking at the top and bottom lip before it fills my mouth.

I moan and press against him, and he turns me with a quick spin, pinning my hips to the kitchen counter with his and twining his arms around my body. I feel…enveloped by him, snuggled into his warmth, and lit on fire by the rub of his body on mine.

I press against him and tighten my hands in his shirt, because if I don't they'll slide down his hard chest and under the waistband of his loose jeans. They'll pull his face closer and knead at his neck. They'll claw at his back and squeeze his ass. And once my hands go crazy over his body, I'll start begging. I know myself so damn well. I'll beg him to take me up to that king bed. I'll beg him to rip his shirt off of my body and run his tongue over every inch of my skin. I'll plead with him and try to convince him to do things that will fill us both to the brim with shame in the morning because I selfishly want this release tonight.

I know that, and that's why I twist into him, drive my hips against the hard length of his cock, kiss him with my lips pressed to his and my tongue eager and quick, but I never move my damn hands. Because once I loosen my grip, I'll freefall so hard and fast, neither one of us will have the chance to look back even if we want to. Even if we need to.

Everything he's doing simultaneously satisfies me and lights me on fire with pure desire for more. I want exactly what I'm getting and exactly ten times more. And tripled.

I have total control over my hands, but Cohen doesn't. His rove down to my breasts, which he squeezes and pulls at through the thin cotton of his shirt. My nipples harden under the rasp of his palms, and I arch my back. Both hands slide down to the white hem of the shirt we're sharing. One hand slides under, skims over my belly, up my ribs, and hits the bare skin of my breasts. My neck goes loose and my head dips back. I can't believe what a difference a fraction of an inch of fabric makes, but, good Lord, it makes all the difference in the world. His fingers find my nipples and tug at them until my breath explodes out in frenzied pants.

Just when I'm sure there's nothing else he can do to make me crazier, his other hand slides to my back, traces down the line of my spine, and skirts under the line of my underwear, curving with quick possession over my ass.

"Cohen," I gasp, and his fingers squeeze harder on my skin.

Like he can read my mind, he swings his arm around my waist just as my knees buckle under me. He has me on the cool granite of his counter and is tugging my underwear down farther, leaving me exposed and ready.

Ready for him

Ready for anything he wants to do, any depth he wants to sink to with me.

His mouth falls to my neck and he sucks at my skin with gentler and gentler pressure. His hands stop their persistent search of my skin and don't pinch and pull in that way that makes my every pore scream with need.

I whimper because what the hell else can I do? He's pulling away from something we never should have done in the first place.

His hand pops out from under the cotton of our shirt and

his other hand drags out from under my waistband.

No, no, no, no!

"Cohen?" My voice shakes, and I just don't care.

"Maren." He drags me off the counter, his dark eyes flickering with a thousand emotions I can't pinpoint. "Damnit, go to bed."

"Come to bed," I counter, my voice attempting bravado but undermined by a crazy shake.

"No." He shakes his head, a piece of dark hair falling in front of his eye. I want to push it away, but, though he's been massaging my tits and ass for twenty minutes, I don't feel like that's within my rights.

Weird doesn't begin to describe this all.

"I want you there," I say, finally letting my fists fall from his shirt. The material is puckered in an exploded star pattern where my hands had balled it tight.

"I want to be there," he says, rubbing a hand over his face roughly. "But I can't."

I wrap my arms around my waist and nod, my eyes brimming with tears. What the hell did I just do? What did I screw up? And why, *why*, do I always manage to screw it up with the good guys, the ones I should hold onto tight?

"I get it," I say, testing my first step back with my heel. I'll take three of four careful steps backward before I whirl around and sprint to my room.

His room

Fuck.

Fuck me.

Can tonight get any worse?

"Maren?" His voice interrupts me when my toes are into my third step back. I'm almost gone.

"Yeah?" I don't look at him because it's hard enough to accept that I fucked up and he's going to be gone. I don't need to stare at what I'm losing.

"I want to get in that bed with you and…" He rolls his neck back on his shoulders, then stalks a few deliberate feet in my direction.

I'm a step and a half away from running to freedom, but I freeze ice-still in my tracks.

"I want to get in that bed with you," he repeats, his mouth close to mine. Kissably close. "I want to. Good fucking God, Maren, I can't even say what I want to do to you, but it's every damn thing, and I can't. I can't while you're with *him*." He spits the pronoun, like even referencing Jason is too much for him. "I don't want you to be some fuck…" He tips his mouth close to my ear, his hair tickling my cheek and says, "Though, make no mistake about it, I want to fuck you. Badly."

I listen to the steady inhale and exhale of his breath, smell the salty bite of his skin, screw my eyes shut and wish I wasn't such a heinous, loathsome coward, and then I turn on my heel and make good on my original plan.

I run away from Cohen, pound up the stairs, and slam the door loud enough that it should wake anyone, including my stupid boyfriend. Except he's too sloshed to register the sound of his girlfriend escaping the arms of the man who's going to steal her away.

I climb under the sheets that don't, I decide finally, smell nearly enough like Cohen to satisfy me. I roll on my side and stuff a hand down low, rubbing with an intensity that's ferocious and guilty. I want *him*, and I have no idea if our few minutes of stolen perfection in the kitchen got us closer to that goal or ruined my chances completely and forever.

"Cohen," I groan, my voice so quiet, I'm not even positive I uttered the word I want to say every minute, every second.

When my body shakes and shudders with its final release, that's the only thought I can register. *Cohen. My Cohen.*

I clamp one hand tight over my mouth and listen, hoping to hear him turn the doorknob and come into the room with me, but it doesn't happen. He doesn't read my mind, he doesn't rip apart the ridiculous fears that hold me back. He

DEPTHS

goes to sleep in his guest room and leaves me alone in his huge bed with memories of the perfect heat of his lips on mine.

Torturer.

9 COHEN

A thousand times, I think about going into the room where Maren is sleeping, my t-shirt barely covering her sweet curves.

And a million times, my brain snaps and snarls at my hormones, insisting that it would be the fucking dumbest idea ever. Which it would be.

What we did in the kitchen, what I said, what she said back, all that was bad enough. I need to get her out of my damn head, get all of them out of my damn house, and find a way to move on that doesn't involve a girl who I work with on a daily basis and also happens to have a boyfriend.

Even if he is a fucking dickhole.

It's not like I expected to have some incredible night on my shitty air mattress, but I guess I assumed I'd get more than a few minutes of sleep.

No such luck.

My body is rioting with need for Maren.

I loved being with Kensley, but it was never like this. I can't get physically comfortable, and my mind sure as hell won't shut down.

Like a middle-school kid, I take matters, *ahem*, into my own hands. When I'm done, I assume sleep will hit me, finally, but it's not in the cards for me tonight. I'm now left with a feeling of half-fulfilled aggravation and a mind that's wide awake and focused on the girl I can't have.

It's so fucking stupid to even think of her.

I work with her. And she's an amazing asset. There's reason number one I need to keep my hands off.

Number two? He's snoring in my office. Even if he is a total douche, he's her damn boyfriend, and I shouldn't be sinking to that level. There are plenty of unattached girls, so why am I screwing with one who has a boyfriend?

Third? I've known her for one day. One. Okay, maybe we've talked dozens of times, but that was mostly about furniture. And I get it *felt* like I knew her so much better than I did, but, the truth is, I just got out of a crazy emotional relationship built on my own hype, and I don't need to construct a whole new one.

One day is not enough to get all physical with some girl. Even if her body curves in all the right ways. And her mouth tastes like sweet heaven. And the way she moans makes me harder and hornier than I ever imagined any single sound could.

All of that is physical rebound bullshit that I feel guilty as hell about.

What the fuck was I thinking backing her up against the

counter while her boyfriend slept a few hundred feet away?

If I'm being honest, I was thinking that I wanted way more than I got in my kitchen. And if I give myself and extra shot of honesty, I'll admit that I'm a fucking dumbass for even thinking that way.

I'm up before the dawn, because I never went to sleep. I step out of the sliding glass doors and walk down to the sandy beach outside my house.

It hits me daily how lucky I am to have the ocean outside my house.

Though, the peace I usually get to enjoy is ruined by the ghost images of Maren walking with me on this sand, going too deep into that water, coming back into my house and my bed. So close to being the perfect scenario, and also so completely far.

I sit down, the wind whipping every cobwebbed, sticky thought out of my head, the crashing waves smoothing out my frayed nerves. I tilt my head back and draw the clean scent of ocean deep in my lungs.

"Hey." A quiet voice shakes my pre-dawn calm.

"Hey." I crane my neck and take a long look. A little piece of me is sad to see she's back in her own clothes, my white t-shirt discarded. "Wanna sit?" I pat the sand at my side, and she plunks down, wringing her hands in front of

DEPTHS

her.

"Um, I'm…uh, I'm so sorry, I just want you to know that," she says, her words gulping out nervously. "Last night? I was such a mess. I never drink that much. Lame excuse, right? So damn lame. Fuck. I know this sucks. I feel like a huge ass. For even saying this."

She stops, and I can't help it. I laugh. "Maren?"

"Yeah?" She looks at me, all eager blue eyes behind the dark streaks of hair whipping in the wind.

"Shut up, okay?" I smile, and her smile is shaky, but it's there. "Just…I know what you mean. And don't worry. We were both off our asses last night. Let's just forget it, okay?"

Her eyes go wide, like she's shocked, and I feel a deep, stupid regret.

"Yeah. Forget it," she echoes uncertainly.

I want to say anything to break the tension, but Jason's voice breaks through our awkward pause before I get a chance to. "Hey, Maren, get your ass moving! I'm golfing with my boss at noon, and I need a shower and some espresso. C'mon!"

We turn at the same time to look at the empty deck. Jason is already gone, back in the house. My house.

God, I want to beat the shit out of this guy so fucking bad.

147

"Well, my prince awaits," Maren deadpans, rolling her pretty eyes. "I hope it won't…you know…be weird? Between us?"

"Weird," I scoff, like it would be crazy to imagine us feeling weird about being nothing more than co-workers, now that we've kissed like we wanted to tear each other's clothes off and have sex on my kitchen counter. "Why would it be weird? It's gonna be just fine. It's all gonna be fine." I can't believe how cool and collected my voice sounds.

I'm such a good liar, I'm actually scaring the shit out of myself.

"Cool." She stands and brushes the sand off her shorts with the flats of her hands, and she never makes eye contact. "Well, thank you so much for letting me sleep in your bed. And…um, thanks for the eggs."

The eggs.

The fucking eggs.

This is what it's come to?

I'm standing by her, my hand an inch from her waist, my mouth a half foot from hers, the words I need to say on the tip of my tongue, when Jason bursts back out on the porch.

"Jesus, Maren, are you deaf? I. Have. A. Meeting. With. My. Boss! Quit fucking around with Carlos and let's get a move on!"

DEPTHS

She looks at me, her eyes begging me to ignore her douchebag boyfriend.

I have a feeling I'm going to wind up beating the shit out of this tool at some point, but now isn't the time.

"You don't have to go with him," I say, and her eyes have this hopeful gleam. "I have another dozen eggs." It's a joke. Clearly a joke.

But my timing sucks.

Her face falls and she shakes her head. "I have to go. Of course. I need to. But thank you. So much."

She turns and flees like a deer running from a hunter, the way she did last night in the kitchen, and my heart has the same nasty emptiness it had last night.

I trudge through the sand and stop short on my deck. I can see them all through the sliding glass doors. Maren is rooting through her purse, and Jason has a hand on Ally's waist, his head is bent close to hers, and he has one finger pressed to his lips, in the classic 'shh' signal. When Maren turns around, he lets go of Ally and pulls Maren close, kissing her on the mouth.

Where I kissed her last night.

The way I kissed her last night.

Ally looks like she's contemplating murder. I bet she and I could be mistaken for twins based on our expressions

149

alone.

He finally pulls back from Maren and shoots a look of triumph out to me, like he knew I'd be watching like some damn tool. Maren presses her fingers to her lips.

My heart shreds. I feel a distinct, shitty hollowness that I have no clue how to begin filling.

If I had a cyanide capsule in one of my teeth like James Bond, I'd so crack that bitch open and end my misery right now.

10 MAREN

I stare at the caller id on my office phone, like I have every day for the last week when Rodriguez Furniture shows up on it. Debating whether or not to answer, like I even have a choice. It's an internal call. It could be anyone in the company.

Still, I half hope it is Cohen, and half hope it isn't.

So far, it hasn't been.

The store he works at is having a massive tent sale, so I tell myself that's why he hasn't called at all. He's just busy. Though, I know more than likely, it's because I was basically naked with him, begging him to sleep with me that night at his house, and then I left with Jason in the morning.

"This is Maren," I say, clutching the phone with my sweaty, nervous palm.

"Hey, Maren, it's Cohen."

Cohen. Sweet, sweet Cohen. I feel like I can taste his delectable mouth through the phone.

"Hey. What can I do for you? Do you need the count for the rugs that are being shipped to you guys tomorrow? I heard you were running low. I figured you'd be calling about it; actually, I probably should have already called you or sent over the specifics. Sorry about that." Sorry about so many things…

"Rugs? Yeah. Um, how many are we getting? I'll make a note for Gen, you know how she loves specifics."

"Right," I say. I tap away at my computer, making mistakes with every keystroke because I can't keep my hand from shaking. This is absurd. It's just Cohen. Cohen who smells like the surf first thing in the morning. Whose kisses were so surprising, so passionate and animalistic that I'm wet every time I think of them. I've got to stop this. I clear my throat, dislodging the lump that's stuck there because my body aches for Cohen to be near me. "Okay, so it looks like you should be getting fifty of the Moroccan Trelis rugs, twenty-five shags in assorted colors, ten Chevrons, and ten florals."

Silence. Except for the sound of his breathing. I close my eyes for a few seconds, and picture the way that vein on the right side of his neck pulses with each breath. How can a single detail be so incredibly sexy?

"Cohen?" I clutch the phone tighter. "Did you get that?"

"Huh? Yep. Ten florals." His words are tight and clipped.

"That's it. They'll be there within a few days. You should have enough in stock until they arrive. If not, let me know." I blush when I remember how close I came to going through

DEPTHS

with my hare-brained plan to screw the order up, just so I'd be sure to get Cohen on the line to help untangle it all. Pathetic.

His voice gets soft on me, making me have to catch my breath. "Will do. Thanks, Maren, fixer of all things."

I feel the warm blush that always burns my skin when he compliments me creep up my neck and stain my cheeks. Not that I need a 'thank you' or his sweet words anyway. Because I love when I make things easier for Cohen. I love feeling needed in a positive way, not in the way that my father needs me around.

But that's exactly the point: I like to keep things easy for Cohen.

Me in his life, wouldn't be that. Cohen wants something completely uncomplicated, and I work for his family, which makes things uppercase COMPLICATED. I just have to accept that and remember that I'd be a hiccup in the well-oiled machine that is Cohen Rodriguez's routine. He would lose patience with me for having to sneak out in the mornings to make sure dad hadn't passed out somewhere in the house, and that he had groceries in the fridge, and that he hadn't gotten his electric cut.

Hell, it annoys me that I cancel plans, cut corners, and tell lies on a daily basis on the off chance that my dad will spring up, his debilitating alcoholism magically cured by my martyrdom, and I can start living a full, normal life again.

If I can remember how to do that, of course.

It's so easy with Jason because he doesn't care much about any of that stuff. If I'm honest, Jason doesn't care much about *me*. The fact that his eyes have been glued to Ally's rack every single second I've seen them in the same space proved that implicitly. And it's fine, because I don't expect anything else from him. Jason fits my temporary state perfectly: he's not the kind of guy you marry. He's the kind of guy you waste time with. That's exactly what I need right now, when things are so damn up in the air.

And he's fine. He's not the love of my life, he's not so amazing, but I like his company most of the time, and we do generally have a pretty good time. He's ridiculously good in bed. I can't imagine sex getting better than it is with Jason— though Cohen's kisses tell me I may be dead wrong about that theory.

"Oh, before you go. This is going to sound weird, but I also ordered a seven-by-ten teal and gray area rug. I, um, I sort of thought it would look great in your living room," I say. It sounds ridiculous now that I've said it outloud. Who am I to pick home furnishings for him? "It's gorgeous, but if you hate it, I'm sure you could sell it in the store anyway."

DEPTHS

"You picked out a rug for me? That's—"

"Creepy?" I stifle a hysterically panicked laugh.

I am a colossal, ridiculous idiot.

"Cool. I was going to say 'cool.'" His voice sounds anything but cool. The way it rasps against my ears is magma hot, and it burns right through me the exact way his hands and kisses did in his kitchen the other night. "Thank you, Maren."

I close my eyes and wish I was brave enough. To tell him that I think I could make him so happy. Someday. If he can wait, we might be amazing together.

But that's the stupidest thought I've had yet. Cohen is right for a life I don't live. And, even though I hate to admit it, I may never live that life. I care about him. I want more for him. So I need to stop being an ass and picturing our life together, because that's just asking for an ocean of heartache.

I keep it short and platonic. The way it should be.

"No problem. We'll talk soon."

"Bye, Maren."

It's fine that it hurts to let go. That little jab of pain reminds me to keep my distance.

***

"Dad? You home?" I ask it, though I know he is. Of

155

course he is, where else does he go? I set the bag of groceries on the counter and turn to preheat the oven. It's meatloaf night.

"Mare, is that you?" My dad's voice booms down the narrow hall. I close my eyes and suck in a quick breath and hold it, trying to put myself in the right frame of mind before I see him.

The frame of mind that isn't full of bitter resentment.

"Pop, I'm in the kitchen," I say, stacking the cans of vegetables neatly in the pantry. Dad probably won't eat them, though he should. I stopped wasting money on the fresh ones since I caught him feeding his meals to the neighbor's schnauzer or hiding them in the bottom of the garbage can, covered up with plenty of napkins—just like a guilty child would do.

Which is exactly what my father feels like to me.

Once upon a time, my dad was lead singer for a semi-successful punk band. They opened for early nineties acts like No Use for a Name and Blink 182. Girls threw themselves at him like he was a huge catch, and, I guess, he had his moment when he was. But once my mom got pregnant with Rowan and forced him to marry her (his words), his life went downhill.

He tried.

I think he really did.

For years I remember the gardening and baking and being a family. But somewhere deep down, he couldn't handle feeling tied down, he couldn't handle the restricted tour schedule, and not being able to go out afterward with the band like he used to. When Mom started her business and poured every ounce of her energy into making it a success, he felt left behind. He'd long quit the band because mom told him to, and then she finally found her dream in owning a bakery. When she eventually left him, after she'd made him toss out his own dream of making it big one day, any other aspirations of ever being a productive member of society went down the drain.

It's so damn cliché, but for some reason, women seem to have a thing for rock stars. I guess their crazy lifestyle and talent is a turn on or whatever. What they don't see is what happens after the fame goes away—when the has-been is living with his twenty-something daughter, unemployed and underdressed.

"Can you put on a robe or something?" I ask. Dad is shirtless, that six-pack in the old photos replaced by a bulging belly, likely full of cirrhosis.

He ignores me.

"What's on the menu tonight, kid?" he asks back,

stretching his arms over his head and grunting like he's just woken up. At six o'clock at night.

"Meatloaf and green beans," I announce. "And don't argue about the beans. You need to eat more green things, Dad. Doc Snyder says so."

"That doctor is a pompous moron." He runs his hand down his long, gray beard. He looks less dapper, more Unabomber with that thing. I've begged him to shave it. Offered to pay for it, even at that stupid barber shop where the 'barbers' wear short-ass skirts and serve you whiskey while you get a shave. I'd do anything to make that scraggly mess go away. I've explained to Dad that no one will ever hire him with that thing. I think that's probably part of the appeal.

"What'd you do today?" I ask. Dad's been living with me for two years, since his workman's comp for that BS pulled back claim he made ran out, he lost his apartment, and he didn't have anywhere to go. When I took him in, it was supposed to be temporary, just until he found work. But he's never tried. So, I support him, because what else am I supposed to do?

Mom lives in St. Helena, right outside of Napa in Northern California. It's a day's drive away, but neither one of us makes the effort much. She's long washed her hands of this mess. I'm all that Dad has, and I think she resents me for not walking away from him like she did.

"Looked at some jobs online," he says, filling a plastic cup with whiskey.

I frown.

Not because I care one way or another if he drinks anymore. It's just that everything that he does makes me a little sad. It's why I tolerate him mooching off of me. It may not be right, or ideal, but I could never sleep at night knowing he was out there on his own drunk, hungry, and all pitiful like. So I let him stay and buy his food and cook his meals and pay his cell phone bill like I'm the parent and he's the teenager.

"Anything promising?" I grip the countertop, because I know there isn't anything new to report. There never is.

"Nope. Bunch of idiots out there. They all want you to have a bachelor's degree just to flip burgers! It's ridiculous. And I ain't busting my ass for some minimum wage job, either."

"Dad, the economy is shit, what do you expect?" It's harsh, but truthful. He hasn't worked in years, and he isn't exactly what HR would consider well qualified for most positions. "I can check with our warehouse department again and see if there's anything open for you. Even just a night stocking position would be great, you know? They have really decent benefits. You've got to do something."

Dad takes a long gulp from the cup, sets it down on the counter and walks away. He just doesn't do well with tough love.

I toss the remaining groceries in the cabinets, unwrap a frozen pizza and toss it in the oven. Maybe Dad will smell it cooking and come out of his room, maybe not.

Either way, I'm leaving.

***

Jason's condo isn't far, but the differences between the places we call home make it feel like a different county. My apartment is basic, small, worn, and lived in. Jason's condo is modern, sterile-feeling, massive, and pristine.

The first time I came over, I made the mistake of asking him where he bought this heavy, twisted white vase. I may have mentioned that it was sort of hideous. It was some kind of Bohemia Porcelain that he'd inherited from his great-grandmother. The vase happened to be a century old…and worth almost five-thousand dollars. I remember carefully setting it back on the bookshelf and making a mental note to never touch anything in his apartment again.

It is the opposite of the comfort and safety that I felt at Cohen's place.

And yet, I'm constantly running to it when I'm upset.

"Hey doll," Jason says, opening the door and pulling me in. His tie is loose around his neck and his top two buttons are undone. I admit, he can be an asshole, but he's hot. And right now, that's all that matters.

"You just get home from work?" I ask.

"Mmm hmm," Jason says, and his lips are already pressed to my neck, hot and hungry. I work on the remaining buttons on his shirt and push it over his shoulders, running my hands up his back, as he reaches behind me, unzips my dress, and lets it fall to the ground. I step out of the black wool sheath that made me think of Cohen when I put it on this morning.

The sensible, modest dress concealing my daring thigh highs and lacy thong…that's the vibe Cohen gives off. So strict in his work, but Jesus once I got a taste of him at play…I haven't been able to stop thinking about him since.

"This is fucking hot," Jason says, slipping his thumb under the miniscule band of my thong.

I kiss him hard, trying to feel a fraction of what I felt with Cohen in the kitchen, but it isn't there. It just isn't. I push myself closer to him and will myself to feel comforted by his touch like I used to when I'd had a bad day, but I don't.

I think about asking him to slow down, but it's nothing

we haven't done before, and I'm standing here in nothing but a scrap of lace, feeling every inch of his hardness against me.

"Let me go grab a condom," he says. I nod, toss my thigh-highs aside, and lean back on the leather sofa. Jason will probably pull me onto the floor with him rather than risk making a mess on his couch.

"Fuck. Fuck. Fuck," I hear him say from his bedroom.

"What's wrong?" I yell back.

"Condoms. I'm out of condoms. Do you have one?"

"Jason, what grown man runs out of condoms? Exactly how much sex are you having?" I laugh, and as the casual joke slides out of my mouth, I know the answer.

That it's definitely more sex than I'm having. It's definitely sex with more people than just me. Ally, no doubt. But does it stop there?

I lunge off of the sofa and grab my dress from the floor, tugging the zipper up my back. I twist and turn like Gumby to get it zipped just as Jason stops in the doorway between his room and the living room, his gorgeous eyes cold and narrowed to slits.

"What are you doing?"

"What does it look like? I'm getting dressed."

He pulls his brows together. "I see that. But why?"

"Um," I say, balancing on one foot to pull my sling backs

DEPTHS

on. "Because we aren't having sex."

"Oh, hell no. You came all the way over here, wearing those sexy-ass panties, and now you're leaving? I'll run to the convenience store down the street, baby. It's all good." He closes the space between us, his voice diving down to a place he thinks is low and undeniably seductive.

It just grates against me, because I know it's the voice he used for every other girl.

Those many girls who helped empty the enormous condom box that was definitely full a week ago when I was the one who grabbed a condom out before we had sex.

He isn't super good at taking cues, especially from me. Especially when I've gone back to him so many times. So he tried another smooth line. "Let me make you feel good."

Too bad for Jason, I'm way beyond his schmoozy bullshit. I've had real. I've had Cohen. And, even if I can't have him for good, I'm sure as hell not going to be able to settle for Jason now.

"I don't think so." I grab my purse from the floor by the door where I dropped it when I came in.

"Okay, you're ready right now, can't wait. I get it. Let's just, just this once, forget it, okay? How long have we been together? You don't trust me? I'm clean, I swear."

He's cocking me that arrogant smile, the one he always

flashes just before he talks someone into letting him have his own way.

"I just..." I fish my keys out of the bottom of my purse. "I just can't do this right now. Anymore. Ever. With you. I can't."

The cocky expression melts right off his face, leaving behind a look that reminds me of a toddler about to throw a tantrum. Or my father when I ask too many hard questions. I can't believe how incredibly sick to my stomach that look makes me.

"Maren, what the fuck?"

Probably on some level, I've been itching for this to happen. I don't feel disappointed like I should.

I stand up straight in his cold, ugly condo and look him right in the eye, the way I never really have before. Maybe because I always knew if I really looked, really stood up and focused, I'd see just how much I don't like him.

And if I admit that, I'll also have to admit that, low as I might be right now, even I have too much self-respect to stay with a guy who disgusts me.

When I take a good look at Jason's incredibly handsome face, I realize that something in me changed. That night in Cohen's kitchen gave me a taste of something so good and right. And now I have no appetite for the junk Jason's

DEPTHS

offering. Frankly, I'd rather be alone, no matter how scary that is, than know there's someone as amazing as Cohen out there while I waste my time with someone as selfish and ugly as Jason.

"I'm just done. And the short answer, is no. No, I don't trust you. Like, at all."

11 COHEN

"Are Deo and Whit going to make it to dinner tonight, sweetie?" my mother asks, her wavy brown hair pulled back in the tight bun that means she's cooking some serious Jewish/Mexican culinary masterpiece.

"I think they'll be a little late, but, yeah, they're planning on showing up." I hand her the potatoes I just peeled for the fiesta latkes. You wouldn't believe how some corn flour, cilantro, and lime can spice up your average potato pancake.

My youngest sister, Genevieve, comes in with the almonds Mom got from a neighbor, shelled and hand slivered, ready for the chocolate nut torte.

"So, is the wedding in the works for those two?" Genevieve asks, trying to keep the sour out of her voice. My little sister has had the world's biggest crush on Deo since she was in second grade. I'm pretty sure she had a scary altar set up in her closet where she lit candles and tried to cast Santería love spells based on the misinformation of her best friend, Charity.

"They're not in any hurry," I say, but when my sister's expression brightens, I add, "Well, Whit isn't. Deo would kill me if he knew I told you, but he's been talking to florists and looked into getting this big, like, coach to show up with white horses…whatever. I think it's so damn weird."

I can hear the hostess in my brain announcing, *Bitter, table for one.*

So maybe the mushy lovey-dovey behavior that I used to find mostly pretty sweet is now driving me fucking out of my skull. And maybe that has to do with the fact that every time I see Deo curl up with Whit or laugh at one of her acerbic jokes or get excited to talk about reception venues, my mind goes right back to Maren and what I'm missing not being with her.

But I realized something important. As hot as she is, with her wide blue eyes and her soft brown hair, all curves and smiles and some kind of innate, intense sexiness that I can't quite put my finger on, she's. Not. Real.

Not as someone I can date, anyway.

She's just a figment of Cohen Rodriguez's intensely overactive imagination peppered with a liberal spicing of rebound desperation, and garnished with some good old-fashioned drunkenness.

In short, I am a fucking idiot, and Maren is best kept at a distance.

I know this. So why do I keep thinking about her?

"I think a horse-drawn carriage sounds very romantic,"

Mom says, one hip braced on the counter, wooden spoon twirled dreamily between her fingers. "But Deo was always a romantic like that."

"I know," Genevieve sighs, her eyes all soft and dewy, her hands balled in tight fists. "I've always known that."

My older sister, Lydia, busts in and rolls her eyes at Genevieve before she even knows why she's doing it. "What have you 'always known'?" she demands.

She's been bossy as hell since we were little kids, and she still thinks it's up to her to know everything about every one of us. It's pretty damn irritating.

"Nothing," Genevieve snaps.

"Lydia! You made it! You've been so busy at work, I didn't think you'd be able to get time off," Mom cries, opening her arms and pulling her down for a hug. Other than being five inches taller than our mother, Lydia is her spitting image. Mom also loves her bossiness and take-charge attitude, so she spills the beans before Genevieve and I can make our escape. "We were just talking about how romantic Deo is."

"Deo?" Lydia scoffs, patting her French twist and raising one over-tweezed eyebrow. "I guess if you think sharing a hand-rolled joint on the beach is big-time romance, he's the winner." She holds up her hand and twirls her finger around.

"Do you try to be such an asshole, or does it just come naturally?" I ask.

Mom clucks her tongue and Lydia shakes her head, eyeing my sister and I with a condescending little smile. "Sooo sorry," she says with saccharine sweetness. "I forgot I'm in the midst of the Deo Beckett fan-club." She narrows her eyes at Genevieve. "What do you look so pissed about? I thought you got over your big crush back in high school. Please don't tell me you still hold a candle for that slacker."

Genevieve slams the knife she was using to cut up cilantro down on the counter and glares at Lydia, her eyes brimming with tears and her voice hoarse and choked. "I bet it feels so damn good to be perfect all the time, right? No wonder you can't keep a damn boyfriend. You can't see past your own huge ego to notice if anyone else would meet your ridiculous standards." My baby sister trembles with fury, but my older sister just crosses her arms coolly and shakes her head from side to side, pursing her dark red lips.

"Better to be picky and alone than willing to spread my legs for any guy who so much as blinks my way. I bet it sucks when the majority can't remember your name the next day."

My mother's wooden spoon clatters to the counter, and I reach for Genevieve, who pushes past me and tears down the hall, her sobs already spilling out.

"Damn it, Lydia!" I yell. "You're home for thirty seconds and you have Genie crying? What the hell is wrong with you?"

"Lydia." Mom, who almost always takes Lydia's side, is using all of her control to get her words out in a level voice. "You *never* speak to any of your siblings the way you just spoke, do you hear me? Look at me!"

Mom's controlled fury is a thing to cower over.

Lydia raises her hands in defeat and huffs, but Mom's ferocious look stops her in her tracks, and she back-pedals. "I was just playing with her," she whines, smoothing out her suit and jacket like she's trying to reassure herself that, yes, she is better than the rest of us, and how can she help it. "I love how she can dish it, but she can never take it. So typical Genevieve! You think it doesn't hurt to have her throw it in my face that I've been single for so long?"

Now it's Lydia's turn to get all choked up, and Mom sighs and opens her arms again.

I don't doubt that Lydia is upset, but it's just like my sister to manipulate any situation and turn it into something about her. She's got her cheek leaned on our mother's shoulder and is blubbering about her 'biological clock ticking' and her 'inability to find a man who can accept a strong woman' while Mom clucks and comforts her, forgetting Genevieve completely.

I leave the kitchen and hesitate outside Genevieve's door, wanting to go in and tell her that things will be alright, but not really wanting to get bogged down in my sister's drama. The smell of smoke from across the hall is a huge relief, because it means the sanest of all my siblings, Cece is home.

It's no surprise she chose to stay holed up in her room while all hell broke loose in the kitchen. I'm serious when I say she's the sanest of us all.

I cross to the door that used to be mine, and knock lightly. "It's me, Cece."

I hear her stop fumbling to hide her cigs on the other side. The mattress creaks and her footsteps run across the floor. The door opens and she jumps in my arms. "Cohen! Please tell me you already peeled all the potatoes?"

"Done, slacker. How do you always manage to wiggle out of every damn chore?" I demand, coming in and flopping on her bed. I hold out my hand and she reaches out the window, pulling in her ashtray with the smoldering cigarette and hands them to me. I take a drag and blow out a long, lazy stream of smoke.

"When you're writing your thesis paper on fourth wave feminist poetry, you'll be able to forgo potato peeling duties too." She grins at me, and I raise my eyebrows at the ashtray, full of butts.

"So, I guess Spirit cigarettes are pretty poetic and all, but how is actual paper coming? Haven't you been working on it for, like, two years now?" I hand the cig over and she takes a drag, brushing the tangle of chin-length curls away from her face.

"Shut up, please. Not everyone majored in finance. You have no idea how much I wish I'd just chosen something I didn't have to...*think* about so much." She takes another drag and grins, smoke coming through her teeth. "No offense. You know I think you're brilliant."

"None taken. Sorry the fourth wave is kicking your ass and all." I look around her room and try to ignore the morose faces of Virginia Woolf, Audre Lourde, and Maya Angelou glowering at me from the posters on her wall. I can remember when there were only surfing posters and a few Sports Illustrated hotties gracing these humble walls. I'm sure Gloria Steinem would have a heart attack from her spot on the bookshelf if she knew how many centerfolds used to occupy wall space in here. "So, I feel like I haven't talked to you in weeks."

"I know." She sighs and pulls her boney knees up to her chest. "I feel like I haven't even really been home, ya' know? I've just been trapped in my own head. But enough about me. How is everything going with you?"

"Same old," I lie.

"You're lying to me, little brother." She pokes me with her toe. "Still stuck on Kensley?"

The thing I love about Cece is that she can push away her own feelings when it comes to helping me out. Because she hated Kensley with an open ferocity that made it hard for them to be in the same room together. But, since we broke up, Cece hasn't uttered even one shitty word about her. Even though I know she's got an entire arsenal hidden behind her cheerful smiles.

"Not at all." I lean back on her bed, arms behind my head, and stare at the ceiling I stared at for so many nights growing up in this house. "There's this girl…"

"The girl in the band?" she asks, her voice low and gentle.

Now I feel like an even bigger asshole for attempting to bring Maren up. Cece and I have barely talked in the last few weeks, but I already cried about Kensley *and* Tracey to her. I'm obviously an asshole who can make myself fall in love with any girl, no matter how un-mutual the feeling is.

"Never mind," I grumble.

She stubs the cigarette out and pushes up the sleeves of

her hideous alpaca wool sweater. "Oh, Co, did you fall in love again? Don't look all embarrassed. You've got a good heart."

Worse even than having my sister realize what an asshole of love I am is having her imagine that I was thinking with my 'heart' when everything went crazy with Maren.

"It's fucking idiotic, is what it is," I finally admit. "And it's not a good heart. It's an insane heart, and it's getting my ass in trouble left and right. I'm done with girls for a while."

She snorts and hides her pack of cigarettes back under her mattress, then leans over me to put her ashtray on the huge window ledge and tosses a Lifesaver in her mouth before she throws me the roll.

I bite into the minty ring and ask, "What? You don't think I can swear off girls?"

"You swearing off girls is as likely as Genie swearing off sex. Or Lydia swearing off being an asshole. I heard Genie's door slam. I assume Lydia said something douchey?" Cece sighs when I nod.

"Nail on the head. And Mom was pissed for all of two seconds before Lydia managed to turn it all around and make it about her shitty life." I pop another Lifesaver in my mouth and crunch down. "Is Enzo making it for dinner?"

"Enzo is, I think, at some film festival with that

girl…what's her name again?" Cece scrunches up her nose like she can't remember our brother's girlfriend's name. "Bambi? Is that it?"

"Just because you think she should be dancing on a pole doesn't mean you can rename her," I say, but I can't help laughing. Cece has always been protective over me, Enzo, and Genevieve when it comes to dating, and she's driven away more boyfriends and girlfriends than we can count. "Her name is Fawn."

"Ah. Fawn. I remember now." She holds out her hand and I pull her to her feet. "Spicy latkes?" she asks.

"Yup. Not that you should get any, lazy ass." I start towards the kitchen, but Cece stops short and points to Genevieve's door.

"I'll take one for the team," she whispers. "Consider yourself lucky that you got to peel potatoes instead." She turns her curly head to the door and puts a hand on the knob.

I book it down the hall, leaving my sisters to deal with all that emotional craziness together. I may get a little down, but a few beers on Deo's couch is as far as it goes. I don't envy Cece right now. Genevieve takes things hard, and I bet she's a crying, snotty, broken mess at the moment.

Damn Lydia.

"Cohen, I was just going to call you!" Mom cries when I

get back to the kitchen. "Deo and Whit are on the back porch with Lydia. How is Genevieve?" Her eyes go soft, and I almost feel bad about snapping at her. But this always happens in my family.

"She's okay. But you could have gone to check on her instead of letting Lydia steal the show as usual."

She turns to the stove and clangs the pots on the stove. "I swear to God, you kids will be the death of me! I never had all this trouble when you were younger. You turned into adults, and you all went into your second infanthood. I'm done! Go on the porch with your friends, Cohen. I want to be alone for a damn minute!"

I don't say another word. The hilarious irony of the entire situation is that Mom is just as emotional and frail as Genevieve. I don't get why they can't understand each other more, but maybe the answer is obvious: if they're so similar, they probably don't see their own ridiculousness.

I'm glad to get to leave my sister's tears and my mother's moodiness in the house. Outside, the sun is just about to set, the breeze is sweet and cool, and Whit holds out a beer for me with a smile as Deo and Lydia discuss the tenants of the new apartment's downtown.

"….and they were supposed to be for the grad students in the law school, but they don't have the money for them, so it's all these coke-head rich brat drop-outs whose parents use the address to pretend their little losers are still in school." Lydia takes a tiny sip of her white wine and gestures with the glass angrily. "It just pisses me off."

"What do you care?" I demand. "You don't live there."

"But I *looked* at those apartments. And I work right around the corner. It's just shady." She sits up straighter, and I look for some sign that my sister is feeling bad about being the world's biggest jerk, but she just looks full of herself. As usual.

"Hey, you never finished telling me how your date with Maren went," Deo segues quickly. He knows when a Rodriguez throw-down is coming from years of watching them unfold, and I assume he doesn't want to shock and horrify Whit.

"It was a date with Ally," I grit out. "And there was no chemistry."

"There was no chemistry?" Whit asks, smiling as she takes a long pull of beer and adds, "Or there was no chemistry between you and *Ally*?"

I should be pissed at Whit, but I have a hard time ever being pissed at her.

"Look, whatever there was, it was stupid. Maren has a boyfriend. Some finance douche who's this big hot shot at fucking Bingham and Walters, Jason, and—"

"Jason Nucci?" Lydia interrupts, practically spitting her wine out.

"Uh, actually, I think that *is* his name," I say, realizing my sister probably comes into contact with all kinds of finance assholes like Jason since she works for one of the county's most powerful law offices. They share a glass high-rise with several financial firms.

"I hope they just started dating, like, yesterday," she says, crossing her legs and smirking.

"Why do say that?" I ask, my voice reined in. When Lydia gets that look on her face, it's because she knows something that's shocking as shit.

I both want to know and don't want to know her big Jason secret.

"Well, it's a rumor, of course. But it's one that I've heard from *very* reliable sources. The talk is that after he slept with pretty much every girl in his office, he got one of the college interns pregnant, and there was this whole hush-hush abortion scandal." My sister's eyes are wide when she tells this, like she gives a shit. But I know she's just totally excited to have a juicy gossip bone to chew on.

Usually I can ignore her love of talking shit about everyone under the sun, but this time, it's about Maren.

DEPTHS

It was obvious he was screwing around on Maren. But now he may have got some girl pregnant? Was it Ally? Was he with Maren when it happened? Does any of it really matter? The bottom line is, I now have another reason to hate this guy, and I can't just ignore them.

Whether I want to date Maren of not, I don't want to think of her being used by this fuckhead.

Genevieve stomps onto the deck just then, Cece behind her. Cece hugs Whit and Deo, and Genevieve gives them a tight smile. They both glare at Lydia, who sighs and crosses her arms.

"You okay?" I ask Genevieve lowly.

"Yeah." She smiles, her eyes puffy and red. "I'm fine. Are you? You look like you're ready to murder someone."

"Cohen went on a double date with Maren, from the warehouse," Lydia says. Genevieve waters down her glare so she can get more information. "I just told him that Maren's boyfriend is, like, the biggest skank in the world and knocked some young girl up after sleeping with everyone in the law district." She shudders. "What a creep."

"You went out with Maren?" Genevieve asks, her face suddenly brightening. "I love her! I love you two together—"

"We're not together," I cut in quickly.

179

Too quickly.

Which Deo makes obvious to everyone by clearing his throat loudly.

"Oh." Genevieve pushes her long hair back off her shoulders, the better to show her tiny little dress off for Deo's benefit, I'm sure. I try not to judge my baby sister, but, damn, Whit is standing *right there*. Lydia may be a bitch, but sometimes she's painfully right: Genevieve needs to calm her ass down around guys, Deo especially.

"I went on a double date," I explain, relieved that Whit doesn't seem to notice my little sister making an ass of herself and glowering when Deo wraps an arm around Whit's shoulders. "And I'm upset because Maren is awesome. As a friend, of course. I didn't get a good vibe from her boyfriend, and now I realize my gut was right."

"You need to tell her," Genevieve says, her face going all loopy and glowy even as I shake my head. "You should get together with her and tell her to her face, Cohen. She's so nice. I love that girl, and I hate to think of her getting used like that."

I lean back on the deck railing and remember the way I jumped Maren in my kitchen, like I was a damn panther in heat. I've managed to avoid her for a week, and that's been working for me. The last thing I need is to be calling her with some rumor my sister told me about the guy she knows damn well is a tool.

Cece tugs Genevieve away from me. "Genie, I definitely think she needs to know, but maybe Cohen's not the best person to tell her. I talked to her a thousand times when I used to do the shipment coordinating for Mom and Dad. She was always super friendly. I could ask her out to lunch if you want."

This is why Cece is hands down my favorite sister.

"Perfect," I say at the same moment Genevieve wails, "No!"

Deo grins at my little sister, not realizing that she's going to take that little look of comradery and weave it into some whole hidden love story. Can my life get any shittier?

And then it does.

"Um?" Everyone looks at Whit, who hasn't said a word this whole time. "I've been trying to place the name since Lydia said it, and now I remember. Rocko was telling me that this asshole came in with the ugliest design for a tattoo of his *own* name. He said he was surprising his girlfriend with it for her birthday. I remember because I double-checked the books for Rocko. He asked if I could be there and just make sure the girl actually wanted to get it done once her boyfriend surprised her. Rocko hated the idea that she might get it just to make him happy or whatever."

I'm shocked the bottle in my fist doesn't crack apart.

"He's going to give her a fucking tattoo of *his* name after he treated her like total shit?" I growl. "When the hell is her birthday?"

"Wait." Genevieve is scrolling through her phone. "Maren is my Facebook friend. Um, it's Wednesday." She raises her big doe eyes at me, and I have the worst thought ever: I think about how Genevieve would probably be awed enough by someone wanting her to get a tattoo like that, she'd go ahead and get it.

I don't *think* Maren would be crazy enough. But I don't know. Girls are weird about romantic gestures. And Maren *is* willingly dating a total douchebag.

"Cece, you need to talk to her," I say, and Genevieve looks let down. I don't give a shit.

"Of course." Cece takes most things in stride, but anything feminist gets her fired up, and the idea of this asshole branding Maren with his name has even my usually calm sister pissed.

I look at Deo and we meet eyes. I announce loudly, "Hey, Deo, I gotta give you that board wax. The stuff from Hawaii. It's in my car." The girls look at me in confusion, but Deo doesn't need to hear another word.

He's already kissing Whit on the cheek and heading to the driveway with me. "Be right back!" he calls.

When we're standing in the driveway, Deo holds his hands out. "Alright. What's the plan?"

"I'm gonna rip that asshole Jason apart with my bare hands," I snarl. Unlike the girls, Deo doesn't get all freaked out when I'm pissed. He actually looks fairly amused.

"Dude, you get so fucking Incredible Hulk when you're pissed. This is exactly why you've got to let it out more often. You know? You're always so damn responsible. You need to be crazy once in awhile." He leans back on his Jeep and jerks his thumb at his board. "Remember when me and you said we'd shred it in New Zealand?"

I nod. Maren told me to make a bucket list, right? I guess I've had a partial one for a long time.

"Right. We fucking should." I clench and unclench my fists, wishing I had something to punch. Like Jason's smug-as-shit face.

"Top five things you gotta do before you get settled down and turn into an old, fat Mexijew, and say them without thinking too much. Go." Deo points at me and I don't think, just say what comes off the top of my head.

"Beat the shit out of someone." I hold up one finger.

"Easy. I've even got a name for that one. New Zealand. Let's do it. Your bachelor party, alright? I know you're not gonna be able to wait much longer to make an honest woman of Whit. So that's two. Uh, huge tat, and it's about damn time. That's three. Four? I want to cliff dive. Yep. Alright, one more?"

I'm going to say that I want to climb some badass mountain or skydive or something, but Deo cuts in.

"Seriously, man? Five is get your balls in order and ask Maren on a real date once you beat her boyfriend to a pulp. Then you two fuck like crazy animals for, like, five days straight. Because, I don't want to know your business with Kensley, but I don't believe a girl that incredibly stupid in every way could have been good in bed. Sorry. I'm just not buying it." Deo's shaking his head like he feels bad for me.

"Are you kidding me? Kensley and I had sex all the time," I protest.

"I never said you didn't have a lot of sex. But, c'mon. Admit it. It was subpar." He raises his eyebrows and shakes his head. "Tell Papa Deo. Your sex was shitty for, like, five years. I know it because Tracey rocked your world, and that was just a one night thing. You didn't even know that girl."

Tracey? How crazy is it that I thought she was the one? As good as the sex with her was, it didn't even begin to do to me what some heavy making out with Maren did: which was throw me into a fucking crazed state of near-constant lust. And, Deo's right. Sex with Tracey was better than it was with Kensley.

If kissing Maren was better than sex with Tracey, which was better than sex with Kensley, what the hell would sex with Maren be like?

It's like some kind of pornographic Algebra problem, and it makes me feel like a total sack for even wondering.

"I…it's not like that, alright? She's…Maren is…" I can't find the words.

Deo unfolds his arms and his jaw goes slack. "No shit. No fucking shit. You already screwed her? You sly fucking dog!"

I rub a hand over my face. "How do you always manage to be a bigger dick than I imagined possible? I did *not* have sex with Maren."

"You did not have sexual relations with that woman?" Deo laughs. "You're so full of shit. I can see it on your face. I know you, man. I even know your lies."

"I know you think you know everything, but…you don't, asshole. We, uh, we may have fucked around a little, no sex, though. But we were so damn drunk. And we both admitted it was a mistake." Or, in my case, I told a really solid lie about how it was a mistake, and she seemed relieved to have me say that. Much as that sucked, it was probably for the best.

"You're so into this girl. Just go for it. She's your number five." Deo grins and rubs his hands together. "And I need to get you to New Zealand. This is the perfect way to guilt Whit into pushing the wedding up."

"You're so damn romantic. Did you ever think there might be a reason she's running away from this wedding? Like maybe she's scared to be Mrs. Beckett?" It sounds dickish, but it's fairly impossible to get Deo down.

Which he proves by snorting at my suggestion. "She's dying to be Mrs. *Deo* Beckett. She's just like you, man. Love-scared. Not me, though. I'm a natural born lover, and I will snare Whit in my love web. Mark my words. Natural. Born. Lover." He points his thumbs at his chest.

"More like a natural born asshole." I toss him the board wax that I really did need to give him. "So, if I need bail after I kick Jason's ass, you got me, right?"

Deo throws an arm around my shoulders. "As long as you don't tell Whit about the Mrs. Deo Beckett joke, we're solid. She's all 'empowered woman, not losing myself, yaddayadda.' And remember to keep your awesome fury in check, Hulk. You wanna scare the asshole, not kill him."

I nod and we head back into the house where Whit and

my loud, obnoxious family wait to eat with us. Conversation bounces from one subject to another like mad, and the food is beyond delicious, but I feel like I can't hear or taste a thing.

My mind keeps flipping between two scenarios. In one, I'm beating the shit out of Jason Nucci and making damn sure he doesn't think about hurting Maren again.

In the second, I'm doing wild, crazy things with Maren for hours on end in my bed.

I can't keep this girl out of my brain, but I realize it's probably because it's been so long since I got laid. I mean, I guess it hasn't been that long in the grand scheme, but sex was pretty much a daily thing with Kensley, and now it's been…too long. Much as I think I want her, I know any relationship is probably the recipe for rebound disaster. Good thing that by the time I make scenario number one happen, scenario number two will probably be out of the picture.

But I tell myself I don't care if Maren will most likely hate me for kicking her boyfriend's ass. I can acknowledge that dating her is a stupid idea, but there's no part of me that can be okay with seeing her get hurt.

I make a decision to get going on my damn list so I can keep thoughts of Maren as far out of my head as possible.

I'm wishing myself a lot of fucking luck on that one.

12 MAREN

I pull the large spiral-bound pad out of my bag and open it to the first page. The pages are heavy and still stiff because, even though I bought his sketch book two years ago, it's the first time I've taken the time open it. I clasp a binder clip to the bottom of the pad to keep it open in the persistent wind and pull out the fresh pack of oil-based sanguine pencils, taking the time to roll one back and forth in my palm, feeling the familiarity of the rough wood before poising it to the pad.

I used to draw daily, once upon a time. It was something I'd done since I was a kid. Almost every photograph from when I was a little girl features me with a crayon, paint brush or pencil in my hand, creating something.

But then real-life happened and the instances of me feeling creative, or even thinking about expending the kind of energy creating something takes, just dwindled and faded away. The last time I'd drawn anything at all was first semester, when I still had hope things would change for the better and all my best-laid plans would finally work out. At least while I was still in school, I had an excuse to waste time on things like art. I made sure to work in some art class each semester into my schedule.

Until I couldn't afford those extra classes anymore…and

then had to drop out of school altogether.

I take a deep breath of the thick ocean air and start outlining. A rough uneven line to represent the shore, jagged peaks for rocks and squiggly lines for calm water. The surf isn't great this morning, and one by one, I've watched the surfers give up for the day and make their way up the sand.

I dig my toes in the sand and try to grasp just how much my life has changed from the time when I was a hopeful student with a shiny new set of classes and fulfilling future in front of her to a depressingly single, underemployed loser living with her alcoholic dad. Instead of getting bogged down in the inevitable suckiness of my life in general, I focus on this moment in particular and remember exactly why I used to frequent this spot on the beach when I needed inspiration. It's perfect because the main crowds stay further south since the sand is a little rocky over here, but I don't mind it. I just put down a double layer of towels and I'm good. Alone, peaceful, perfect.

I did second-guess whether I should go to a different beach or even sit up on the pier this morning because now I know where Cohen's place is—it's less than one hundred yards from where I'm sitting now. If it weren't for the huge rock formation next to me, I'd be able to see a straight shot to his gorgeous home.

It was a risk picking this spot. But a calculated one.

Maybe if I run into him, it'll quash some of this awkwardness between us. We still haven't had a normal conversation since his tongue was on my neck and his hands were…Christ…maybe seeing him will only make the awkwardness worse.

I press my pencil back to the pad, but the line is all wrong. It's too thick and dark and heavy handed. I close my eyes and let the wind swirl through my hair, transforming it to a knotted mess, no doubt, but I've got to relax. Since that night at Jason's place, I've been wound tighter than ever. I feel like I wasted so much time on him. And for what? He's called round the clock. He even texted me that he loved me last night, which I don't think he ever said to my face.

I didn't reply.

I can't.

I just want to forget that Jason and that chapter of my life ever happened.

I need a clean slate.

And a fresh piece of paper. I unclasp the clip and turn to the next page in my sketch pad, smooth it down, and re-clip.

"Maren?" a voice I know so well says. I pause for a moment, wondering if I imagined it, but the wet droplets collecting on my towel say that, no, it did actually happen. I slowly raise my eyes, taking in the tanned and toned legs, the abs that no one has the right to have—at least if I can't touch them—and that jet black hair dripping water onto his broad shoulders, down his chest, and... "What are you doing here?"

I swallow hard. "Here? I'm just drawing." I hold the pad up as evidence and start to blab like I'm guilty. It's like I'm outside of my body watching myself act like a huge fool, and there's nothing at all I can do to stop it. "I know you live nearby. I swear I wasn't hoping to run into you or anything. Really, I just—"

"Maren, it's a public beach, you have just as much of a right to be here as I do. Even if your page is blank." Cohen winks at me and I want to crumple myself up like a piece of paper to avoid this particularly hellish embarrassment. "Surf is terrible today. Do you surf?" He graciously changes the subject.

"I do." I watch the corners of his mouth twitch up into a pleased smile and I feel a flash of satisfaction. "I haven't in a long time. Jason—" I start to tell him how Jason thought surfing was only for slackers and people with too much time on their hands. He didn't appreciate how you experience both wild exhilaration and total serenity while in the barrel of a wave. But I decide against talking about Jason to Cohen.

"Never mind."

"We'll have to go sometime. I'm out here almost every morning," Cohen says, running his palm across the smooth surface of his board. I've never wanted to be a surfboard so much in my entire life.

"Absolutely. I'd really like that," I say, keeping my voice steady and hopefully concealing the raw lust bubbling up inside of me.

I hold my hand up in an attempt to block out the rising sun when Cohen locks his dark eyes on mine. We stare at each other for what should be an uncomfortable amount of time, but it isn't, because I'd love to stare at him longer. All the time.

"Listen, Maren. I need to talk to you about something and—"

"Please don't…" I pause and let my courage build for a few seconds. Which is totally necessary when I'm being faced with Cohen in all his wet, sexy glory about to tell me that the little perfection we had wasn't good enough after all. It's the last damn thing I need to hear today. I take a deep breath and dive in. "Don't say that you regret the other night. Don't say how it was a mistake, because I can't take hearing that right now," I confess.

Maybe it's too much honesty to lay out here, on a sunny

public beach so many nights after our amazing, hot stolen moment, but I can't keep it inside anymore. He's got to know.

"I wasn't—" Cohen pauses to clear his throat. "I promise you I don't think it was a mistake." The sincerity in his voice, combined with the way his eyes rake over me, instantly convinces me that he doesn't regret the scene in the kitchen.

I nervously pull my bottom lip in, waiting for him to finish.

"Can we just go somewhere and talk? I have some dry clothes in my car and there's a place right up the beach with amazing Mexican food if you're game. I'd really like to buy you lunch." I let my eyes wander one more time on his exposed stomach, dreading the minute he pulls a shirt on, and nod. "That sounds good."

The restaurant is uncomfortably packed. They've crammed us into a booth that should maybe fit two toddlers, not full grown people like me and Cohen. Still, being close enough to smell the sand and ocean on him isn't exactly a negative.

I tap the edge of my cardboard coaster onto the mosaic table top.

DEPTHS

"Well, what's good here?" I ask.

Cohen presses his back against the booth and stretches his long legs out. One of his knees knocks into mine, but neither one of us flinch away from the touch. "Their enchiladas are killer. Not as good as my mom's, but still awesome. The flautas are pretty bomb, too. What do you like?"

You.

I shake my head at myself and smirk.

"What? What'd I say?" Cohen asks, propping his elbows on the table and leaning in close to me.

Bad idea, Cohen. You're hard to resist from afar, this close makes it almost impossible.

"Nothing." I shake my head. "I think I'll just get the quesadillas. That sounds safe, right?"

I love being here with Cohen, I do, but part of me feels like this is a really bad idea. I've been trying to convince myself to stay away from him, and then I all but stalked him out and now we're at lunch, and it suddenly feels like I've maybe made this happen and it shouldn't be happening.

Cohen lets out a laugh that smoothes the creases in my mood.

"I'm sure they're great. Do you want a drink?" he asks, as the waiter approaches.

"Bottle of Sapporo?" I ask.

A smile stretches across his face. "Ah, that's my girl. Good choice."

I know he doesn't mean anything deep by it, but it feels good to know that he approves.

Cohen orders for us, and it doesn't feel possessive or weird. It feels like it should. Like a gentlemanly gesture. We both nurse our beers a bit before he finally speaks again.

"I meant what I said on the beach." His voice drips raw sexiness over the words that he says without a hint of hesitation. "What happened at my house, that wasn't a mistake. At least not for me."

I glance up from the label on the bottle I've been picking at. I open my mouth to speak, but he isn't finished.

"You, Maren. You are so not what I expected to fall into my life right now. You're beautiful, and smart, and you just *get* things... and Christ you're so damn sexy." His voice goes rough on the last few words and parts of me start throbbing that shouldn't while in public. "I just... I don't want you to think that that night in the kitchen was some rebound thing for me, because it wasn't. You aren't. But I get that, for whatever reason you're with Jason, so I am sorry if I stepped out of line."

"Jason and I broke up," I spit out.

Cohen jerks his head back in surprise and then relaxes a

bit and takes a long pull from his beer. "Why?" It's a single word tight with control.

"Isn't it obvious? He was a complete douche. I don't know why I was even with him for as long as I was. I mean, I guess I do, but still…"

"And why was that?" Cohen asks, looking me in the eye. Forcing me to expose things I don't want to, but I know I will because it's *Cohen*.

"Because it was easy. Safe."

Cohen shakes his head and scoffs. "Maren, what about Jason screamed safety to you?"

I mull the question over for a minute while I pick apart a tortilla chip, feeling a little embarrassed. "I guess I mean that my heart was safe. Jason wasn't always terrible to me like he was at the end, but he was never great. He was just enough. And it was safe because he couldn't break my heart…because he didn't have it."

Cohen nods knowingly, and I can't help the relief that washes over me when our food arrives and puts a nail in the talk about Jason. For now at least.

"Good?" Cohen asks, as I stuff a bite of tortilla and cheese into my mouth.

I nod. "So good. Yours?"

"Excellent. Always is. Genevieve used to date the cook

here. I'm seriously glad he doesn't hold a grudge, because I eat here at least once a week."

I love knowing little things about Cohen like this. Pointless things maybe, but still, it's more information about him and what he does outside of the confines of Rodriguez Family Furnishings. Getting to know these little facts make me all tingly and fills me with an ache to be a bigger part of that outside life.

"Speaking of exes—" he starts.

I roll my eyes. "Please not this again."

He swallows hard and puts his food down, like he's not remotely comfortable saying what he's about to say. "I just have to tell you something, and I'm so glad to know that you aren't together anymore for so many reasons...but this one most of all."

"What?" I lean in, unsure if I want anyone else in this establishment to hear whatever horrifying thing Cohen is about to tell me about Jason.

"So, Deo, my best bro, his girlfriend is Whit, and she works at a tattoo place. Anyway, she put two and two together and realized that she's actually met Jason before. I mean, I was just mentioning you and..."

I feel a warm blush creep over my face, knowing that he must have been telling his best friend about our semi-hook-up. "It's fine, Cohen, go on."

"Anyway, turns out Jason had been into Rocko's tat shop a couple of weeks ago, prepaying for a tattoo. Of his name...for you."

I spit my beer out. I can't help it. "Oh, God, I'm so sorry!" I say, grasping at the stack of cheap napkins and blotting every surface. "So, so sorry."

Cohen chuckles. "It's fine. Don't worry about it."

I'm mopping up the mess I made, and he's helping, looking a little confused and relieved, and I have to explain things. Because Cohen needs to know that I may have been in a shitty relationship, but I always had boundaries. Firm ones.

"Cohen, I would never. Ever. *Ever* in my life tattoo any man's name on me, especially that slimy prick's. I can't even believe that he would think that I would want that. I just..." Even as tears stream from my eyes, and other patrons of the restaurant stare, I can't control my maniacal laughter.

"That's good. Good. I'm glad to hear that. He said it was going to be your birthday present." The relief on Cohen's face is priceless.

I know I made the right decision when I walked away from Jason, but it's moments like these that reaffirm just *how* right a decision it was. "My birthday present? That's insane. That's the last thing I'd ever want. He really has no idea who I am at all. I guess he never really wanted to know."

"I want to," Cohen says, his words suddenly making the tone of this conversation more serious than it has been before.

"W-what?" I stutter out.

"I want to know you, Maren." The entire place just recedes, and it's like all I can focus on are the words coming out of his sinfully perfect mouth.

I grasp at frantic straws, trying to make sense out of what he's saying, but not daring to hope he might mean what I think he means. "You do. We talk every day."

Cohen sighs. "Right. We talk about recliners and spreadsheets and both of our exes, but I want to know more about *you*."

"I'm not so interesting. What do you want to know?"

Cohen rubs his hand across the scruff of his cheek and I fight back the urge to lick my lips.

"For starters? Why someone so freaking intelligent and beautiful allows herself to basically be held hostage by her father. You have so much to offer and you're just stifling yourself and your dreams to take care of your dad. I don't get it."

"That was harsh," I say, pulling back. This conversation right here is why I was with Jason. Because I never had to defend or explain myself or my choices to Jason. He didn't ask complicated questions and he didn't care. It was easier that way.

"I don't mean it to be. I'm just curious. What makes you feel the need to take that on? It just seems to me that you're too young to have that kind of load on your shoulders." He slides his hand across the table and almost grabs mine, but not quite.

Which is good. It's hard enough to resist the urge to leap over the table and onto his lap, even when he's butting his nose in where he has zero right. If he touches me, I know I'll lose my will and just give up trying to resist him.

I shrug, not all that excited to delve into the extremely tangled mess that defines life with my father. "I guess so. But he just doesn't have anywhere else to go. I feel like I can't let him down. I'm all he's got."

"Fair enough. But do you know what I think?" He leans in, and I feel like I might be getting slightly hypnotized by him. I hope he doesn't think I should get up and cluck like a chicken or something, because I don't know if I'll be able to deny whatever it is he thinks I should do. "I think you should make this year the year of Maren. The year you figure out what *you* want and only do what makes you happy."

His request actually makes a public display of the chicken dance sound like a fun time.

"That sounds like a dream." It's cornball to put it that way, but that's the sad truth. *Just* a dream, I should add. And one I'm not about to torture myself with. Real life is hard enough without lost dreams to make it more unbearably depressing.

Cohen reaches across the table and brushes his thumb across my bottom lip. It's a soft touch that's over way too quickly and leaves me aching for more. "Make it happen."

The words sound like a demand, but the tone of his voice makes it more like a mantra, like advice or just plain old encouragement. God, what a simple thing encouragement is. Until Cohen said those three words, I didn't realize just how little of it I had in my day-to-day life.

In fact, it's almost like the people around me have been dragging me down, drowning any hope before I could reach out and grab onto it.

"I'll try." And I mean it. Cohen is right, and I've known it for a long time, long before he spoke up.

Something has got to change with Dad. I love him, but our relationship is so unbalanced and one-sided. I can't spend my entire life taking care of him like he's an invalid.

DEPTHS

Cohen clears his throat and interrupts my thoughts of evicting my dad.

"So, since you won't be getting any ink for your birthday, why don't you let me take you out tomorrow?"

I suck in a quick, nervous breath. "I don't know..."

Cohen drags his eyebrows down and looks disappointed. "What makes you unsure? Like you just said, we know each other, so it's not like going out with a stranger. You've been to my place; I'm not a crazy ax-murderer. It's just me and you and some good food and wine. I know a place, or, my sister recommends a place, that's supposed to be amazing."

"You talked to your sister about this?" A tingle of warmth travels through my limbs and fills me with bubbly hope.

He shakes his head. "Not about you, just asked for some dinner recommendations. Just in case."

I cut my smile short by catching my bottom lip between my teeth. "If we didn't run into each other today—"

He doesn't try to hide his smile. "It's like you want to make me say it. Alright. The answer is 'yes.' Yes, I was still planning to track you down and ask you out. What do you say?"

And then that awful saying, *be careful what you wish for*, singsongs through my brain. Is this not what I was hoping would happen? Isn't this even better than what I was hoping for?

But, the weird thing is, with Cohen I don't mind telling him what scares me. So I do. No matter how terrifying it is.

"I'm scared. I'm scared of how I feel for you now, and can't imagine how much more I'll feel if we go out-out."

Cohen nods like he understands, then reaches across the table and clutches my forearm. My heart skips and thuds at his fingers on my skin.

"I'm taking chances here too, Maren. But you've got to give me one."

I could drown in those eyes, big and bold and dark. But, with Cohen, it's like I'm okay with letting go and diving deep. Maybe because I sense that he's going to show me how to swim out of the shallows and grab for something more.

His voice coaxes me. "Come on, it's your birthday. Let me take you out and show you a good time."

13 COHEN

"This place is great." Maren looks around at the brightly painted red walls of the little Thai place Lydia swears has the best pineapple fried rice she's ever tasted. Plus they fresh make their own Panang sauce and rice noodles daily.

I feel like maybe I got the vibe wrong. Maybe it's too impressive. Maybe I should have just bummed out a little, the way I usually did with Kensley. But I realize this isn't about my own damn comfort. It's about effort.

Awesome as I thought things were with Kensley, I never tried things that were new and different, and I think that might be because I was fine with just settling when it came to her and our relationship.

But Maren makes me brave. She makes me want to try new things. With her. For her. And that's gotta be a good thing.

"I'm glad you like it."

I'm glad she's here with me, her skin glowing, her eyes shiny, like she's got some kind of happiness running like sunlight under her skin. I'm glad she wore the dress she picked. It's the same deep blue as her eyes, and the top dips a little low, letting a tiny bit of lace bra show every now and then when she leans toward me. One strap is looser than the other, and it keeps sliding down her shoulder. I don't know what the hell it is about her outfit exactly, but she somehow looks sexy and innocent at the same time, and it's a huge turn-on.

We order too much food and wine that's so expensive, I have to work hard to keep from looking panicked when I order it. But when the waiter pours a few deep red splashes into her glass and she takes a sip, I know it was worth every dollar. The face she makes is exactly the face I imagine she'll make when we finally wind up in my bed together.

It may be unromantic as hell, and I don't mean to sound like a pig, because it's not like that with Maren, but getting her in bed with me has definitely made it to position number one on my bucket list.

"So, your sister was telling me you've got this big New Zealand surf trip planned?" she asks, adjusting the strap on her dress. I keep one eye on that creamy shoulder, just so I can enjoy watching the fabric slip down her skin again in a minute.

"Deo, he's been my best friend since we were in diapers, he's marrying this awesome girl. And he's not into strippers or Vegas or any crap like that. We've surfed together since just after we learned to walk, pretty much, so I thought it would be cool to go to New Zealand and have one last major surf while he's still a bachelor." I move my feet under the

DEPTHS

table and love when my foot brushes hers. More than that, I love that she rubs her foot up and down along my calf in a slow, gentle motion. "It's partly your fault."

"Really?" She squints at me. "I'm pretty sure I never told you to pack up and head to New Zealand." The way she smiles behind her wine glass, kind of shy and sweet, yet so damn sexy? It makes my head go places it definitely shouldn't.

"You suggested I get a bucket list going. And you were right. I need to stop being so predictable. I need more adventure in my life." I look at Maren, biting her lip and toying with her napkin across the table and feel a sense of pure determination. I want to keep her interested in me. I don't need to make the same mistake I made with Kensley.

"I know I said that." She looks up, her blue eyes wide and serious. "But, you know that I meant you should do what you need to do for yourself, right Cohen? I mean, I think New Zealand is an amazing idea, and I love that you're making these goals and lists. But you? *You* are perfect the way you are. You're not predictable. You're *dependable*. And, look, I get that I'm a huge nerd and I say things that only further prove it." She grins and leans forward, and, like we're connected by an invisible string, I move forward too. Her voice caresses my ear. "You *are* adventurous. You don't need to be racing motorcycles and diving with sharks to prove that. Everything I do with you feels like an adventure." She laughs to herself and ducks her head like she's embarrassed. "So, do things that make you happy. No question. But don't you dare change." This time her expression looks ferocious and her voice matches it. *"Don't change."*

I can't help smiling at her when she gets all tough like that. "I don't think you'd be so sure that I should never change if you got to know me better. Deo always says I'm the biggest tightwad. He might be exaggerating a little, but I do kind of worry. Maybe I over-worry."

She closes her eyes like she's savoring my words.

"Worry?" She shakes her head, her dark hair shining in the light of the flickering candles on the table. "Do you have any idea how perfect that word is? Do you know how incredible it would be for any girl to have someone like you *worrying* about her? I feel like my entire life is comprised of people who don't worry about anything except themselves. And I feel like I'm left doing all the worrying for everyone. And it sucks. I'd love to worry *with* someone."

Our dinner arrives before I can say anything, and we sit in comfortable quiet for a few minutes while we ingest the most amazing food that's ever hit my mouth. Damn, Lydia was right for once. In a big way.

"This is amazing," Maren moans, wrapping her lips around a forkful of gai pad king. I never imagined watching a girl take a bite out of her dinner could feel like foreplay, but I'm ready to push my plate away and take her home right now.

"I'm so glad you like it. I was hoping you'd be happy with everything tonight." I start to eat, but stop when I notice she's laid her fork down and is just staring at her food like she has no idea what it is. "Maren? Are you okay?"

She pushes her plate and the candle and wine to the side and leans over the table, grabbing my collar and yanking me close to her. I'm half out of my chair, her hands coming up soft on either side of my face.

"I'm not ready for you, yet," she whispers, her lips sometimes brushing mine. "I want to be. You have no idea how much I want to be."

I would worry over that cryptic message, but I don't have time to think. Because her mouth presses against mine, hard and hot, sweet and soft, her tongue licking the seam of my lips and dipping into my mouth with possessive flicks that drive me fucking crazy.

I'm about to rip the table cloth off and throw her on the tabletop without giving a damn who's watching or what they're thinking, but she pulls back, her cheeks pink and her lips so gorgeous, puffy and a deep red. She leans back against her chair and presses a hand to the place where her blue dress dips low, just over her heart, and tries to catch her breath.

I sit back, too, not bothering to right anything because I like the fact that she roughed me up. That she wants me as much as I want her.

"I just..." She rights the tablecloth with a dainty tug, rearranges her place setting, and shoots a sheepish smile at the other couples gawking from the surrounding tables. When she looks at me, there's this complete satisfaction that, I swear, changes the color of her eyes and the shape of her mouth. "I just wanted to thank you. For an amazing date. For being so amazing. For being you."

She takes a long, thirsty sip of her wine, and I try to collect my thoughts, but I'm so rock-hard and turned on, I don't know what the hell to do. She gestures for me to eat, so I do that, breathing slow and focused to try to get my body back under control. The problem is, every time I look at her, I start to feel wild again.

I mean, I guess it's a problem. Or maybe it's just a problem I don't want to find a solution to any time soon.

I've never experienced anything like this. I'm

overwhelmed by incredible food, but I don't want another bite. I want *her*. I love that there's this elegant atmosphere here, the good music underlying all the chattering conversation, the smiling people making everything feel at ease, but I want *her*.

She's all I want, and I want her *now*.

"What are you thinking about?" she asks, breaking through my thoughts.

Part of me wants to tell her. Why the hell not?

Because I'm not a complete dick.

"Just thinking about what you said, about going away with Deo. About life changing so fast, I feel like I can't even keep up." It's an improvised answer, but it's not all that far from the truth.

"It must be hard." She scoops up every last scrumptious bite of food on her bone-white plate. "Since you and Deo were so tight for so long. It must be hard to suddenly have to get used to someone else in his life."

Her eyes are heavy-lidded and sad with that obvious remorse that comes from knowing how it feels to constantly not be included. I hate that she spends so much of her life on the outside looking in. I hope I can start making that change.

"Not at all," I correct her gently. "Deo and Whit...they make so much sense together. She loves him exactly the way he is and, it's like, if I could have picked a girl from all the girls in the world to be Deo's soul mate, I would have picked Whit." And I admit the thing I've never really told anyone else, because it's half-embarrassing. "Plus, I kind of love being around her. When I broke up with Kensley, I had a pretty shitty opinion of girls in general, but being around Whit gave me hope I'd find someone amazing. Someone who I click with the way she clicks with Deo."

Maren runs a fingertip over the scroll pattern on her fork. "Mmm. So you have a crush on her?"

I laugh and rub my neck. "Wow. Way to make it awkward, Maren." She looks up, surprised, but I wave off her shock. "I'm joking. But maybe not totally joking. Because I guess I did kind of have a crush on her. Or, maybe not her exactly. It was more like I had a crush on what she and Deo had together. And…I know this sounds stupid, but it made me embarrassed to be with Kensley when I saw how right they were together. Like I was the world's biggest fraud."

Maren leans forward so far, I can see all the lace edging the top of her bra, her eyes big with excitement, her lips parted to spill her eager agreement. "Not stupid at all. I used to watch other couples who were so nice to each other, so in love, and I'd point them out to Jason, like maybe he'd be…I don't really know? Inspired maybe? It's like I could see what I wanted, but, even though I knew damn well I didn't have it, I was so sure I could just make him be that way. Because I was scared out of my mind to let him go." She clamps her mouth shut and blinks too fast.

I wonder if she misses him, and I hate myself for hating him so much, I want to break something.

"Why were you so scared to let him go?" I demand. "He was pretty much a douchebag to you in every way imaginable."

When she looks up at me, the sadness in her eyes knifes me directly through my heart. "I guess Jason was fucked-up enough to never really notice my fucked-upness. And I've been lonely. My dad isn't exactly the best company, and I dropped out of college, so I had no friends after I moved into this new apartment. Jason was just a warm body, but sometimes you need that. I mean, I'm human. I can't go without other humans, even kind of shitty ones."

I push back from my nearly empty plate and wish we'd never started down this path. But, fuck it. Maybe first dates didn't have to be all schmooze and romance. Maybe it's better if they get real fast, because then you can see if the person you think you might want to make forever happen with will even be able to handle your shitty past and present.

"Deo hated Kensley," I admit. I've never told anyone that, though anyone who knew the both of them would have guessed it in a second. "He thought she was shallow and a user. He thought she had no sense of humor. That's pretty much the kiss of death, right? No sense of humor? What could possibly be worse?" Maren opens her mouth, all sweet pink lips and eager eyes, but I don't give her a chance to answer. "You know the craziest part? If Deo gave me his opinion about a taco stand or a wave or a shirt or a band, I'd listen to him no question, because he's pretty much the best person I've ever met in my entire life. But I never listened to him about Kensley, the girl I planned to marry and spend my life with, and he wound up being totally right."

She reaches across the table, but there're too many plates and glasses in the way, and she never quite connects her fingers with mine.

"I get that. I lost a lot of friends because they just couldn't stand Jason. And worse than all that?" She takes a deep breath and lets it leak out in a wobbly whoosh of breath. "I knew for myself, in my own gut, that Jason was no good. I knew that. So why the hell was I with him as long as I was? When did I become the kind of girl who just stayed with a guy because it was easy?"

Her face has so much self-hatred plastered on it, it makes

me pissed.

"Hey. Hey. Look at me." When she looks up, I don't let her look away again. "You don't have a fucking thing to be embarrassed about. He was an asshole, you got caught up with him, and now you ditched him. Good for you."

She doesn't seem like she took my rousing speech to heart, and I follow her eyes when they get wide and take on a forlorn look, all orphan-like.

"Speak of the devil." She puts a hand to her throat and gulps the last few sips of her wine quickly.

Jason comes in with Ally at his side, looking pissed as hell.

Fuck! I should have known if Lydia recommended a place it would wind up being douchebag central. But why *this* particular douchebag on tonight of all nights?

Much as I hate his damn guts and would love to let him know it, I'm hoping he just moves on to his table and leaves us the hell alone. I want tonight to be special for Maren, and having Jason here is not going to accomplish that.

But it's like his hate is looking for a target, and when his eyes scan the trendy crowd and come to rest on Maren, there's a little gleam of glee in them.

Despite my Jedi command for him to back the hell off, he heads to our table, bumping a few people in their chairs on the way over. By the time he gets close to us, his heavy breath gives away what his uneven steps had me guessing: he's drunk as hell.

"Maren," he says, drawing her name out like a forbidden word. "Fancy meeting you here. I always thought you were more an obscure taco stand type girl. I actually remember inviting you here and you said, and I quote, *'Fuck you and your show-off hipster bullshit.'*"

Maren's eyes meet mine, and she begs me to forgive her as she flicks her gaze to Jason.

"I've been dying to eat here. I said that because you had zero interest in taking me until you read some stupid blog about that ridiculous foodie event, which was the same night as Rowan's birthday," she says, her voice so cold it could frost the wine in the glasses.

Jason sways a little on his feet and grips the back of her chair with white-knuckled fingers, his hand almost touching her back.

"Well, whatever-the-fuck the reason was, you never wanted to come here with me, but now you'll slum it with Carlos? Is that why you weren't into it when I was down to fuck the other night? Your taste got darker?" She gasps and bites her lip, and he seems excited to see her uncomfortable. "Aw, did I hit a nerve? You know what's funny? That's half the reason I was so into you. Being with you felt like slumming it a little, and that was exciting as fuck. All these uptight professional women, they don't let me do the shit to them you begged for, Maren. I miss all those nasty little—"

They both jump when I topple my chair back standing up. It's probably not fair that Jason is as drunk as he is, but any sympathy I may have had for his incapacity went out a smashed window when I heard what he said to Maren.

"Shut your fucking mouth and leave this table right now."

I know he's not going to back down, so I cuff my sleeves up as he opens his mouth to say something I just *know* is going to give me good fucking reason to land a punch on his pretty boy face.

"I can talk to Maren anywhere, anytime I please, asshole. I've got first fuck claim on her. Here's an idea? Why don't you stop sniffing around my leftovers and find some nice Mexi—"

It was going to go on and disrespect Maren more, it was going to get racial, and I wasn't standing for a single fucking second of it.

Pulling my arm back feels amazing. Maren's shriek doesn't feel quite as good.

But then my fist slams into Jason's mouth, and that feels beyond fucking incredible. I'm stoked that he isn't so drunk that he can't swing back, and swing he does. A nice wide arc of arm slashes my way and his fist hammers under my jaw and detonates an explosion of sparks behind my eyes, then his other fist wails up and whacks me square in the nose, giving me the perfect excuse to punch the bastard back.

His efforts throw him off balance and he knocks over a chair at the table next to us and topples back. I hurl him up by his collar, because I don't hit an asshole when he's down. When he sways back and forth on his feet, I slam into his nose twice, fast, and smash the side of his face.

For a single, spectacular second, there's just the slow motion twist of his body and the fine spray of blood as he drops to the floor. The entire scene has a dreamlike quiet.

Then the sound and action rushes back at hyper speed. Maren is beating on my back, screaming in my ear. The manager and several staff members are rushing forward. Ally, all her pouting forgotten, races on too high heels to Jason's side, where she sinks to her knees and sobs over his moaning form.

The manager is screaming and pointing at me, and it's then that I realize I might be in deep shit. Luckily, Jason sits up woozily, helped by Ally's frantic arms.

"I'm fine!" Jason yells, holding his gushing nose. "He took a cheap shot. Just get this fucking border jumper out of

DEPTHS

my face."

I lunge at him again, but Maren yanks my arm back, and the manager sicks two dark-skinned busboys on me. Luckily, their investment in causing me any harm only goes as far as getting me to the doors, where their boss can still see them.

"Good fight, man," the younger one says in heavily accented English. Jason picked a particularly stupid slur. If he stays at the restaurant, I'd wager he'll ingest a pound or two of scorned busboys' bodily fluids hidden in his food. "You beat the piss out of that asshole."

The other claps me on the back. "That guy is such a fucking *pendejo*. He can *besa mi culo*. He had it coming. Nice job."

I gasp and nod, thanking the guys between wheezes. I'm glad when they walk back in and I can try to catch my breath in private, until I realize I'm all alone with Maren, and she looks totally, absolutely disgusted by me.

Shit.

Some girls love a guy who fights. Kensley would orchestrate fucked-up scenarios just to see me throw down, but Maren is obviously more dove than hawk.

I lean over, blood dripping out of my nose and onto the sidewalk. I glance up at her, my hair in my eyes. "He shouldn't have talked to you like that," I argue, though she

219

hasn't said a single word.

Her mouth opens and shuts like she's searching for something to say back to me, but she settles on just shaking her head. I want to pull her close, tell her that I'm sorry I messed things up on our first real date, but my nose is still spurting blood, and I feel a little bit like I might pass out any second.

"Give me a minute. I'll take you home." I tilt my head back and feel Maren's cool hand on my neck.

"You stupid ass," she mutters, bending my head forward with the gentle press of her fingers. "You're just making the blood drip down your throat. Tilt forward."

She leads me to the curb and we sit. Her fingers come close to my face and she clamps them at the bridge of my nose, tight.

"I'm sorry." I try to look over at her, but her wrist blocks my view of her face. A few long seconds tick by. "Apology not accepted?"

Her sigh shifts her entire body. "I don't think you should try to make me feel bad about not accepting your apology, because I don't think your apology means a damn thing." I can barely catch her words, like she's looking away from me. From us. From this disaster of a date.

"I mean it," I insist. Her second sigh is deeper and way

more irritated. "I mean it because I really am sorry that I ruined our date. I was having a great time, and I hate that it got fucked up."

"Or that you fucked it up?" she corrects.

"That's kind of cold. Jason deserved it." But I sound petulant, even to myself.

"Okay. Maybe he did. He's had that coming for a long time. And it's not exactly wrong that you kicked his ass. It's just…look what we traded for it." She's got this wistful tone going in her voice, and I hate it. I fucking hate it. "I'll always think of our first date now and remember Jason."

"So?" I loosen her fingers from my nose and pinch it myself, because it's driving me insane to not be able to see her. Funny how I haven't been able to see her for all of five minutes, but the second she's back in my line of site, I'm shocked all over again by how damn gorgeous she is.

Those big blue eyes blink with confusion. "So, I don't want Jason to have anything to do with the new part of my life. I want him to be part of my past, period."

I start to laugh, but stop before I dislodge another blood clot. "I don't think it works like that, Maren."

"Like what?" She straightens her back and squares her delicate shoulders, getting even more gorgeous as each pissed-off second ticks by.

"Like, you don't get to move on and just blow your past away. Everything you do, every new move you make is all tangled up in everything you did." Her eyebrows slam down over her eyes because she clearly hates what I'm telling her. "I'm not saying you don't move on and grow. Just, you can't disconnect yourself from who you were."

"But what if who you were was just who you were being while you waited to become the real you?" She turns her head and looks at me intently, like she wants me to give her an answer. Not just any answer, either. The right answer.

In the name of saving this date, I'd be happy to do just that. But I have no clue what she wants to hear. I doubt it's what I'm going to say.

"Um, I think this is pretty philosophical for a guy who just answered a couple of insults with his fists, but I can tell you what I think. I think you are who you are. There is no waiting. There's no pausing any of this. And if you feel like you're on a break or whatever, okay. But you better get back to it. Life goes fast, and who wants to sit any of it out?"

She presses a hand to her eyes and lets out a little shuddering sound.

"Maren?" I take her free hand, and, when she doesn't pull away, I wrap an arm around her. "What's wrong? I promise you, if it's this whole bullshit fight, I'll march back in there with my damn tail between my legs and make nice. You're right. I *am* an ass. Even if that tool deserved it."

Her laugh borders on a wet hiccup. "It's not that. I mean, yes, you are an ass, but, yes, also, Jason deserved every punch he got. I just..." Her voice wobbles as she tries to get the next words out. "I just want this part of my life to be over for good sometime soon. Erased. Gone."

I could totally tell her that she can do that if she wants. But I don't.

"Why?" I ask instead. "That's me erased, too, at least partly. That's me and you talking on the phone all day at work, watching baseball together, hanging at the beach, making out in my kitchen...all that. You want it gone?"

She shakes her head and rubs under her eyes hard with her fingers. "No. No. I don't want to erase anything about you. But everything else?"

"Jason is a dick, but would you really want to not remember anything? If you magically got to cut him out of your memory for good, you might wind up with someone like him again, right?" I can't believe I'm defending Jason's right to any space in Maren's brain, even hypothetically.

But it's not really that. It's more like I'm trying to let her know that it's totally okay to fuck up. More than okay. It's normal. Our fuck-ups make us who we are, and if we don't accept that...well, there'd be nothing but more potential fuck-ups in our future. Or, worse, we'd just freeze up and stop doing anything at all.

"I just need...a clean slate I guess. I just need to fix this all and be free to start over." She looks up, her makeup smudged, her smile shaky, and touches my nose gingerly. "It hurts like hell, right?"

I nod.

"See? Wouldn't it be great if you could make it go away?" Tears slide over her lips.

I shake my head.

"No?" she double-checks.

"I wouldn't change a single thing about tonight. I know it's not right that I liked kicking his ass, Maren, and I am truly sorry that it ruined the night for you. But no one is ever going to talk to you like that in front of me. I know you want me to say that I won't do anything like that again, but I can't." I let go of my nose, which seems to have stopped spurting blood, and hold her hand, still damp from mopping up her tears. "I care about you. I'm not going to let anyone walk all over you. Not happening. Ever."

She pulls her hand away from mine and nods tightly, like she's done with me. Sometimes I wish I was a better liar.

Then she turns, grabs my face in her hands gently, and

kisses me. It's light at first. I did just get my face half bashed in, and I guess she's trying to be careful.

But I have her. In my arms, the scent of her surrounding me, her body pressed on mine. And, more importantly, I have her happiness to be with me, her forgiveness, her excitement. So I kiss without worrying about my smashed nose, and every time I think the pain is going to get so extreme I honestly might pass out, I run my hands over her, let my fingers get lost in her soft hair, run my tongue over hers, and readjust so she's pressed closer to me, twined tighter around me, and let my mind jump wherever it wants to go. Which is some pretty lowdown, awesome places.

"Thank you," she whimpers, pulling away.

"You're welcome," I say, dragging her closer, rubbing my hands over her shoulders. "What are you thanking me for? Because I kind of feel like *I* should be thanking *you.*"

She cups my jaw, running a thumb over my cheekbone, her nose rubbing my against my face as she breathes me deep. "For taking care of me. No one, seriously, *no one* does that for me. I'm sorry I was mad at you. I'm just so used to being ignored. I'm so used to being the one taking care—"

She interrupts her own ramble, which is breaking my damn heart, and kisses me again, harder, with little nips of her teeth on my lips, and nuzzles her face against my neck.

My hand drags up her dress, making the skirt ride high on her thighs, then heads up along her stomach, over the bumps of her ribs, and between all that lace that's been teasing me through dinner. I brace my other hand at the small of her back as I run my thumb over the soft curves pressed high in that sexy bra.

She feels so good through the fabric, but I want my hands on her skin. I want her naked. I want her moaning. I want her all.

"Come home with me," I say softly against her ear.

She bucks and rubs closer, letting out a long, "Mmm," that lets me know she's at least tempted.

And that shred of temptation is all I need.

"Come home with me because I want to strip you."

14 COHEN

She stops moving against me, and I wonder if I pushed it too far already, but her hands squeeze at my shoulders expectantly, so I tell her, in plain words, everything we've danced around and hinted at for all the weeks we've wanted each other so badly. "I'm going to strip every last shred off of you, Maren, because just thinking about seeing you naked gets me hard."

Her fingers dig into my shoulders and she moans, making me feel brave enough to say more, to let her know how sexy she is and how turned on I am around her.

"And once you're naked, I'm not going to stop kissing you and sucking on you until you come for me."

Her breath catches in her throat and she rocks against me so softly, I don't even know if she realizes she's doing it. I unleash the words I'd hold tight unless I was in the dark, secret confines of my bedroom. I do it because I have a hard time containing anything I feel for her.

"And I don't mean once. I want it over and over, so you're slick as hell. I want you to come when I lick you and when I'm inside you."

She presses her face closer, until her mouth is right up against my mouth. She's not thinking about my nose and how much it hurts, and I don't blame her. The promises I'm making are pushing me right through the pain.

"I want to touch every inch of you. Do you want that?"

She nods, her hair rubbing against my face, the coconut-sweet smell surrounding me.

"Now?"

It's the only thing she's said since I told her what I want, but it's all I need to hear.

Without a word, she stands and tugs my hand. I help her into my car, and the longest ten minute drive in the history of my life begins. Every curve of the road I have to slow down for or residential reduced speed section makes me frustrated, but maybe it's good to have something to focus my aggravation on. Because when I glance over at her, she looks so nervous, and so damn completely gorgeous, I don't know…

I grip the steering wheel hard. Is this too fast? Too crazy? The wrong time?

I don't know. I don't know the answers to any of those questions.

I do know that I just gave her a big, bold speech on the usefulness of mistakes. And I hope with everything in me that the two of us and what we're about to do will never wind up labeled a *mistake* by her.

I know I could never think of it that way.

Things with Maren were supposed to stay neat. We both like things in their own little compartments. But I can't promise any of that anymore.

In fact, I can pretty much guarantee the opposite.

But she scrambles out of the car before I can open the door, and she's already kicked off her shoes by the time I catch up. She runs the bottom of her foot over the sandy step of my front porch, watching the key slide into the lock with an intensity that makes my hand shake.

We don't say a word as we make our way into the house, Maren ahead of me. I shut the door and she turns, her eyes fixed. On me.

I try to get a handle on my body, suddenly shaky and unsure.

She puts her hands at her hips and grabs fistfuls of fabric on either side of her skirt. It inches up, exposing more and more leg, and I'm so focused on every revealed bit of her, I'm blindsided by the way she drags it over her head and drops it on the floor.

The bra is a little bit of scrappy purple lace. Her thong matches. She's still in her heels. Her finger is crooked.

At me.

There's no way in heaven or hell I'm not going to follow.

She paces backward as I walk her way, stopping when

she hits the steps.

It's been ten seconds, a half-dozen steps, but my body reacts like I'm an hour into the world's sexiest striptease.

Like she can hear my thoughts, she turns her back to me and presses down one bra strap, then the other, and pulls her arms out, one hand moving to the clasp in the back.

I lock my breath in my lungs and wait for the fall. It's excruciatingly slow, like that lace is clinging to her skin the way I want my hands and lips to be. Then the tiny bit of fabric is floating to the stairs and Maren backs up, climbing with careful steps.

"Do you want me?" she asks, her voice husky, her dark pink lips trembling.

"More than I've ever wanted anything." I make sure my words are clear, that I say it so she'll have no doubt whatsoever.

Her thumbs hook in the waistband of her thong, and she slides it down an inch, then pulls it back up, down and up, her fingers playful against her own skin.

I pull my shirt over my head, kick off my shoes, and unbutton my pants. I half-think she'll stop or get spooked, but her hands run up from her waist, lingering under the swell of each of her perfect tits. She brushes her thumbs over her nipples and they stand at attention, ready.

So am I. Holy fuck, I'm so damn ready.

I tug down on my fly and step up two steps. She's higher than I am. My mouth is level with her nipples, and I make use of that particular vantage point, catching one lightly between my teeth and sucking in with firm pressure, licking at it until she grips the bannister and her head drops back. I switch to her other side and let my hands run over the soft fabric of her thong, my fingers dipping in under this last shred of lace that barely covers anything and pulling back out before I go too far.

Maren leans forward and down, pressing my face against the soft, sweet swell of her tits. Her hands grab at the waist of my pants and push so hard, my boxer briefs half go down with them. She braces her hands on my shoulders and looks over my head and down my back, where my ass is half-exposed by my falling clothes.

She pushes my face away and steps down, crouching on the step I'm on, her face eye level with my dick, which is still held back by the thin cotton of my half-on boxers. And then, with one more yank, I can step out of everything and appreciate the way her lips barely brush the skin of my upper thighs and my eager, over-stimulated dick.

"Wow." She eyes it and lifts a brow.

I'm so hot, I wouldn't doubt it if my face was bright red.

"Don't be embarrassed," she says softly, cupping the tip in her palm, her fingers brushing along the shaft with slow, steady motion.

I reach down and pull her up to eye level. "I'm never embarrassed with you, Maren. I've never been so comfortable with anyone. Never. I feel like…I've known I wanted you since the day we met. It's weird, but I feel almost like we need to hurry up and have sex so we can just seal it all, make everything between us official."

Before she can respond to everything I'm saying even though I shouldn't be, I scoop her into my arms and hold her tight to my chest. She lets out a little gasp, then rings her arms around my neck and grabs on to me. I walk to my room, the same room I left her alone in the night she slept here. The same room I imagined barging into so I could rub against her sweet, curving body all night long.

This time I barge in with her in my arms, and she giggles as I set her down on the bed.

"This place looks familiar," she says with an impish smile, falling back on the blankets, her dark hair spread around her, her arms at her sides. She rubs them over the covers, palms down, like she's making a snow angel on my sheets.

I watch her snuggle and roll on my bed like it's hers, and

I feel a kind of crazy-possessive happiness well up in me. I don't get to just ogle for long, though. Maren suddenly stops and looks up at me, shakes her head, and clucks her tongue.

"I don't want you all the way over there," she says and rolls to the side, patting the bed. "I want you here."

I'm not an idiot. I'm on that bed so fast, it makes Maren giggle again.

"You're pretty eager, huh?" She reaches one finger out and draws it across my left shoulder, my chest, my right shoulder.

It's barely even any contact, but we're both breathing hard when her finger completes its trek.

"Eager like you wouldn't believe." I roll her under me, my hands quick and sure on her skin, bringing out her moans and making her pull her knees up and spread them wide, inviting more touching, deeper.

I tear the last little piece of fabric off of her, bunching it up and tossing it aside. She rolls onto her back and I straddle her, gripping her hips on either side and relaxing my hold so I can push the flat of my palm up her body. She arches into me as my fingers climb, finally tangling in her hair, the hard length of my dick pushed in the apex of her thighs, my face low over hers.

Her mouth reaches up for mine, and I pull back just to

relish one more second of seeing her lips puckered toward me, hungry for me. When I skim my mouth over hers, she lets me know she's done being teased by nipping at me and turning her face away.

I thread my hands deeper into her hair, netting her close to me, and holding her still with gentle pressure so I can finally kiss her mouth again as long and deeply as I need to. She opens her lips and flicks her tongue into my mouth. I relax my weight on top of her, letting her eager hands pull at and reposition me until she's comfortable.

But I don't let my mouth leave hers again. Her tongue is a silky soft slide in my mouth, and I plunge deep to get every taste. She's sweet and a tiny bit bitter in unexpected corners. I refuse to leave a single spot unexplored.

When I'm sure she's not going to pull her mouth away again, I slide my fingers out of her hair and trace them down her arms, pulling her hands from their current position, cupping my ass, and threading our fingers tightly together. I press her hands up along her hips and ribs and shoulders and then over her head, forcing our bodies into two long lines pressed hard at every matched juncture; sliding heat against sliding heat, firm press to firm press, hard length against hot, wet depth.

Her skin is velvet under mine, but every single place it

DEPTHS

rubs against me shocks through my body like an electric jolt.

And there's so much touching, it's like a velvet-wrapped electrocution. A sweet torture I never want to end.

I kiss down her mouth and along the line of her neck, loving the strain of her hands against mine and the wild buck of her hips, pressing me so close, but not nearly where I need to be.

I kiss down, tugging her hands with me. She lets out little mews and groans of protest any time my mouth leaves her skin, switching to sighs and moans when I suck her nipples in with frantic pressure, lick her skin in a long line down her body, and finally wind up at the place that's wet and ready.

Her arms are stretched down, and she tugs for me to loosen my hold, but I pull back so she's sitting up, at first all the way, then back on her elbows. I let go of her hands, but hold up a warning finger to let her know I'll trap her again if she doesn't listen.

"Spread your legs," I tell her.

She closes her knees instead and asks, "Why?"

I put a hand on either knee and test them open with gentle pressure. "It's your birthday. Spread your legs so I can lick you into a happy one."

"It's already a happy one," she protests, closing tight against my hands.

I pry her knees open again. "You think so because I haven't stuck my tongue in you. Yet. Now trust me. And. Spread. Your. Legs. *Please*."

She wiggles up and lets her knees fall open, biting her lip and pressing her eyes closed as she does. I slide my tongue in a long, wet lap that shakes an instant moan from her.

I pull back and spread her folds with my fingers, letting my index, then my middle finger dip into her slick, tight depths. "That's it. Let me touch your pussy. Let me lick you. I want to hear you moan. Will you do that?"

"Yes," she gasps, and I tip my head back down, licking with quick, short flicks that have her pumping her hips and pressing toward me. "Please, Cohen, please."

I suck against the wet bud of her clit, and the long pull of her moan lets me know I'm doing something right. I lick again, tasting the salty sweet of her, using my fingers to set up a rhythm deep in her, and every once in a while I pull back to tell her to moan for me or ask for something I know she wants. Maren is more than willing, and I love the way her back arches against my mouth.

"Tell me where to lick it," I tell her.

"Here." Her hand slides down and her fingers press against the spot where she wants my mouth. I follow, my tongue tracing over her fingers as I focus on the sweetest center of her. "Faster," she gasps.

I slow down.

She laughs.

"Jerk." She runs her fingers through my hair and presses at the back of my head with her hand, getting bolder when she feels my moan against her skin. "Faster. Faster, *now.*"

I listen to her, even though I'm barely holding on to my sanity by taking things nice and slow. I flick my tongue, she pumps her hips, my fingers press and pull against her, until just when I'm positive I can't stand it a second longer, she shudders against me, pulling up on the back of my head with her hands, clamping her thighs tight to the sides of my face.

"Cohen! Holy shit, Cohen!" she cries, running her hands up and down over her body before she falls back on the bed, limbs spread in a lazy jumble. "Cohen?"

I army crawl up the length of rumpled covers to get closer to her. "Good?"

She turns her body tight to mine and crushes her arms around me. "A-freaking-mazing!"

"Happy birthday," I say, nuzzling her neck.

15 MAREN

"That's not it, is it?" I ask, pressing my sweat-damp hair back off my face. My body is humming, my blood singing from the way he touched me, the way he talked to me, the way he looked at me. I feel energized. I feel sexy as hell. And I'm not remotely ready for this to end.

He shakes his head and grins, his fingers trailing up and down my body lazily. "Nope. But you have to let me rest for a second."

"Hmm." I get up on my knees, loving the feel of having him spread out, all beautiful boy, all mine. "I'm not really into the idea of you resting."

I swing one leg over his hips and sit across his muscled thighs, straddling him. I reach over to the bedside table and open first the top, then the bottom side table drawer, determined not to end my search until I find what I'm looking for. And it takes two seconds for me to find what I need and pop back up, triumphant, with a condom in hand. I roll it over him, admiring how gorgeous he is in every way, and laugh a little when his eyes roll back.

He reaches his hands up my body and runs them over my thighs, making goosebumps prickle up and down my legs and right to my toes.

"It's *your* birthday," he points out, as if I didn't know.

"And I love being on top." I squirm a little, just to make him moan, and let the laughter bubble out of my throat when he does, exactly as I expected. "If you want to switch when you get your strength back, I'll consider it."

And that's where all our conversation stops. Because I press up on my knees, take him in my hand, and slide down over him in one tight, slick press of my body over his.

"M-m-Maren," he stutters, and I feel another burst of pride. One second in, and my sex is making him stutter. That's pretty nice work if I do say so myself.

I put a hand to my lips because the pressure is so good, I'm afraid I'm going to get loud and crazy fast. I rock my hips back and forth to test the best position, and pull back up slowly, then press down, repeating this whole crazy, sweet, wet motion that steals my breath and voice and mind.

There's nothing but the perfect stretch of me around him and the rhythm that starts out manageable, then spirals into a quick, maddening frenzy.

I'm panting and he fists both hands into the sheets, gritting his teeth in an effort to keep some semblance of control.

But I'm having none of it. If I'm about to go over the damn cliff, he's coming with me, no exceptions.

"Your hands..." I manage to gasp out, rocking harder, spreading my legs wider. "Your hands...need to be...on *me*. Now!"

He lets the sheets loose and half sits up, rubbing his big, rough hands up my legs, around to my back, down to cup my ass like he's trying to slow the tempo. I hold back at first, but eventually agree to his suggested pace when he tilts me forward, and I feel my body working itself into the tight flex and pulse that precedes a spine-tingling orgasm.

He slides his hand between our bodies and his fingers press and rub on the peaked, sensitive place where I'm starting to come undone quickly.

"Come for me," he says, kissing my mouth when it bumps up or down near his face.

I'm losing my rhythm because he's touching me in a way that makes it hard to do anything but feel his hands on me and the length of him in me. I can't even kiss him back, because I'm in some kind of zone. Every cell in my freaking body is driving with wild intent towards one explosive goal, and I'll be damned if I deviate from that goal for a single second.

I adjust once, then again, but I can't seem to hit that exact place I need to. Suddenly Cohen rolls me under his body, and I wrap my arms and legs around him tight when he does.

DEPTHS

He presses into me as deep as he can, rocking in and out until he hits that exact point as familiar as the click of a key in a lock.

"Mmmm." I'm thinking so many things, so many sweet and nasty things I want to whisper in his ear but he's unraveled me, left me panting and breaking apart in the most knee-knockingly, breath-stealingly delicious way.

I covered my mouth before, but by now I just can't care. He slides in and out, and I finally can't feel him, can't feel myself, don't know what's happening, and don't care.

I reach my arms up for what? Nothing. I want to let go. I'm not doing this for any kind of shallow cheap thrill. I'm in this to rip through to the shuddering depths.

That's where it starts. My orgasm builds from somewhere so deep and dark, and it crashes over me like a tsunami wave, making me buck from shoulders to hips, making my voice tear and scream from my throat in a jibberish of raspy syllables that end with the only word there is for me.

"Cohen! Cohen!"

His face is perfectly twisted, unable to contain another second of composure, and that's good. I scratch my fingernails down his back, buck my hips against him, let him feel every quiver and slick wave of pleasure he's giving me. I've never wanted to share sex the way I do with him. I've never wanted to drag my partner in and let him see every last wild thing.

He jerks in and out, buries his head in the crook of my neck and shoulder and lets out a long, shuddering moan.

"Maren," he bites out, and I feel the lock of his shoulders and stiffening of his back as he drives his hips against mine hard and gives in to his release.

For a few minutes, there's nothing but the sound of our ragged breathing, the damp smell of sweat, tinged with the sharp scent of latex. I can hear the crash of the waves outside, and start to get confused between their rush and the thud of our hearts.

I twist against him, my hair tangled around his arm, smudges of my lipstick on his neck and chest, my fingers twined around his. I didn't even remember making a move to hold his hand.

He rolls over and takes off the condom, and I have this dreadful fear that he's just going to get up and walk away. But he turns on his other side and reaches a long arm out, dragging me close.

"Get over here, birthday girl. When you blew out your candles did you wish to strike a man dead with pure sexiness? Because you almost achieved that."

I nuzzle his neck and suck on the salty skin. "I would

definitely not want you dead. Maybe maimed, but only so that I could keep you locked away to use as my sex slave."

He presses my hair back off of my face and rubs his thumbs in circles over the curves of my ears. "How did this happen? How the hell did I get lucky enough to convince you to get into my bed?"

"You actually weren't all that convincing." I kiss the tip of his nose and bite back a sigh when his hands bump down over my shoulder blades and back to cup my ass, squeezing appreciatively. "I was just super horny."

"Should I feel used?" He smiles and drags his fingers up and down my back with excruciating lightness.

"Well, I guess so. I did use you, after all." I drop my mouth to his shoulder and blow a raspberry, loving the way he laughs, loving that we can transition from passionate to goofy to honest without any hiccups.

"Do you promise to use me again?" he asks, his low voice rasping over my ears and somewhere in me. Somewhere a little deeper than I'm totally comfortable with.

But that's not all that surprising. I've been wading in the shallows for so long, the depths freak me out.

"I promise." I brush his hair back and love that I can. That he's mine to groom as I please. "But maybe not until later. I have to go check on my dad soon."

His lids half close and his mouth does this adorable pout. "Maren? I know you hate talking about your dad and your family in general, but maybe we need to talk about them a little."

I tense up. Instantly. My muscles have gone from jelly to stone, and I hate that it happens so fast. I try not to also hate Cohen because his words brought it on, but I want to lash out at something that won't lash back for once. And he's just lying there.

Why is he doing this right now? I want that to be the last thing on his mind. I guess I should have never even mentioned needing to leave.

Cold, slicing words are on the tip of my tongue, but there's something about his face, so open and sweet. I can't. The anger stops boiling, and I lay my head on his chest and count back from ten before I say anything.

"I hate it because it's not fixed."

"Fixed?" His voice echoes in his chest, where my ear is pressed. "What does that even mean?"

"I'm not crazy," I insist, looking over at his nipple as I talk. Funny how comforting it can be to talk to a guy's nipple. Way easier than looking him in the eye for sure. "I know we'll never be a real family again. Mom and Rowan never forgave Dad for falling apart and not even trying. And

DEPTHS

I know they love me. They just work hard: they don't have time to deal with anything other than the bakery. But I know Dad can get back on his feet."

He strokes a hand through my hair, gently untangling the knots our crazy sex made. "I think you have an amazing heart, Maren. And I'm not telling you to stop believing in your dad. People turn their lives around every single day, right? But, it's got to come from him. No matter how much you want it to happen, it's got to be from your dad."

"I know that," I rush to explain, tripping over his words in an effort to get mine out. "I do. Seriously. But he does want to, that's the thing. You don't understand how depressed he is. How much he wants something else."

"I believe he's depressed." Cohen pauses, and I can tell he's choosing his words with care. "But depression…that's, like, it's a thing that needs to be dealt with, Maren. Professionally. And if you're around him all the time, it's going to start pulling you down. Don't get upset, but it kind of has already, right?"

I push off his chest and yank the sheet up to cover my nakedness, getting ready to present to him the same argument I've argued to myself every time I think about leaving.

"I'm so young, Cohen. I can go back to school anytime.

He needs help now. And if I don't stop and help him, I'm scared…" The words are in my mouth, but I'm having a really hard time forcing them out. "I'm scared he'll *die*, Cohen. And I'm not being a drama queen. I'm afraid he'll have a heart attack or puke in his sleep and choke on it. So I check on him and make sure he's okay, the same way he did for me when I was growing up."

He nods. "I get it. I do."

That's not all he has to say, I can tell. "But?" I press.

"But what?" He hooks his fingers around mine and pulls me down close to him again. "If you don't want to talk about it, we won't."

I lie down next to him and press my face in the sheets. "Jason grew up with his mom. He never even knew his dad. And he and his mother talk, like, once every two months, maybe. So he never got it. But I thought you would get it, since your family is so important to you. So, I guess I don't get what you don't get. If that makes any sense."

He rolls over so I'm trapped under him, his arms on either side of me. "I get family. I get they can be a pain in the ass. And sometimes you need to give more than you really want to. But no father can expect his daughter to just give up everything and care for him when he's perfectly capable of caring for himself."

DEPTHS

I turn my head to the side to avoid his eyes, so focused and severe. "I could never be that selfish."

"There's such a thing as not being selfish enough, Maren. And, I know you don't want to hear this, but your dad is being super selfish. To you."

He sighs when I press at him, trying to get him off of me. I want to throw my clothes on and stomp away for a minute, but I can't.

I left the vast majority of my clothing in the foyer and on the stairs. There is one tiny ball of crushed lace that would be more embarrassing to pick up and try to untangle and put on in front of him than to just be naked. I try to pull the sheet, but he's wrapped in it.

Jason would have laughed at my stupid situation before he rolled over to take a nap.

Cohen gets off the bed, pads to his dresser, and pulls out a t-shirt. I take it from his hands and stuff it over my head, glad it's a little long, because I don't absolutely need to have underwear on with it. I am not going to be able to effectively state my case concerning why I need to take care of my father first right now with my ass hanging out in the breeze.

He pulls clothes on and says, "Would you like to sit on the deck?"

I nod and he leads me to the small wooden deck just off

247

his bedroom, already set up with two chairs. The sun is just setting, making the sky so neon bright, I can barely stand to look directly at it. The hiss and crash of the waves is an awesome antidote to the jumble of thoughts piercing my brain like a bramble.

I don't notice him leave, but when he comes back, he has two beers in his hand.

"Thank you." I take a long sip.

"I love having you here," Cohen says, squinting into the light. "You know, when I got this place, one of the main reasons I picked it was because I could picture having a wife here and a family. Eventually. And I thought I was going to marry Kensley. Bought her a ring and everything."

I curl my legs up and drink more, not sure I want to hear this story.

"I stand by my first thoughts on her," I confess. "She's an idiot, Cohen."

I think back to what he and I just did in that bed, and I try to imagine just walking away from it for no good reason. She must have been out of her damn mind.

"Thank you." His smile melts me. I expect him to look sad when he revisits his break-up, but he seems okay. "I thought it was all figured out, right? And I was pretty upset when she first left. But I realized something that now seems pretty damn obvious."

When he doesn't make a move to finish his sentence, I prod him. "Okay. Tell me what you realized."

He takes a long pull of his beer then looks out at the sun, now falling like a neon disk into the ocean. "You know, I'm a guy, so I was thinking of Kensley from a guy's perspective. She was good-looking, she was into the idea of being married, we had fun together."

I make a noncommittal sound. I so wish I could be more mature, but I want to drag Kensley around by her hair and scratch her stupid eyes out.

"But the person you marry, she's going to be your family. Maybe even more than the family you're born to, right? And when I started to think of Kensley as family, not some girl I was dating, it just made no sense to me. She and I made no sense on that deep a level." He looks at me like I'm supposed to get it, but I don't get it.

"What are you saying? Why wasn't she family?" I ask, feeling like I've just cracked open a fortune cookie but have no idea what the little scrap of paper is trying to tell me.

His smile is slow and sweet. "I don't know why. I guess I wasn't comfortable. I guess she wasn't right. I guess I didn't want to change for her, and she sure as hell didn't want to change for me. But, you?"

I put my hand to my chest when he says 'you,' like I'm making sure I'm still here, sitting in front of him, not faded and blown away. I'm here because Cohen sees me and points me out.

"Me?" I repeat.

"You." He puts a hand out and traces the line of my cheek with his finger. "Every single thing feels right with you. You make me want to change. I feel like you want what's better for me. And I want that for you, Maren. And anyone who doesn't want to let you change into the best version of yourself? They're not worth being with."

"My dad," I say hollowly.

He shakes his head. "I wasn't talking about him. I was just making a general statement, okay?"

I'm irritated at him. I'm irritated at me. I'm irritated at my dad.

How did things flip so quickly?

Then he pulls me into his arms and everything flips again.

"I don't want you to leave, but that's not for me to decide," he says, his voice a rumble over the sound of my own heart pounding in my ears.

"I don't want to leave," I say, turning my head into his shirt. "I don't want to lose you."

DEPTHS

He pulls back, and I half expect to get booted out. But he's smiling like I just said something incredibly funny.

"Lose me?" He cups my face in his hands. "If it was up to me, I'd never let you out of my damn sight, Maren. You can go wherever you need to, for however long you need to, and I'll be here waiting when you get back." His thumbs brush back the tears I didn't even realize were sliding out of my eyes. "You never have to worry about losing me."

"I do have to leave." I can hear the wariness in my own voice, and it makes me tired. I'm so tired, and I feel like I haven't slept for months on end, but tonight I got to take a half hour nap in his arms, and I need more. My body needs more. My heart needs more.

"Okay." He kisses my lips softly. "You're welcome back whenever you're ready, alright? I hope it's soon, because I miss your fine ass already."

In my chest, it feels like my heart is bursting, blooming. I feel...hopeful. For the first time in so long, I feel like things may be possible. Like I can stop treading in the shallows and explore the depths.

"I have to go," I repeat, my voice shaky.

"That's fine," Cohen whispers, kissing me harder, with more urgent passion. "And I'll be here." His hand slides under the cotton of my shirt. "But first? Come to bed with me again."

Even though I tell myself it's okay, I'll be able to come back to him soon, I follow him to bed and make love like it might be the last time.

Which gives me courage to make damn sure it's not.

***

I hate to bug him when he's so content, gorgeous and sprawled on the bed.

"I need a ride back home." I expect an argument, a grumble, but he gets up and dressed without a single complaint.

On the ride back to my shitty apartment complex, he reaches over and keeps his warm fingers twined with mine. By the time we're in the parking lot, I want to tell him to take me back to his place, only this time, I'm not leaving. Ever.

But I know I have to check on my father. I can't just leave him alone, even if Cohen made some good points. Which I know I need to take seriously. He wants to walk me up, but I convince him to just watch me until I get in.

He doesn't make it easy, kissing me in the dark interior of his car until my head spins. When I finally manage to pull back, I practically jump out of the door, because I know if I don't leave immediately, I'll follow my heart and go home with his wildly sexy, sweet guy.

"I'll be back as soon as I can. It might be a while," I warn him as I lean into the car.

"I'll be waiting," he promises with a reassuring smile. "Call if you need anything, Maren. I'm here for you."

I hold my breath, hurrying out before I change my mind, hoping, this one time, things will start to work out the way I need them to.

***

The TV is glowing in the living room when I quietly push through the front door. Dad is kicked back in his recliner, eyes closed. I quietly set my purse down, and catch the lingering smell of Cohen on me when I turn. I pad lightly across the carpet, not wanting to startle Dad, lean over him and flip the TV off. He's snoring soundly, but I still tiptoe as quietly as I can to my room to gather up some clean clothes and take a shower.

The water both soothes my chilled body and leaves me a little melancholy, knowing the places that Cohen kissed and sucked and touched are all washed clean. I haven't even been away from him for an hour, and I already ache to be near him again.

It's crazy how he's been in my life all this time. Every day. Just not like this.

I shiver thinking of the way it felt to have Cohen so damn close. Moving inside me, holding me tightly with those arms that I never wanted to leave. But I had to…because, even after our talk, I still had to come home to check on Dad.

I towel dry my hair, and then make my way to the kitchen. The fridge is already nearly empty, even though I just went shopping two days ago. I let it slam a little too hard with frustration, and Dad stirs in the recliner.

"Mare? That you?" he calls.

I close my eyes, purse my lips, and silently count to ten. Willing myself to have patience with him. I don't want to get into anything with him tonight. I don't want it to ruin the high I'm flying after my night with Cohen.

"Yep. Just me."

The old chair that he's had since the late eighties is stained with beer and still holds the smell of clove cigarettes. It creaks and pops as he rolls to his side to see me. "What time is it?"

I glance at the clock on the decade-old microwave. "It's just after two."

"In the morning?" Dad says, knowing the answer even in his permanent state of whiskey-induced numbness. "Where've you been?"

I let out a small laugh, laced with annoyance. "I was just

with a friend, Dad."

I feel gross having just diminished what Cohen actually is to me for the sake of an easy ending to this conversation with my dad.

"You didn't come home for dinner," he says with a deep huff. When I look over the high counter top, I see his arms are crossed over his chest.

"You mean, I didn't come home to cook you dinner? Sorry, Dad, I had plans."

"Could have told me so."

"Dad—" I start, and then let my mouth clamp shut again. I'm not going to do this right now. I'm not. Now that I know he's okay, I want to go to bed and not have to dwell on an argument with my dad as the way my night ended. "I'll give you a call next time."

"You probably need to up my minutes on my phone."

I grip the counter top. "Why is that?"

"I've been talking to a friend of mine a lot more than I thought I would be, and I just don't want you to go over on the minutes." He says it like he's so courteous. Like he's doing me such a huge favor by letting me know. "And you need to get to the store. We're out of yogurt."

"You don't even eat yogurt," I say, rolling my eyes.

"And maybe some of this." He holds up the empty bottle

of whiskey, and it's the final straw.

"Dad, I'm not buying you anymore booze."

"What's that supposed to mean?"

I shoot him an incredulous glare. "It means I'm done. With all of this. With buying your booze. With paying your cell phone bill. With cooking your meals. With leaving an amazing night with someone who is so important to me to make sure you haven't drowned yourself in a pool of your own filth. That's what it means."

I slam my palm down on the counter for emphasis. Dad doesn't flinch.

It isn't exactly how I planned this talk in my head. At all.

"Maren, I'm sorry. I know it's rough—"

"Do you, Dad? Do you really? Because I sort of feel like if you knew how hard these last couple of years have been for me, that you might do something to change the way things are. Unless you just don't care."

"I care. Pumpkin Pie, I care." His brows pull together in a look of guilt. "You've just got to give me some more time. I just need a little more time, is all."

I let my shoulders fall in defeat. This part, this is precisely how I figured things would go.

"I was out late because it was my birthday. Did you even know that? Do you know how many birthdays you've missed?"

"Aw, hell, Mare. I'm sorry. You know I wish I could give you something nice—"

I shake my head. "I don't want gifts, Dad. I want you to remember dates like that because they're important to you. Because I'm important to you. But nothing, *nothing* measures up to the importance of that bottle."

"Don't say that, kid."

I know that I'm his daughter. I know that I'll always be, but man it works my nerves when he refers to me as a kid.

"Dad. I love you. That's why I've done this crazy thing for years. That's why I cook your meals and pay your bills. I do it because I love you so much, and just want you to feel better. But you just aren't. And I… I really don't think I can anymore. I don't think I'm helping you…or me." I let the last two words slip out in a whisper.

Dad nods his head slowly. He looks small. I pity him.

I don't want to pity my own father.

"I understand, kiddo. Just give me six more months and I'll get it together. With your help, I can get a job. You said you'd look into the warehouse thing, right? Could you do that for your old man?"

"Dad." I pause to pull in a breath and work up my nerve. "I think you need more help than I can give you. Like, professional help."

"I'm not talking about this with my daughter. You're a child, Maren. You don't understand things—"

"How can you say that? What do you think I do all day? What do you think I worry about all day? You! I take care of you. I worry about you, Dad. I understand plenty. I understand that it's not okay for me to be raising my father." I grab my keys off of the edge of the counter.

"Where are you going? You're gonna say all that and just leave?"

"I can't do this right now, you're not even listening to me."

"Fine," Dad says. He throws his hands up. "You want to put on your big superior attitude and run away like your mom, great!"

But I'm not running away this time.

I'm running to something.

Someone.

16 COHEN

I'm just falling into that perfect state where you're half asleep-half awake and can hear everything going on around you, but you're so relaxed it's like you're paralyzed and you don't even care. My head is swimming with thoughts of Maren moving on top of me, her expression so intense and gorgeous.

But, damnit, there's a knock at the door. Without moving, my eyes shift to the clock on the nightstand. It's almost four in the morning.

My immediate thought is that it's Kensley.

She used to pull shit like this when we were together. Going out with her friends, downing way more alcohol than her hundred and fifteen pound frame could handle and then having her friends drop her off at my place, slurring her words, and horny as hell. There's no way she is pulling that shit with me tonight. But it'd be just like her, to come and fuck with the most incredible night I've ever had with any woman—even her.

I lay still in my bed, until I can't shake the thought that even if it is her, she's out there alone and at least needs a damn ride home. I pull a V-neck t-shirt over my head and make my way to the door, planning what I'm going to say to her to get her to leave without a big scene.

But it isn't Kensley.

"Maren, baby, what are you doing out here?" I barely get the door open the entire way before I'm pulling her through it, out of the wind.

"It just...my dad...fuck!" she says, her voice shaking hard. "Everything is so wrong!"

"Doll, everything is not wrong. Earlier? That was definitely not wrong at all," I say. I help her out of her sweater and scoop her off of the floor and up into my arms.

"Cohen, what are you doing?" she asks, pawing at my chest like she's protesting, but she's not actually pushing away, so I know she digs it.

"Taking you back to bed. It's late."

"I know, but, I didn't come back for...I mean, earlier was nice. So, so nice, but that's not why I'm here." I carry her up the small flight of stairs back to my room.

I shake my head and smile. She's shaken up for sure. It's my job to make her feel better.

"I'm not about to strip you down, if that's what you think. I didn't want you to leave earlier. I get why you said you had to, but I was a sad sack watching you go," I admit. "But now you're back, and it's late, and you look stressed as hell." I set her on the edge of my bed, our bed. "Take off those jeans and top and put this on."

DEPTHS

I pull my t-shirt over my head and toss it to her. She holds the blue shirt in her hands for a minute before shimmying out of her curve-hugging pants and slowly undoing each of the buttons of her shirt. I sort of regret handing her a replacement, because Maren topless is a thing of fucking beauty.

She needs me, and I have to repeat that mantra in my head over and over as I watch her pull the shirt over her head and think of how good it would feel to press my lips to her stomach again.

She needs me.

"Come to bed," I say, patting the space next to me.

She crawls up the length of the bed, perfect ass in the air, and snuggles into my chest. "Thank you," she says.

"For what?" I reach over and flip the nightstand light off, then pull her in even closer, letting the coconut smell envelope me.

"Not asking. Just, you know, just being here."

"No thanks needed, doll. You've got me." And she does. "Maybe you'll feel like talking in the morning. Right now, I'm just so damn glad you're back."

And, Christ, I am. This girl belongs here. It's so damn clear. I don't believe in love at first sight. I think it's horseshit. But love at first phone call, I'd buy. Because from

261

the moment I heard that sweet, sexy voice say my name a year ago, I've thought about her. Maybe not like this, but somewhere in me, I think I hoped. I hoped it'd be more than it was.

And now? It is.

I kiss her forehead and let her weight sink into me, and it feels so right. This girl owns me to the fucking depths of my soul.

***

I stand outside the apartment and triple check the address before I knock. I know her building from dropping her off, but had no idea which exact unit she lives in. I looked it up on one of the computers at work, though I guess it probably would have been less shady if I'd just asked Maren herself. But this doesn't need to involve her. This is a conversation that needs to be conducted man to man.

I'm still in mild shock over the fact that she told me everything that happened when she went back to her place and talked to her old man. Every time I wanted to discuss it with her before, she'd been tight-lipped, and I knew that was something I had to accept. I knew she needed space. So I was pretty happy when, after a long night of holy fucking amazing sex, she snuggled in my arms and spilled her guts.

Told me all about her mom and sister and what made them ditch her dad.

About how she decided, when she was just in high school, to stand by his side. How it had been sad at first, but okay. How they needed to lean on each other, and that worked.

Then she explained how things went downhill. How every day seemed to get just a tiny bit harder, just one more pebble of angst and difficulty thrown on her shoulders day after day, until she was being crushed under a metric ton of stress.

I mopped her face up when she cried and crushed her to me when she told me how badass she had been when she was facing down her father.

But the first thing she did before heading to work was arrange for a neighbor to check in on him.

I realize that I could probably convince her to move in with me, but she'd always be giving so much mental and emotional energy to her father. And that seems crazy.

Maren isn't used to being taken care of. But I'm used to taking care of people, and I want to do this for her. Even if I'm not positive she'll be all that happy.

I have to knock for a while before I hear any noise from

the apartment. The bolt trips on the door, and it opens slowly, revealing one bloodshot eye in a waxy, pale face with a giant gray beard.

"Mr. Walshe? Can I come in for a minute?"

The eye kind of rolls back and forth, I guess trying to check the hallway through the sliver of open door that the chain lock allows him to peek through.

"My daughter deals with the bills. If we're late on something, I'm sure you can take it up with her."

I was planning on using my best respectable-guy manners. I really was. But her dad just pretty much threw her under the bus and left her at the mercy of a hypothetical bill collector he's too scared-as-shit to open the door for.

Enough is fucking enough.

"Mr. Walshe, I'm not a bill collector. My name is Cohen Rodriguez. I'm your daughter's boyfriend." I say it without a pause, like I'm sure of myself and what I'm declaring.

I know damn well it's wishful thinking. For now. But I also know in my guts that, if Maren is willing, this is my chance. She's my chance. And I'm not going to let some aging rocker with a Peter Pan complex fuck that up.

"What's the trouble?" he asks, backing away from the door.

You, you washed-up bastard.

DEPTHS

"There's no trouble. Can I come in? I think we need to sit down and talk some stuff through. Face to face?" I advance toward the door, and he pulls back.

"You got anyone out there with you?" he asks, his eye darting around with nervous quickness.

"No one but me." I try to keep the irritated edge out of my voice, but it isn't all that easy.

The door closes and I hear him slide the chain lock before he opens it, inch by inch, poking his head out and swinging it left and right before he opens the door the rest of the way.

"Come on in." He shuffles into a dingy living room with a disgustingly stained recliner taking center stage.

The furniture salesman in me wants to run his credit to get him a new chair and see if we can arrange for complementary disposal of that rotten piece of crap.

The part of me that can't stand to see Maren shiver in the cold or drop her classes for a dead-end job has to get his rage under control.

The walls are streaked with the kind of yellow stains that only a truly devoted cigarette addiction can bring about, and there is a ring around the recliner spotted with food stains. The carpet is vacuumed, the kitchen looks dingy but scrubbed down, and there are tiny bright spots here and there; a beautiful painting of the ocean with Maren's

265

signature on the wall, some hand-made blankets laid over the sagging couch, a pair of bleached-out curtains hanging over a window with parking lot views.

This isn't where Maren belongs. And I'm sure as fuck not going to let her sit and rot here.

"I came here to talk about Maren," I say.

I wasn't sure how I'd put it all out there before I saw this filth. Now I know that I'll say any damn thing I need to get him to get his fat ass out of her life before he can do any more damage.

"You wanna drink?" he asks, looking sheepish.

Weird that his manners still force him to offer me some booze, even when he has to know from the look of disgust I'm sending his way that I'm giving serious thought to breaking the bottle over his skull.

"It's not even ten in the morning," I say between gritted teeth.

He shrugs. "Habit I picked up back in my days on the road. Guess I never really kicked it." He throws back two fingers of what I think is whiskey, then immediately pours two more.

"Maren's been worried sick about you."

He barely lifts his feet as he drags his ass from the kitchen to the chair, bottle tucked at his side neatly.

DEPTHS

"Sit." He gestures to the couch, and I'm about to tell him to shut the hell up and listen, but I remember that I'm here to get him out of Maren's life. If that means kissing some old rocker ass, so be it.

"Thank you." I wish I had better acting skills, because I know I'm coming off as pissed and uncomfortable.

"I love that kid." He swishes his drink in the bottom of his cup, and his mouth goes soft and wobbly. "Love her. No one in my life has ever stuck by me the way she has. And, no matter how shitty things are, she doesn't leave. That takes a certain kind of heart."

A thousand biting, crazy things bubble up in my mind, but I stomp them back.

"I know." I take a deep breath. "She dropped out of school."

His nod is slow and heavy. "I guess I figured that. She kept packing her school bag up, but I could tell something was off."

Gee, how observant of you, Pops.

"So, now that you know, what's the plan?" I demand.

I like action. I like figuring things out, getting a pattern down.

Watching her prematurely aged, overweight father rock in his gross chair while he lets Maren collapse every

267

opportunity in her life is driving me crazy.

"I'm not really in the position for plans right this minute." He rubs a hand over his disgusting beard. "I told her the other night, I just need six months, and I'll be—"

"Six *months*?" I interrupt. "You realize in six months, it will be mid-semester at her school. Which means she loses another full year of school. Did you know she's maxed out two credit cards and doesn't know how she'll make her next car payment? She told me it might just get repossessed." Obviously, I'd never let that happen, but I like the way her father's face sags with self-loathing.

My goal is to make him so full of guilt, he picks his ratty ass up and leaves.

"What can I do?" His voice warbles.

I pick up a stack of pamphlets and toss them his way. "These are three detox programs that have open space and offer services for people who don't have insurance. They're pretty good."

He rubs a hand with long, dirty fingernails over his face. "I've never been big on those programs. Just a bunch of assholes and their psycho babble."

Frustration cyclones through me. No wonder Maren feels like she's on a downward spiral. This guy is stubborn about his own demise. Which is fine; if he crashes and burns, it's

DEPTHS

on his head. I just refuse to see him take Maren down with him.

"Here's the thing, Mr. Walshe: my sister has some ins at the local college, and she's helping get Maren back into some of her classes. Her professors agreed to excuse her absences and give her an extension...*if* you go into an approved rehab and we have documents that say Maren was caring for you during the time before you came in."

It's a half-truth. Cece already told me that if Maren explained her situation, she'd vouch for her at the dean's office, and she was positive it would work out. Good thing my sister tutored the dean's sons through high school.

But why should I make it easy on Walshe? Maren deserves a shot at doing this without having to run back and forth to make sure he didn't fall asleep with a still-burning cigarette in his fingers.

She needs peace of mind.

"They'll let her back in if I do this?" he asks, thumbing through the brochures.

"They *won't* let her back in if you don't," I say, then get up and hold my hand out.

Walshe stares at it like he doesn't know what to do. Finally he puts the pamphlets on the arm of his dirty recliner and shakes, his overlong fingernails biting into my skin.

"Well, I'll think about it, Carmen," he says.

I swallow back the urge to throttle him. Also, what the hell is so complicated about my damn name?

"Think fast," I say. "Part of Maren's deal is that she'll live on campus and take a work study job. The rent on this place is paid through the next three weeks, and then you're out."

I enjoy the look of panic in his eyes. I'm not a total asshole, but he's been making Maren squirm and worry for years. He needs to man up and get his ass in gear, and I'm not above enjoying the show while he does.

Even Maren doesn't know this next piece of the plan to get her life jumpstarted. I owe Cece big time for setting things up, which probably means being the male guinea pig for a bunch of terrible gender studies interviews and studies.

Whatever it takes, even if it means mainlining nights of feminist slam poetry. I'll do it for Maren.

I'd do anything for Maren.

I turn to leave, and he's already pouring another glass, the neck of the bottle smashing on the side of the rim.

17 MAREN

"It's going to be fine," Cohen says, his big, safe hand clutching at mine as we walk up the driveway to his mom's house. "More than fine. They already love you."

"They 'work' love me. I'm a freaking amazing employee, Cohen, and there's no doubt that I'm an asset to them, but that doesn't mean they want me seeing their son." It still gives me a little thrill when I realize that I'm actually, officially dating Cohen Rodriguez.

"You know what I think about your assets?" he says, raising a dark eyebrow and patting my bum. I lean into him and hope he's telling the truth. That this is going to be a good day. No complications. But I can't help but feel nervous about meeting his entire family in one place. "Anyway, Deo and Whit will be here and they'll like you for sure. It'll make up for the sharks that my sisters can be."

"Cohen!" I swat as his arm with a pleading expression. "You're not helping."

"I don't get why you're so worried. It's just my family. You've already met some of them. What's the problem?" We stop on the porch that's full of plants near death and a massive stone religious statue that I don't recognize.

I want to explain that I know he's never brought anyone here but Kensley, and how can I replace her? That sisters never like me. That his family is so close that I feel like an intruder. I open my mouth to speak, but he pulls me close and covers my mouth with his. His tongue silences me with its gentle path along the inside of my mouth.

He pulls away, taps my nose with his fingertip and says, "You're beautiful. It's going to be great." Cohen winks in that adorable/sexy way that makes everything okay in a more personal way than his laugh used to on the other end of the phone. "Ready to get your mexikosher on?"

We turn toward the door and I smooth my tiny, floral skirt just as I notice there's an elderly woman standing behind the dark screen.

"Jesus Christ," I gasp, jumping back.

That's got to be strike one, right?

Cohen chuckles and pulls the door open. "Hey, Nana," he says, leaning in to kiss the woman on her cheek. "Way to make your presence known. Maren, this is Nana, my mom's mom."

"It's nice to meet you," I say, extending my hand, but Nana tugs me to her, wrapping her arms tight around me.

"You're too skinny. But you and my Cohen will make beautiful babies," she says, grabbing at my hips with warm, bony fingers all decked out in gold rings.

I choke.

DEPTHS

"Easy, Nana. You're going to scare her away," Cohen laughs. "Let's get inside and meet everyone else."

Gulp.

As soon as we walk through the door, it's chaos. Chaos that smells like heaven. There are people everywhere, dishes full of delicious-smelling food on almost every surface.

"This isn't all for me is it?" I lean in and whisper to Cohen.

"You're a big deal. But no, this is every damn week."

In the kitchen, a woman with dark, glossy hair leans over the counter to set out yet another dish and catches my eye. I recognize her from photos on the company website. Mrs. Rodriguez, Cohen's mom. I've met his dad before, but never his mother.

"Maren?" she says, rounding the corner into the living room. She and Cohen share the same nose, down to the adorable little curve in the bone in the middle. She smiles broadly and it feels like this is actually going to be okay based on that look alone. Mrs. Rodriguez clutches at me the same way Cohen's grandmother did, and it's warm, welcoming, and feels like family should. "It's so nice to finally meet you. I can't believe it's taken this long. How long have you worked for us?"

"Ma, she's not here as an employee," Cohen says,

wrapping a protective, sturdy arm around my waist.

Mrs. Rodriguez pulls the dishtowel that's slung over her shoulder and swats at Cohen with it. "I know that, son, I just meant—oh, never mind. Maren knows what I meant."

I nod politely. "It's really nice to meet you, too, Mrs. Rodriguez."

"Oh, please, call me Dinah."

"And call me Daddy," a male voice pipes in at the same time I feel his arm slip around me and shove Cohen's away.

"Deo, don't start off being an asshole," Cohen says, shaking his head. "Maren, this is Deo. My best friend. Apparently, I wasn't the smartest kid. I picked this one pretty much before we could walk and haven't been able to ditch him since."

"Please. I have the legs of a Rockette. You'd miss them if you ever left me," Deo says, pulling his board shorts up to expose his lean, tan legs.

I love him already. I love how he jokes and loosens up the straight lines of Cohen. I love how in the two minutes since I've met him, I already know that Deo is just as much Cohen's family as the rest of the Rodriguez clan.

Who, I realize suddenly, *all* have their eyes set on me.

I channel my panic into smiling widely at the Deo as he keeps speaking. "And this is my much, much better half,

DEPTHS

Whit."

He pulls a gorgeous girl with serious eyes but an easy smile into his side.

"Hi," Whit says, ducking out from under Deo's arm and giving me a small wave. "I'm so glad you came. Deo's been chomping at the bit to meet the new girl Cohen's been laying pipe with."

I can feel myself turning a shade of red that matches the paint on the accent wall as Cohen reaches over to intertwine his fingers with mine, steadying me.

"Whit, really?" Deo says, grinning. "Exposing our classlessness the first time you meet the girl? You've been hanging out with my mother way too much lately. That's clear as the awful sex euphemisms in your normal conversations. Apologies, Maren."

"Sorry, Maren, but if you hang out with us jerks long enough, you'll see that's just the way we are." Whit shrugs. "And also, I'm so, so glad you didn't get that douche's name tattooed on you. And we really, really are glad you're here."

I snort-laugh. "I'm glad, too. For all of those things."

"Table! Food's getting cold!" Mrs. Rodriguez calls.

The rest of Cohen's family is charming. I've met Genevieve once before, Cece is a doll, exactly the way

275

Cohen has described her and someone who I'd love to get to know better, and Lydia I think will be a completely decent human being once she gets laid. She's polite, but sort of resembles that damn grumpy cat hating life on all of those memes.

The food is delicious. Carnitas and rice and all sorts of things I didn't even know could be made kosher.

"Maren, I wanted to thank you for the excellent order of the rugs last week. We sold every one of them and still had additional orders after sell-out. Incredible," Cohen's dad says.

I love how the two of them look side-by-side. Cohen is a taller, younger version of his dad without the neatly combed black moustache.

"You're so welcome. Glad I could help." I can hardly chew around my smile.

"Pop, let's not talk shop, okay?" Cohen sighs and squeezes my knee under the table.

His dad huffs and shakes his head. "I was just saying—"

"I got a promotion!" Lydia interrupts in a squeal. "I've been trying to keep the news in until they wrote a press release, because, then it's so much more *real*, and then Enzo didn't show again today, but I just couldn't wait to tell you guys any longer! I made junior partner! Can you believe that? The youngest one in firm history."

It's the first time I've seen her smile since I've been here, and it's radiant.

"What? When did this happen?" Mrs. Rodriguez asks. She claps her hands to her face and her eyes fill with tears of pride. Mr. Rodriguez tosses his napkin onto the tabletop, then rounds the table to kiss Lydia on the temple. It's a beautiful moment. Except for the furtive glances across the table between Cohen and Cece.

I reach under the table and run my palm across his thigh, and he covers my hand with his. Something is up.

"Good job, sis," Genevieve says.

"Cheers," Whit says, tipping her bottle of Corona back.

"Thank you," Lydia says, smoothing her hair and setting her face back to what I gather is its usual, miserable expression. "I'm hoping with the extra money I'll be making, I'll be able to afford to move back closer to you all. I mean, I didn't fall into a small fortune, so I probably won't be able to swing a place on the water like some people, but I hope to still be close."

I feel Cohen squeeze my hand tighter, but he doesn't give Lydia the satisfaction of a response to her passive-aggressive dig.

Deo clucks his tongue and wags his finger in Lydia's

direction. "Aw, c'mon, Lyd, don't be all angry because Cohen and I have mad diving skills. We worked—"

Cohen finally looks up. "Deo it's fine. Happy for you, Lydia."

"Well, I think it's time I get the desserts, don't you?" Mrs. Rodriguez says, standing and smoothing the apron that's tied around her waist.

"Ma, wait just a second. Sit," Cohen says.

Something is definitely up.

"I'm glad Lydia brought up my good luck, because if it weren't for that dive, I wouldn't be able to live where I do, or drive the car I do, or be able to take care of this woman the way I hope she lets me," Cohen says. Everyone at the table turns to look my way. An involuntary chill quakes through me at his words. "I especially wouldn't be able to do any of that if my only income was from the shop."

"We know that, son. We appreciate your hard work." Mr. Rodriguez's words are firm. He means what he says.

"Please, I do most of the work," Genevieve laughs. Cohen shoots her a quick glare and she straightens her smirk. "I was just kidding, geez."

"My point is, that money from the dive isn't going to last forever. And I can't live the way I want to live, and be who I want to be professionally working at the store." Cohen's jaw is set and his mouth is just a slice across his face. He's not enjoying delivering this news.

And I'm pretty much too shocked to react. Rodriguez's without Cohen?

My throat tightens when I think about what my day-to-day will be like without him.

I glance around the huge oval table and watch the elated smiles that glowed from Lydia's news melt right off of the Rodriguezes' faces.

"Are you really doing this right now?" I lean in and whisper.

"So, what are you saying? Do you need time off to go on more dives?" Mr. Rodriguez's voice is tight.

Cohen shakes his head. "I'm saying that I have an interview with an accounting firm in LA. They'd let me telecommute most of the time, the starting salary is amazing, especially considering what the economy is like right now—"

"You don't have to tell us what the economy is like, Cohen," his mother says, her voice fluttering. "That's why you offered to help us in the first place. Because sales aren't what they used to be and having to hire outside of the family…you just…you have so much. And you're just going to leave us?"

279

Cohen stares down at his plate, and then lifts his eyes, his expression determined. "What about Enzo? Why can't he ever step up?"

Mr. Rodriguez is scary quiet. I'm not even sure he's breathing. His face is red, his livid eyes trained on Cohen.

"He isn't qualified like you, Cohen! He wouldn't know the first thing about how to run our store! That's our family business you're talking about. Don't you care about that?" His mother slaps a palm on the table and we all jump.

"I know, Ma. I wanted to help, and I think I did. I put a lot of years in, and things are running really well. I'd be happy to stick around and train whoever takes my place. But right now, now, I need to get my own life straight. It's just time." He nods like he's hoping everyone else will nod along and get what he's trying to say.

All eyes on the table shift to me again.

Crap.

"I think…I think I should step out," I say, my voice gasping out like I just finished a sprint.

Cohen clutches onto my forearm, but I pry his fingers off and storm out the front door without looking at him.

I can't *believe* he didn't warn me about this.

I can't believe he brought me into this today, knowing how it would go.

I can't believe he's been looking for a job, and never mentioned it.

He's always been so focused on me and my dad; he never told me how he felt about his own family situation. This whole thing is bullshit, and I feel so blindsided, I'm shaking.

"Don't think that's because of you, in there." Deo's voice scares the crap out of me. When I turn, he's sneaking up behind me and taking a seat on the wicker chair next to mine.

"Of course it is. It's all about me," I say, tugging the band out of my hair and letting it fall free onto my shoulders. It's a habit when I'm frustrated: it's like my equivalent of breaking something. "It's like he had to prove to me that change is easy because I'm so scared of making it in my own life." I run my fingers through my hair, feeling shut-down with frustration.

Deo shakes his head and takes a sip from his beer, and I wonder why I'm spilling all of this to a virtual stranger.

"Nah, Cohen's been wanting out of there for a while. You just gave him the push. You gave him the reason."

"I knew I'd screw things up. I knew I'd just complicate things for him. That family...that family is amazing. They all love each other so much and now look at them. They're probably in there screaming because of me."

I point to the front door of the house that was filled with so much love and happiness. Before Cohen brought me in and dropped his 'life-changing' bombshell. He doesn't realize what he's throwing away.

And he has no idea how lonely and full of regret he's going to be about this. I could tell him all about that.

Deo's laugh breaks through my misery. He shakes his head, his eyes crinkled at the sides from smiling so hard.

"Come on, all families fight, right? Even my hippy-dippy mom rides my ass some days. Trust me, I've known the Rodriguezes my entire life. They fight hard. They fight dirty. And yeah, Cohen is probably in there saying things he'll wish he didn't tomorrow. But tomorrow, it won't matter because you're right: they are tight as hell and there is not a damn thing in this world that'll ruin them. Trust me. It'll blow over."

Deo's words are reassuring to a degree, but I still feel a huge knot pitted inside me. "I just feel like it's my fault."

Deo waves that off like I'm being crazy. "Cohen is doing this because he wants to. Because he wants *you*. Dude's crazy about you. Why do you think he went to talk to your dad? He wants you both to have a fresh start."

I jerk back and feel my mouth fall open. Are there any other goddamn surprises I need to know about before this hellish evening is over?

Deo lets out a long breath and bangs his head back against the porch railing. "Oh, shit, I'm sorry. I guess you probably didn't want me to know about your old man. Listen, my lips are sealed. Not even Whit knows, and she'd have to do dirty, dirty things to me to get me to tell her," Deo says with a wink.

"My dad?" I say, my brain still fuzzy and shell-shocked. "He went to see my dad?"

Deo blinks three times. "Oh. Uh, shit. There goes my fucking big mouth again. Yeah. He did, and I'm sure he has a good reason for not telling you."

"Like he didn't tell me he was looking for a new job?" The anger in me is vicious.

My dad. He went to see my dad? When? Why? What happened? How the hell could he keep this from me?

I'd had this idea in my head that Cohen was one-hundred-percent 'what you see is what you get,' and right now, this instant, I feel like I don't know a single thing about him. The anger and betrayal is swirling in my stomach, and I just can't be here anymore.

I start toward the car when Cohen flings the screen door open and comes stomping out.

"Are you ready?" he asks quickly. He already has his car

keys in hand.

Deo meets his eyes for a split second, and they must communicate telepathically, because Cohen stops walking down the driveway and looks at me.

"Maren? You okay?" He stoops down a bit so that he's eye level with me.

"Just take me home," I try to glare at him, but I'm too full of too many emotions to put the effort into being pissed at him. I mostly just feel numb. And disappointed.

"See ya, bro," Deo says as Cohen opens the passenger side door for me. "And Maren?" I turn and Deo holds his hands at his sides, like he's asking for mercy. "Remember, he's crazy about you."

18 COHEN

"I'm sorry I dropped that today, I wasn't going to say anything to them until I had an offer in the bag, but damn Lydia—"

"What about to *me*? When were you going to say something to *me*?" It's the first things she's said since we left my parents' house, and honestly, I don't have a spectacular answer.

I wanted to tell her, but I felt like I needed something more concrete. I wanted to have a good, stable job, then ask her to come and stay with me. To move in with me. It sounds crazy. It sounds way too fast, and I'm too damn nervous to explain all of that to her and scare her off.

I downshift, slowing the car to make a turn, then reach over to rub Maren's shoulder.

"You're going the wrong way," she says, her words biting out.

We just need to be together, to be alone. We need to talk, we probably need to fight. We hopefully need to crack the headboard having makeup-sex after. I glance over at her, pissed but so damn sexy, it tears at me.

"No, this is just a shortcut to my place."

She whips her head my way, and her eyes are fiery. "I said to take me home, Cohen. Take me home."

Whoa.

"Maren, I get that that wasn't the best first meeting of the parents in the history of time, but trust me, we get over stuff quick in my family. By next Sunday, they aren't even going to mention that. Their first reactions are always to freak out. But once they think about it, they'll be happy for me. I'm positive. Don't worry."

I reach a hand to touch her because I want so badly to fix this. But I decide to wait for some reaction from her, some indication that wants me to touch her again.

Silence.

I take another swing, desperate to get things back to right. "Plus, this way I get you home and to myself quicker, anyway."

Nothing.

The warning look that Deo gave me before we climbed in the car suddenly makes much more sense. Something went down between them when I was still inside battling with the parents. She knows.

"Maren, what's going on? Talk to me."

She shifts in the seat. Away from me.

Fuck.

"How could you go and talk to my dad? And then keep it from me?" She shifts in the seat, irritated by the seat belt holding her in, pressing down on her sexy little skirt with frustrated swipes of her hands. When she looks back at me, her eyes are snapping. "I know we slept together, but that doesn't give you a right to stomp in and talk to my dad, who I didn't even get to introduce you to yet! You don't get to make my decisions for me, Cohen. I can take care of things myself."

"I know that." It's crazy how I imagine my voice staying calm in my head, but when it comes out of my mouth, I'm practically shouting. "You are one of the most generous, caring people I know. I talked to your dad because I knew you've tried before, for so long and didn't make any headway. Okay?"

She crosses her arms. "No. Not okay. I have no idea what he'll be like when I get home. Trust me, Rowan tried the tough love crap a million times, and it always made it worse. Which I would have told you if you'd bothered to discuss it." She pushes her hands to the side of her face, her dark hair falling over her fingers. "You should have talked to me first."

I grab the steering wheel hard. "I may have helped, you know."

She leans her forehead on the window. "I guess." She doesn't sound like she has any hope that I might be right.

"I wanted to help, Maren. It's not like I have some hidden agenda. I wanted to help you do all the things you told me you wanted. I swear, I'm on your side." I manage to take my voice down a few notches when I say this, and it seems to take the wind out of this argument's sails.

She turns to look at me, and I hate the way she looks so exhausted, her eyes ringed in dark circles, her skin pale. I guess all I noticed when I went to pick her up was how gorgeous she looked. It sucks, because I honestly thought I was helping lighten her load, but I just may have made things worse.

"I appreciate you trying to help." Her words sound wooden. "But I can handle this. I want to. I don't want anything anyone else to destroy my relationship with my dad. I can do this on my own."

"So, you can do all of the helping, but no one can ever offer you a hand? That's insane, Maren." We're pulling up to her complex's parking lot, and I wish I'd driven slower. I wish I'd stalled more at my parents' house. I want more time, and now I may not get any.

She puts a hand out and grabs mine, pulls it to her mouth, and kisses it. "I know it sounds crazy. I deserve that, I guess. But it's the way I need it to be right now. So, you need to back off. Okay?"

DEPTHS

I want her to pull me closer. I want her to wrap herself around me, tell me she chooses me over her boozing dad, tell me that she's thankful for what we have and doesn't plan on letting me go.

But she gives me a sad smile, the kind of smile that makes my heart seize.

Fuck.

Is that a good-bye smile? Not yet. Holy fucking hell, please not good-bye.

She licks her lips. "I'll call you." She switches from foot to foot, and I hate that she's nervous. I hate that there's not a damn thing I can do.

I nod and grip the steering wheel hard. I hate to have things out of my hands. I hate to have things unknown. I hate that my only real chance at keeping Maren is letting her go without me.

"You better call," I say and try to smile at her. "I'll be waiting for you. Whenever you need me. Remember that."

I don't know if I'm just imagining that her eyes are full of tears as she rushes back to the shadowed, dim apartments.

I sit in the parking lot for more than half an hour, staring at my phone like I can will it to ring with her number on the screen. Finally, I go home to wait some more, hoping like hell I haven't screwed this all up.

19 MAREN

"Dad! I'm home!" I swing the door wide open and look around, but he's not in the recliner, and my lungs freeze. I know what this means, because I've played out the nightmare a thousand times in my brain. To prepare myself.

My first instinct is to call Cohen, because I don't want to find my dad's body alone. But I can't waste the seconds. What if I can still save him? Do I remember CPR? I run down the short hall to the bedroom where Dad has a bed he hardly ever sleeps in, but it's empty. I'm about to rush to check the bathroom when I turn on my heel, my brain whirring.

My hand taps on the wall, painted a glossy, harsh yellow. When my fingers find the light switch, I flick it on, the room comes into focus, dirty and exposed. My eyes do a quick sweep, but I can't make sense of what I see.

The bed is made. As usual.

The closet is ajar, and I can't see anything hanging in it.

Is he…he wouldn't have…

I tiptoe to it and take a few gulping breaths before I push it open and collapse against the frame with relief. It's just emptier.

The side table is missing the framed photo of the four of us from the Christmas I was eight. It's Dad's favorite

DEPTHS

picture. My heart is pounding so hard and loud, I feel a few gasps away from fainting. When I cross the narrow hall and turn on the bathroom light, rage and confusion and laughter all fight for a place in my chest.

The remnants of my dad's gnarly gray beard are in the sink, the garbage can, on the floor, and even stuck to the always-mildewy tiles. His shave kit and toothbrush are gone.

I make my way back to the living room, but something catches my eye. There's a phone bill envelope with a note on it lying on the scratched kitchen counter.

Hey Pumpkin Pie,

You know I love you more than anything. I'm no good at saying good-bye. I was also scared I would keep making excuses if I tried to do this while you were home. I can't promise anything. These programs don't always work. I'm an old guy, set in my ways. But your boyfriend came by. He's right. The paperwork you need will be in the mail once the shrink they got to work on my head stamps it all. That will probably be on Monday. Take care of yourself for once. Your old man will make it fine.

Love,

Dad

Next to the envelope is a business card for St. Monica's By the Sea, an addiction rehabilitation center.

I slide to the floor and sprawl out on the linoleum, the neon light buzzing overhead.

So.

My dad did exactly what I wished he would do for years.

Why do I feel…so drained?

I tilt my head back against the old almond fridge and want to cry. I think. But my tear ducts have gone dry. So has my throat. So has my brain and my heart.

Dad left me?

I always imagined when it happened, *I'd* be the one leaving *him*. I had run the entire scenario through my head a million times, because I knew it would happen at some point, so it was like doing a test run in my brain to make sure I didn't break down when it really happened.

I'd drop him at the facility, and there would be crying on both sides. And hugging. Lots of promises, lots of apologies, and forgiveness. I imagined him crying as they led him in, because my father is chronically over-emotional. And I imagined sitting in my car, forehead on the steering wheel, bawling my eyes out from relief and sadness, hoping I wouldn't get crushed again.

It's not that I wanted to see my father in pain. I guess I just wanted to know that I played a part in helping him. I wanted the release of all this horrible crap that's built up in me for years. I wanted, maybe, a 'thank you' from my dad and the knowledge that he didn't bear me any ill will.

If he could just jump up and shave that damn beard and arrange everything himself, get himself to the center, get documents collected, what the *hell* was I doing all this time? What was my purpose all the nights I scrubbed vomit out of the carpet and dragged his boots off his feet when he passed out?

Why did my tears and sacrifices mean so little, and Cohen's one talk, the specifics of which are still just one big mystery to me, catapulted this entire change?

I get up and grab the roll of paper towels and Fantastik from under the sink, then march into the damn bathroom. I spray until every surface is covered, until the smell of the chemicals is choking me. But no matter how much I wipe everything down, no matter how many times I run the paper over it, there's no end to the little bits of gray hair.

How fucking *selfish* can one person be?

How fucking *shitty* is it for him to have left me here, alone, cleaning up his damn mess?

How fucking *sad* that I'm stuck here, on my hands and knees in this disgusting little apartment with nothing to show for the last few years, and he's gone without even a good-bye?

I don't even realize I'm sobbing until the tears hit my hands, sliding over the knuckles that are turning pink and raw from the harsh chemicals I'm using to clean.

I feel gritty from the inside out. I feel like nothing can make me good or whole, and I just want to erase everything I've gone through and forget. Start over.

Then I hear a mad thumping on my door, like some lunatic is trying to break in.

I jump up, tears still falling off my face, and my fight mode bursts to life. The sad, pathetic 'give-up' feelings that felt so real a moment ago are replaced by a ferocious sense of survival.

No one is going to make this night worse than it already is.

The pounding gets louder, and I rush to the kitchen, grab my phone and a steak knife, and creep to the door.

My heart is thudding so hard, it dulls my hearing, but when I finally press my ear to the chipped paint that covers the metal door, I hear my own name.

"Maren!" Cohen's voice screams. "Answer this door right now, dammit!"

I drop the knife to the floor with a clatter and whip the door open. He stumbles in, and when he sees me, he growls and grabs me around the waist, running his hands down over my hair and holding my face tight in his hands.

"Where the hell were you? I called your damn phone a million times!" he yells, squeezing me to him, crushing his arms around me. I rub my face into his shirt and grab onto the back of it with both fists.

I should ask him what he's doing here. Why he came back. Why I matter so much. But I'm too spent. So I just fall into his arms, the one safe place I have.

"Dad's gone," I choke out. "He went to rehab. What did you say to him?"

"Maren." Cohen's eyes flash to a bleak, hollowed black. "I'm so sorry. He never said goodbye?"

I shake my head, my misery skidding back now that I know I don't need to use my energy to fend off a murderer.

"What did you say?" I repeat, the tears making my lips slippery and my words muffled.

"Cece can help you get back into school, this semester. If that's what you want. I told your dad that it was what you wanted, and that it would be easier if he was getting himself help." He runs his thumbs over my lips, his eyes wild with sadness. "I know it must feel harsh that he left without saying goodbye, but he did it because he loves you. You can't doubt that, not for a second. He's not strong right now. If he could have done it right, I know he would have. And I know it hurts, but you need to be thankful that he did it at all."

"Okay." I hiccup.

He waits a second, then a tentative smile tugs up on his lips. "Okay? That's all?"

That's not all.

I grab him at the hips, my fingers digging into the bunched muscles of his abs, and stand on my toes, drag his neck down, and kiss him, sweet and deep. His mouth opens and he licks at me with a quick, hungry tongue. His arm curves under me and he hikes me up, carries me fully into the room, and presses me against the wall, his hands hot as they slide over my back and around to the buttons on my tissue-paper blouse.

"I want you," I whimper against his lips. "But not here."

He kisses me quiet and moves his hips against me with quick, gentle thrusts. "My place?" he asks, his mouth sliding over my neck and drawing a long moan out of my throat.

"Or your car. Or the beach. Or anywhere you want. Just not here," I beg, pressing my hands into his soft hair and yanking his face back to mine.

"You need shoes," he whispers, his voice rough with need.

I shake my head. "Not for what I want to do with you, I

don't."

He kisses me for a few more frantic, hot seconds, then flips me into his arms, strides into the hallway, kicks the apartment door closed without even locking it, and heads to his car. I tighten my arms around his neck, not giving a damn that I'm barefoot, that I left my apartment unlocked, that my father wasn't remotely as brave as I thought he was, that I have absolutely no clue where my life is going.

I'm in Cohen's arms, and that's all that matters.

He sets me in the passenger seat, and there's not another word until we pull into his driveway. We start for the house, and I have plans to head to his bedroom, but I get pulled into the living room for some reason.

I realize that the reason was a flash of color. A splash of teal.

"The rug." I stand stock still as Cohen kisses along my neck and down my shoulders.

"Mmmhmm," he murmurs. "I snapped it up the minute it came in. You have awesome taste. In rugs and men, I might add."

"You like it?" I pull back and his face looks confused.

"I love it. Thought, to be fair, I'd probably love anything you picked." He watches as I bend down and run my hand over it.

"It's soft," I whisper. "It's beautiful. It fits here."

"Like you." He pulls me up and wraps his arms around my waist. "Soft. Beautiful. Fits here."

"I didn't say something when we were at my place." I take his gorgeous face in my hands and smile because he's so damn amazing and so completely mine. One hundred percent mine, no questions this time.

"Okay." He grins and kisses my nose. "Say whatever you want."

"I want to tell you thank you." As soon as the words leave my mouth I feel a hundred times lighter. "Thank you."

He kisses behind my ear. "You're welcome. So welcome." He clears his throat. "I noticed you eyeing the rug."

My smile goes wicked at the suggestion in his voice. "It does seem really soft." I back out of his arms and lie down, loving the starved way he eyes me from his vantage point, six feet plus above my body. His eyes tear over me like he wants me. Like he can't get enough of me. Maybe, even, like he loves me.

I close my eyes and listen to the jangle of his belt buckle, the whine of his zipper, the whoosh of his clothes hitting the floor. I hear him tear the condom wrapper and imagine him rolling it on. I keep them closed when he lies next to me, but

DEPTHS

I let my hands graze over every tight, hot, naked inch of his skin.

His fingers move slowly on me, stopping to stroke and touch my skin before he peels off my shirt and tugs me out of my skirt. His fingers hook and tug on my underwear and bra, and then it's just me and Cohen on our teal rug, the crash of the ocean loud and perfect outside.

He pulls the back of his hand down my body, every rough bump and stroke making my breath catch.

"I was so happy you came for me," I whisper as his hand turns over and his fingertips tickle along my ribs. I open my eyes and he's looking down at me, a lazy smile on his lips.

"I tried to call you on my way home. When you didn't answer, I imagined all kinds of stupid worst case scenario type things. I didn't even make it home." He dips his head and kisses the skin just over my breasts, his lips leaving damp circles to mark where they've been.

"I pushed you away," I say, tracing my nails lightly down his back.

"Mmm," he murmurs, licking and nuzzling every sensitive place he can find. "I'm tough. I don't mind a little pushing from you."

His hand slides down between my legs and presses them open. His fingers are light over my skin, but I still lift my

299

hips and jerk against his touch. "I shouldn't push you away."

He sucks my bottom lip in and bites down on it gently. "I agree."

I reach down, grab his wrist, and press him closer, his finger sliding inside me and making my back arch. "I won't push you away, Cohen. I promise."

He dips his fingers in and pulls them back out, his rhythm dictating my breathing patterns, my heartbeat, and the pulse of my hips. He draws his fingers up and rings the bead of my clit, wetting it with his index finger and using his thumb to massage a pattern that has my spine arched off the rug, my hand reaching for the length of him.

My fingers circle around his dick, and I draw up, loving the way he sucks his breath in through his teeth. When I press back down, he pushes his forehead against mine and strains his body into my hand.

"Maren," he grits out.

His hand moves faster, his thumb increasing pressure and pace, and my hand moves to match his. We twist against each other, angling to find the position that gives us the most pleasure this kind of limited touching will allow.

His free hand rubs over my skin, playing over my nipples, pressing his palms to the full swells of my breasts, flattening and gliding up to just over my heart. His eyes are wide open and look startled, like he just realized something important.

"I want you in me, Cohen," I whimper, using my hand to direct him to the next place where I want him to go.

"Now?" he asks, his voice a tight snap.

"Right now. Please. Right now. Please," I chant. His hands slide to my inner thighs and knead the skin there. He's on his knees, so long and gorgeous and hard. He presses my legs apart and positions himself where I'm slick and ready for him.

There's a second where we're both balancing on the precipice. In one smooth motion, he'll be deep inside of me, and I'll be completely wrapped around him. But, for now, it's only gut-clenching anticipation.

"Maren?"

I buck my hips his way, teasing the head into territory where I want all the rest of him.

"Cohen," I moan, squirming under his fierce, piercing look.

"I love you."

The words are sharp and sweet, and, before I can respond, he presses into me in one long, smooth slide, and the sensation is so all-body encompassing, I can't do anything but wrap my legs around his hips and urge him closer.

He grabs me tight under the ass and yanks up, and I arch to allow him to fill me as much as he can before he pulls out almost completely. He pulls out and pushes in over and over, his hands frantic everywhere over my skin, his mouth pulled in a tight line as he fights for control.

I sit up suddenly, determined to close the nonexistent gap between our bodies. He rearranges and falls back so I can settle on his lap, my legs twined around his hips, our bodies rubbing from chest to thighs. His arms drape around my waist, mine grip his big shoulders, elastic with bulging muscle. I tilt back and lift my hips, then drive down on him, exploding a long path of pure pleasure through my body.

And his, if his reaction is any indication. His hands squeeze at my sides and drag me closer, press me against him harder. "Maren, holy fuck, Maren."

I arch away from him and feel every inch as it slides out, leaving me with a momentary emptiness I can't stand. Just as he's about slide out of my body, I melt back against him, driving him deep inside me, and loving the way my body stretches to take him all in, make him all mine.

The pace increases, and my control begins to spiral out of my grasp. Sweat dampens my neck and my breath pants out. My body is splintering, about to explode, and I wrap tight around him, letting the words I've wanted to say to him for so long scream out on the cusp of a shaking, tearing orgasm.

"Cohen! I love you!"

I slump against his chest, totally spent by the tremors that just tore through me. Cohen gently flips me onto my back, and continues to press in, his arms pushing his body up on either side of me, so I can see him from the top of his head to the wet, sweet place where he and I are sliding together.

"Come again, Maren," he begs, his voice choppy. "Come on me one more time. Come for me."

And, like his voice has some kind of magic connection to the very center of me, I unravel as he speaks sweet and low, undoing me so fast and hard, my entire body shudders over and over just before his follows suit.

"I love you."

He says the words. Or maybe I do. Our voices are twisted together, our words tangled, spilling and mixing. Funny how a few hours ago, those three words felt taboo, too soon, too strong, and now we're curled in each other's arms, repeating them like we can't stand to not declare it over and over.

He finally gets up to get rid of the condom and brings back a blanket, a wine bottle, and a package of firewood. He stokes the fire, buck naked.

I giggle, and he turns to smile.

"What's all the giggling about?" He throws the blanket over me and hands me the bottle of wine, already uncorked.

"You're like some caveman, starting a fire naked." I giggle again, and he laughs along with me.

"Sex. Fire. Alcohol. All I need is a slab of raw mammoth meat, and this night is a caveman's wet dream."

I roll on the floor, laughing so hard my sides hurt. "No glasses?"

He raises one eyebrow, holds out his hand for the bottle, and takes a long swill. "Glasses? We're barbarians tonight, Maren! Embrace it."

I sit up and wrap the blanket around me, holding one side open so he can snuggle close. We pass the bottle back and forth, taking long sips of the spicy wine while we watch the fire flicker.

"I could get used to this," I say, pressing my nose to his chest and breathing deep that simple smell that's all *him*.

"Um, yeah, you better." He kisses the top of my head. "I tried the whole 'let her go if you love her' thing and almost gave myself a heart attack. I want you right here with me."

We listen to the fire crackle and trade sips of wine, nestled so close, I don't want to bring up the thing I need to bring up.

"Cohen?"

"Mmm?" His fingers trail gently over my warm, bare skin.

"About school? Was Cece sure I could get back in?" I squeeze my hands together, not wanting to get too excited if it's not really possible.

"Yes." He folds me in his arms. "I hope you don't mind, but she checked with the dean using a hypothetical situation that just happened to be yours."

"No. I don't mind. I'm so grateful." I squeeze him tight. "But you got an interview in LA. That puts us over two hours apart, and with traffic? After a long day of work? You're not going to want to commute that."

His kisses climb up along my temples. "About that. Cece told me you could live at the dorms, if you wanted. You could do work study, be an RA or something. I don't want to pressure you, but I think it would be such an amazing experience. I want you to experience all of college. If you want."

I knit my fingers with his. "I want *you*." I curl against him.

"Easiest request ever, doll. You have me, no matter what. You could go wherever, do whatever, and I'd be here for you when you got back. Always." I hear the steady thrum of his heart under the words. He means it. And I love him for saying it.

But...

"You don't think we should, you know, not tempt fate? See if we make it living close by each other before we take a stab at long distance?" I'm trying to sound cool and collected, even if my body is stiff with nervous terror.

I can't lose him this soon after I got him.

But I shouldn't have worried.

When he reassures me, his voice is steady and strong, and it works to instantly calm me.

"This thing we have? It didn't happen by chance, Maren. It wasn't some sort of voodoo or stupid good luck charm hanging in my living room. We go deeper than that."

"Deeper?" I turn in his arms.

"Right into the scary-as-hell depths, doll. You and me, we were both doing our thing in the shallows for way too long. That's not where we belong. We're brave. We're fucking adventurers. And every adventure we have from here on it, it's gonna be more amazing because we'll be together. Even if we're thousands of miles apart. That's how deep we go."

I blink sleepily, staring into the licking flames of the fire. When I yawn, Deo grabs a throw pillow from the couch, but I push it away and opt to lay on the cushion of his arm

DEPTHS

instead, pillowed against his strong warmth.

"I'm madly in love with you, Cohen. To the depths of my soul," I whisper, sleep making my eyelids heavier by the second.

"You're so freaking adorable when you're overtired," Cohen whispers. "I love you to the depths and beyond that. Sleep, doll."

My eyes fall closed and I sink into sleep, cradled in the arms of the man I know I'll love with my all, for our forever, to the deepest depths and beyond.

EPILOGUE

"Do you think she'll show?" I ask, holding the narrow end of his tie and sliding the knot up.

Cohen scoffs. "Of course she'll show. Deo would stalk Whit to the ends of the earth if she left him standing at the altar."

"I know that. I meant your sister, Genevieve." I roll my eyes, center the knot, and pat it. "There. Are we all set now?"

"Unless you want to untie this thing and let me tie you up instead." Cohen raises a single, sexy, dark eyebrow at me like he's not kidding in the least.

"We're not going to be late to your best friend's wedding!"

"Fine. Later, then." Cohen grins as he sweeps his keys off of the counter and shoves his wallet into his back pocket. "And yeah, I think Gen will show."

"I don't know, she seemed awfully…non-receptive at the rehearsal dinner." I slide my feet into my gorgeous silver peep toes, so high I may break my neck, but so sexy, I'm completely willing to take the risk.

Cohen's eyes travel up and down my body with such obvious need, I know he appreciates my efforts. He gives me a low wolf-whistle before he answers, "Girl's got a bad attitude, what can I say?"

"Looks more like a broken heart to me." I feel sad saying it, because, under all the drama, Gen is such a warm, loving person. And, even though I love Deo like the brother I never had, I can understand how falling for him would result in the kind of lovesickness that could make a girl go a little unhinged.

But Cohen laughs it off like the unobservant man he is. "Gen? Nah. It's just a crush. It'll be fine. Besides, Marigold already did some Rose and Water Love Spell and promises this day is going to go off without a hitch."

"Must be so then," I say, swatting at his bum as he holds the door open for me.

He grabs me by the waist as I pass and tugs me into him. "Don't start something you can't finish, woman," he growls into my ear.

This chemistry…this magic….this love…it's been six

months, and it hasn't gotten old. Cohen works long hours at the accounting firm, and I sometimes feel like I need to hoard the moments we have together, especially on the weekends when I stay here.

It's not like I don't love school. I'm acing my classes, and the dorms are actually amazing. I wound up on a floor with so many smart, funny people who are becoming real friends.

My dad and I write letters back and forth. He's not doing as well as we hoped, but he opted to extend the program instead of signing himself out after the mandatory time he agreed to, so I try not to be pessimistic about what will happen when he finally finishes and joins the real world again.

Mom and Rowan came out to visit me a few times. They even provided the refreshments for my dorm's Spring Fling, where they also got to meet Cohen, all suited up and so gorgeous, even my tightwad sister drooled a little. It's way more awkward than I'd like, but it's baby steps. And I can do that.

But, as full as every other aspect of my life is, my heart bucks and strains in my chest waiting for the weekends when

DEPTHS

I go home. To the house Cohen and I are making ours.

It didn't stop with the teal rug. He converted the spare room into an office for the two of us to use, and we spent hours arguing over paint chips and flooring. I bought new decorations for the kitchen, all beachy and gorgeous. And he surprised me by doing the extra bathroom in Angels red. He kind of spoiled that one with Angels toilet paper, telling me the only way he could stand having an Angels fan in his house was if he could wipe his ass with them, but I still love the overall gesture. And him, despite his crappy taste in sporting teams.

"Doll, you all ready? Wanna lock up while I get the gift loaded?" he asks, kissing my neck.

"Sure." I take my key out of my clutch while I watch him wrestle with the enormous Hine Moana statue he found when he and Deo took that trip to New Zealand. She's the Maori goddess of the ocean, and Cohen used his crazy connections to get her shipped over for Deo and Whit's wedding gift.

"Got her in!" he finally crows after struggling with the wooden statue for twenty minutes. He points to the excessive knot of bungee cords and rope he used to get the trunk

311

closed with a confidence I hope is grounded in reality.

"They'll love her," I say, not pulling away when Cohen tugs me closer and kisses me, first sweetly, then with a need that makes my muscles loose and my blood burn.

"I love you," he whispers, his lips pressed to my ear.

"I love you," I answer. "Cohen, we need to go, or we'll be late." I'm begging him a little, because I know how easy it would be for me to just give in and never leave his arms.

But, tempting as that is, we both love Deo and Whit too much to mess with their day, so he lets me go after a few more kisses, and we drive to the site.

The wedding and reception is being set up outside Deo's mother's herbal shop, right on the ocean. There are baskets and bunches and piles of flowers absolutely everywhere, brought from all over the West Coast by Marigold's amazing friends, who all seem to have organic green thumbs. The air smells gently sweet and salty clean. Lanterns swish in the breeze, ready to be lit when the sun sets and we all dance the night away on the dance floor brought in especially for this day. A traditionally decorated, white tiered cake is on a large table, and I smirk, knowing it's likely laced with a little something extra. A band of scruffy, friendly hippies in flowy

DEPTHS

clothes sets up their instruments as Marigold rushes over to us.

"You're here!" She grabs my face, then Cohen's, pressing kisses on our foreheads. Marigold gives me an apologetic look. "I hate to steal him away, but Deo is having a nervous breakdown."

Cohen's dark eyes pop in surprise. "Deo? Deo is nervous?"

He shoots me a look laced with pure panic, and I grab his face in my hands. "Go to him! Of course. You give the most amazing pep talks. You can do this."

Marigold and I watch him run to the house, and she puts an arm around my shoulders and kisses my temple. "You two were made for each other, you know that? I'm so thankful he found you."

My heart is fluttering when she lets me go to chase the caterer down, and I'm left alone among a wonderful, loving chaos. I wave at a few familiar friends and Rodriguez family members, but I never see Gen. I wander to the bar and order a chilled white, when I hear a muffled sob.

Behind a low citrus tree, I catch sight of silky black hair

313

and a tight black dress.

"Gen?" I walk through the roots and leaves carefully, and see Cohen's sister wiping tears from her cheeks.

"Maren. God. So embarrassing." She laughs wetly and lets out a rough sigh. "I'm such an ass. Please, ignore me."

I hand her my wine glass. "Drink, sweetie. You're not an ass. Not at all. And you look amazing."

She tries to smile, but it's weak. "Thank you." She gulps the wine down in two sips. "I'm not crying because Deo is marrying Whit," she says, her voice cracking over the words. "I'm crying because...because does it ever feel like you're just messing up every day for years on end? Like, you're the world's biggest loser, and maybe it's not a stage? Maybe it's who you are?"

I swallow hard against the lump in my throat. "Genevieve, you have no clue how completely I understand that. But I promise you, you are not and this is just a stage, and one day, you're going to be so damn happy and you'll look back and wonder how you ever could have thought you wouldn't be. Because happiness will be part of who you are."

DEPTHS

This time her smile is a tiny bit more real. "Thank you. I'm really happy you're dating Cohen." She holds up the glass. "Do you mind if I get a refill? I think you're probably right, but today I might just need to be tipsy to believe it."

"Go ahead. Be careful. You don't want a hangover tomorrow," I warn. She rubs my arm and throws me a half smile as he walks away, looking smoking hot and devastatingly sad.

The start of the music sends me scurrying out of the shade and to my seat, up in the front. I'm relieved to see Cohen standing with a pale, but ridiculously handsome, Deo at the altar.

The last guests sit, Gen among them, ignoring her mother's scowl as she sips another over-full glass of wine. The violins swell and we all stand and turn.

I take a quick look at Deo first. His jaw swings open, and Cohen slaps a congratulatory hand on his back. Before anyone notices, he wipes his eyes and blinks hard, then smiles and mouths, "So beautiful," to Whit.

Whit looks like an angel. She's wearing a simple ivory sheath that glows against her peachy tan. A long veil with fancy bands of lace embroidery covers her dark hair. She doesn't look right or left. Her eyes focus down the center, directly on Deo. Marigold's husband, Rocko, stands to one side of her, and a beaming, balding man I assume is her dad stands on the other.

When she walks down the aisle, I notice the bouquet of flowers in her hands has a Purple Heart pinned to it, and I choke up when I realize it's her brother's. Deo and Cohen told me how crushed Whit was to plan the wedding knowing he wouldn't be there to celebrate with her, and I catch her running her fingers over the medal before she wipes her eyes quickly.

The vows are simple and perfect, and they make more than a few guests, me among them, cry openly. Cohen catches my eye and smiles, and I know he'll tease me later, but I don't care. When the non-denominational holy woman tells Deo and Whit they can kiss, he tips her back and kisses her with such total passion and love, they get an immediate standing ovation.

"This perfect girl is my wife!" he bellows when they stand back up. "How lucky am I?"

Everyone cheers back their support, and Whit shakes her head and slaps at him, her blush the prettiest thing I've ever seen.

The party whirls around us, and it's a while before I see Cohen, who's being introduced to everyone and keeps getting pulled away every time he makes his way to me.

I finally feel his arms circle my waist and his lips press to my neck. "Come dance with me, sexy lady," he coaxes.

I follow him onto the dance floor and sway in his arms. "This is such an awesome day."

"I know it. I can't wait til we have ours."

We both stop dancing, and I stare while he laughs sheepishly. "C'mon, Maren. You know that's what I want. I've got plans. You know I always have plans." He shakes his head and stops talking, pulling me close instead.

I move with him. "I'm very happy to hear you have plans," I whisper. We're stunningly, happily silent for a few more beats before I ask, "What was Deo so upset about?"

He pulls away and tips my face up under my chin, so we're looking into each other's eyes. "He was scared he wasn't going to be good enough for her. He was scared he rushed her."

"That's crazy talk," I protest. "They're amazing together."

"I know it. I told him that," he says, kissing me softly. "But I know how he feels. You know I worry I'm not enough for you sometimes. You're damn amazing, woman."

I ball my hands in his suit jacket. "Stop that right now. You're the best thing that's ever happened to me."

He kisses me harder, then pulls back, his eyes dark. "So, Deo started this tradition at his mom's wedding."

"Yeah?" I like the way his mouth curves, like he's going to suggest something naughty.

"He and Whit snuck away and had sex. And look how amazing things have gone for them." His fingers bite through the red silk of my dress.

"Well, you know it's bad luck to break traditions, Cohen." I tug at his scarlet tie. "Shall we go find someplace private?"

DEPTHS

He dips me low and his smile is pure love. "I love you so damn much."

To the depths. And deeper, I think.

But I'll tell him that. Soon. As soon as we carry on the Becketts' wedding tradition.

Coming soon in the LENGTHS series....

Genevieve Rodriguez is less than thrilled when her older brother's best friend, Deo, runs off and marries Whit, the girl who doesn't even deserve him. At least that's what Gen believes. And so what if everyone thinks it's just a stupid crush? She's had a thing for Deo for as far back as she can remember.

Freshly heartbroken and downright annoyed, Genevieve is also one 'D' away from getting kicked out of school. In other words, life could be better for the rowdy, youngest Rodriquez sibling. Her only hope of passing physics is her quiet, nerdy tutor, Adam.

Adam isn't her type at all. He's too quiet, too polite, and he'd rather stare at lab charts than bother to notice the bustier top so sexy, it turned the head of every guy in a five-mile radius.

When Adam tells Genevieve that he won't be back after winter break because his visa is about to expire, the words drop out of her spontaneous, heartbroken mouth before she has the time to think... *"Marry me."*

Thinking it's a joke, Adam gives Genevieve a firm no. But when the joke turns into something more, all bets are off and all limits are broken. Adam may not notice a perfect bustier, but he can't resist a good argument. And Genevieve has been arguing to get exactly what she wants her entire life.

LIMITS

by Steph Campbell and Liz Reinhardt

Coming Summer 2013

ABOUT THE AUTHOR'S

Liz grew up on the East Coast, and Steph on the West Coast—and somehow they both ended up making their homes with their husbands and children in small, Southern towns.

Liz loves Raisinettes, even if they aren't really candy, the Oxford comma, movies that are hilarious or feature zombies, any and all books, but especially romance (the smarter and hotter, the better), the sound of her daughter's incessantly wise and entertaining chatter, and watching her husband work on cars in the driveway.

You can read her blog at elizabethreinhardt.blogspot.com, like her on Facebook, or email her at lizreinhardtwrites@gmail.com.

Steph has one husband, four children, and a serious nail polish obsession. When she isn't reading, writing or wiping someone's nose, you can usually find her baking something.

You can find Steph on Facebook, @stephcampbell_ on Twitter, stephcampbell.blogspot.com or steph.campbell@gmail.com

Made in the USA
Lexington, KY
12 March 2013